THE MAPMAKER'S WAR

"A fun read for fantasy lovers." —*Publishers Weekly*

"Beautifully capturing the tone and voice of a classically told tale, Ronlyn Domingue crafts a deeply intelligent, richly enhanced tale of magic, power, greed, and the infinite resilience of the human heart." —*New York Journal of Books*

". . . it'll entrance you." —*The Advocate*

"A bold and innovative tale of a woman fighting for her place." —*The News-Star*

"Journey to the heart of a fairy-tale land with doomed queens, epic quests, and enemy kingdoms. Ronlyn Domingue's jewel of a book has a big canvas, memorable characters, and intimate storytelling. You will be swept away by this otherworldly tale that charts the all-too-human territory between heartbreak and hope."
—Deborah Harkness, *New York Times* bestselling author of *A Discovery of Witches*

"An extraordinary tale of a woman's courage in an ancient Utopian world. Domingue has taken on the herculean task of inventing a new legend, and the result is a remarkable novel at once absorbing and heart wrenching, but above all mesmerizing!"
—M. J. Rose, internationally bestselling author of *Seduction*

"What a stunning, original book this is—restrained and sensual, cerebral and lush, always blazingly intelligent, expansive, yet filled with the most precisely and lovingly observed details. You won't be able to put it down, and it will take you somewhere you've never been, leaving you transformed."

—Carolyn Turgeon, author of *Mermaid*

"This novel is a celebration of brave women and men, of expansive vision, and ultimately, of a humanity not easily denied."

—River Jordan, nationally bestselling author of *Praying for Strangers*

"Evokes not mere fantasy, but the real magic I found as a child, reading by flashlight under a blanket. As then, the story took me by the hand to exotic lands and noble people and held me under its spell." —Ava Leavell Haymon, author of *Why the House Is Made of Gingerbread*, Winner of the MIAL Prize for Poetry

THE MERCY OF THIN AIR

"This is that rarest of first novels—a truly original voice, and a truly original story."

—Jodi Picoult, #1 *New York Times* bestselling author of *The Storyteller*

"Entrancing and ethereal." —*Seattle Post-Intelligencer*

"Through the alchemy of Domingue's rich, lovely prose, we are transported back and forth through time." —*The Boston Globe*

"An amazing first novel. . . . Razi is so enchanting that readers will gladly follow her anywhere. Filled with vivid descriptions of scents, sounds, and marvelous human sensations that people take for granted and that spirits can only wistfully recall, this is a novel that gets under one's skin." —*Library Journal* (starred review)

"Domingue's vision of the shifting, shadowy world of the dead is convincing and surprisingly affecting . . . and stays just the right side of romantic."

—*Daily Mail*

"Blending the practical matters of marriage with the sentimental, Domingue has fashioned an emotionally satisfying story of love and longing."

—Meg Wolitzer in the *Washington Post*

"Domingue weaves a tapestry of lost spirits and misplaced loves."

—*Kirkus Reviews*

"A hopeful, inspired debut that lands Domingue surefootedly on literary soil as a talented young novelist."

—*Hartford Courant*

"Engaging. . . . In each plot, so different in time and place, Domingue takes a probing look at what produces strong and independent women, be it environment, education, or genes."

—*Booklist*

"Luminous, wise, tender, passionate, and compassionate, this book is special. Razi is a rare character, and her story opens like the petals of a flower."

—Posie Graeme-Evans, internationally bestselling author of *The Island House*

"Domingue has a strong and distinctive voice. Razi, so determined, so lovely, is a heroine to cherish. . . . Anyone who's ever fantasized about New Orleans in the '20s will love this book, with its detailed descriptions of the city's bygone glamour and the lives of women of the Jazz Age."

—*The Times-Picayune*

ALSO BY RONLYN DOMINGUE

The Mercy of Thin Air

THE MAPMAKER'S WAR

Keeper of Tales Trilogy: Book One

RONLYN DOMINGUE

WASHINGTON SQUARE PRESS

NEW YORK LONDON TORONTO SYDNEY NEW DELHI

Washington Square Press
A Division of Simon & Schuster, Inc.
1230 Avenue of the Americas
New York, NY 10020

First Washington Square Press trade paperback edition March 2014

WASHINGTON SQUARE PRESS and colophon are trademarks of Simon & Schuster, Inc.

For information about special discounts for bulk purchases, please contact Simon & Schuster Special Sales at 1-866-506-1949 or business@simonandschuster.com.

The Simon & Schuster Speakers Bureau can bring authors to your live event. For more information or to book an event, contact the Simon & Schuster Speakers Bureau at 1-866-248-3049 or visit our website at www.simonspeakers.com.

Designed by Akasha Archer

Manufactured in the United States of America

10 9 8 7 6 5 4 3 2 1

Library of Congress Cataloging-in-Publication Data is available.

ISBN: 978-1-4516-8888-7
ISBN: 978-1-4516-8889-4 (pbk)
ISBN: 978-1-4516-8890-0 (ebook)

TRANSLATOR'S NOTE

This narrative is an exceptional rarity. The source language scarcely has been heard spoken outside its cultural borders. Until the acquisition of this work, the presumption was that no writing system existed for the language. In remarkable condition despite its age, the handwritten manuscript is not only one of the earliest known autobiographies but also one of the first attributed to a woman.

The author's rhetorical structure defies the conventions of any period; she addresses herself throughout and appears to be her own audience. Further, while matters of war and society are so often the domain of chroniclers, historians, and philosophers, this author offers a concurrent, heretofore unknown representation of past events through the story of a participant and a survivor.

Simplified pronunciations of several proper names are as follows. Aoife [ee-fah]; Ciaran [keer-ahn]; Wyl [will]; Aza [ah-zah]; Edik [ed-ick]; Leit [lite]; Wei [why]; and Makha [mahk-ah].

—*S. Riven*

THE MAPMAKER'S WAR

THIS WILL BE THE MAP OF YOUR HEART, OLD WOMAN. YOU ARE FORGETful of the everyday. | misplaced cup, missing clasp | Yet, you recall the long-ago with morning-after clarity. These stories you have told yourself before. Write them now. At last, tell the truth. Be sparse with nostalgia. Be wary of its tangents. Mark the moments of joy but understand that is not now your purpose. Return to the places where your heart was broken. Scars evidence harm done. Some wounds sealed with weak knits. They are open again. The time has come to close them.

Here, choose the point of entry. Any place, any time, right now and you have—

Your small finger in the hearth's ashes. A line appears. You divide space.

Then there were twigs and broom bristles. Scratches and marks and lines until you had the control to create shape. Circle, triangle, square, said your older brother. Ciaran put the first nib under your thumb and first scrap of parchment beneath that. What you drew is missing in substance and memory. In its place, years apart, you transformed the circle into a tub. The triangle was a churn. The square became a table. You marked your spot with an *X*.

Aoife, said your brother, who taught you to draw a map?

The kitchen as it was when you were five. You could render space and suspend time.

You lived in a large cold house at the edge of a forest. The shady quiet lured, then hid, you. Wild child, said the nursemaid. Uncivilized, your mother declared when you returned home dirty with treasures. She tried and failed to tame you. Wait until I tell your father, said she. Next to his chair, you held your breath and your guard. He saw no harm in the fresh air and exercise. Good habit to start now because what man wants a fat wife? said your father. Indulgent, she called him. She stormed off on stout legs.

You had few ordinary interests as a girl. You didn't dress your bronze hair, tend to dolls, or join petty quarrels. This perplexed your mother, who tried her best to create a being in her own image. You soon realized you had to give to take. When you were attentive to your morning girlhood duties, she fought less when you asked for afternoon freedom. You acquiesced to learn how to behave regardless of whether you intended to follow suit. The reward was worth the concession.

With meticulous care, you planned your provisions, though not your expeditions. Adventure wasn't in the hunger to come but in the quest of what to follow. You packed your pouch | nuts and fruit, soft bread and hard cheese | along with parchment and ink, cloth scraps and straight edges.

You mapped the hidden worlds when you were still young enough to see them.

Spiderwebs and honeycombs taught the wisdom of symmetry. To you, everything before your eyes was built upon invisible lines and angles. The very spot where you stood only a point among many. A girl is not always in her place, you thought. A girl can be many places at once. And so you were. When you settled upon a space in the forest or meadow, you made a grid on the earth with small steps and tiny flags until there were row upon row of even little squares. You took your seat within the grid. You moved from square to square, noting what stood still and what passed by. All day long you observed and measured, sketched and colored. That which was off the edges appeared on the parchment as well. There were mysterious realms of bees and ants and creatures never seen before, with tiny castles and bright gardens.

One day, as you traced the uncovered trails of termites, you heard a rustle in the brush. You remained still with hope that the ancient stag or a sturdy bear would meet your eye. What a lovely beast to draw in that place! Instead, you faced a boy with green eyes and chestnut curls. A boy you knew well. Prince Wyl called your name and held up a dead rabbit by its hind legs. You lifted your hand in a polite wave and turned back to your work.

Did you see what I caught? I shall skin it and give the fur to the tailor to make you a fine collar, said Wyl.

It will be cold if you do that, you said.

It's dead. It has no need for fur now.

So literal, Wyl. You mistake my japes.

You meant no hardness toward him. As you looked to the ground again, you smiled. You knew his gesture was an act of affection. Such regard you had neither sought nor earned. His attentions you tried not to encourage or reject. That you two knew each other at all was a matter of circumstance. Your father served as the King's most trusted adviser.

On that day, when you wished Wyl had been the stag or a bear, you realized he didn't ask to see your map. He had on other occasions. You had no way to know that in years to come he would be privy to every chart you made, to the very last one.

See, you became a mapmaker.

Those hours you spent looking at the distance from one point to the next | star to star, rock to rock, blade to blade | were your study of geometry before you ever received formal instruction. You could be both abstract and precise, and sit for long periods. Ciaran gave you lessons in mathematics and astronomy. He had also taught you to read. You enjoyed the challenge of learning. You also liked the attention from your brother, amiable and patient with you. Your mother encouraged the companionship between her children. However, she saw no purpose for the lessons.

You need to know what is practical for a woman, said she. All this effort leads to nothing.

Nothing indeed would have come of it had you not heard your father and brother in conversation.

The kingdom was in a quiet time. For generations before, there had been years of strife, battles to claim land and battles to control it. At last, there was much to manage and little known about the holdings. They discussed the King's consideration to map the entirety of his realm. Mapmakers would need to be hired and some trained.

You almost cried out on impulse. This you wanted to do, although you didn't know why. You banished the thought that you would be denied the training. You wanted to be good at something other than what was expected of you, for life. You threw yourself at chance.

We'll see, said your father when you asked for a place at the apprentice's table. Don't raise your hopes, said Ciaran when you told him of your wish. Your brother, seven years your senior, had begun to serve the King in earnest, the heir to your father's role as a trusted adviser. You had no such secure inheritance. You suspected your name would not receive mention.

Now. Tell the truth.

You turned Wyl's affection to your advantage. The pull between you both served in your favor. You didn't call it manipulation. Perhaps it was. An offhand comment was all it took. *I would like to learn to draw real maps.* With magical speed, there you were in the mapmaker's chamber.

Heydar came from another kingdom with an accent, his instruments, and several bound volumes. His ears sprouted whiskers that reached up to his frantic hair and down to his bushy beard. He looked, and ate, like a lion. You passed the tests he gave you, then he tested your courage because he saw your wits. He didn't care that you were a girl, but twelve. All he cared was whether you could learn the craft, whether you practiced enough. He demanded excellence. You would deliver.

You thought to thank the King for his favor. Wyl arranged a brief meeting. The King said he had been assured of your talents. He said he made exceptions for what pleased him, and it pleased him greatly to have such intelligence, enthusiasm, and tenacity at his service. He gave no mention as to who might have swayed him. Or why he allowed it.

When you sat with your studies at home, your mother bustled to and fro. She stitched and stitched and stitched. She hurried and harassed the servants. She sighed and moaned. You ignored her. She told your father he would have difficulty finding a mate for such a daughter as yourself.

She isn't crippled or ugly, which is good enough, but no man wants a stupid wife, said he.

That was how you became apprenticed to the old man. Why you, with that silent desperation you hoped he could not detect? You sensed if you could do well there, if you were a good mapmaker, you would avoid the inevitable. You knew what happened to girls like you.

You confess that you weren't as smart as others assumed. You were no prodigy at figures and measures. What you grasped you did so with diligence and repetition until it became second nature. There had to be precision in your practice. You took pleasure in it. There was room for error in the Land of the Bees and Outlying Environs but not in the case of territory and ownership.

For four years, you apprenticed with the old mapmaker. Heydar tutored you in the pertinent subjects related to the craft. He showed you how to use all of the instruments. He sent you afield with them | heliotrope high in the hot sun |, then allowed you to practice at his side at the table. He gave to you his insight into triangles. That he brought from his distant land of sand. He mapped with three sides as his center and trained you to do the same. This he claimed proudly as his innovation. You claimed his legacy.

Heydar supervised your work as you charted the castle and its immediate lands. He had done so himself, but this was your final test. He praised your effort. He declared you ready to go on your own. Before he left to return to his homeland, he gave you the waywiser given to him by his adept.

Many distances this wheel has measured with its walks. Remember me in a step once in a while. My time is done, and yours has begun, said he.

The old mapmaker gave his leave and the King his permission. You crossed paths with your brother on his travels from holding to holding. With his group of envoys, Ciaran created lists and tallies. He was to collect numbers of people, animals, and goods. He was also to discern what grievances needed attention, what loyalties called for boons, and what troubles might be in brew beyond the borders.

You were instructed to chart all that could be seen, and that was much. The kingdom was wide and broad. There were mountains and rivers, hills and streams, forests and valleys. Within this were the hamlets and towns, mills and smithies, pastures and arables, roads and paths. Ciaran and you were to note the fortifications. Ciaran, the condition. You, the location.

Many times, Ciaran's work would be done before you finished with yours. He would return to your childhood home, and you would stay behind to tend to the maps, but not only the maps. You explored the nearby regions by yourself. There were birds and plants and on occasion creatures you had never seen. You liked to speak with the people and learn about their customs. They fed you unusual foods and told familiar stories with subtle twists. Sometimes you sketched simple treasure maps for the children and hid coins for them to find.

To you, knowledge of the people was meant to be mapped as

well. For whimsy, you would include reminders on your work for the King. They meant something to you and only you. This was how you entered your childhood again. A hut's roof edged with ribbons for no apparent reason. A place where you ate too much of a succulent pie. A fallow field speckled with blue gentian.

It seemed, though, that just when you had found a comfortable rhythm in your temporary quarters, Prince Wyl appeared with matters to tend on behalf of his father. His presence caused a stir, with people running about to catch a peek at him and share words. He was, in fact, good with the subjects, when he saw them. He exchanged pleasantries. Sometimes he asked questions and listened until the people had had their say. When requested, he touched the crowns of children's heads with gentleness. But, more often than not, Wyl was within your sight. He rode his horse around the place where you were at work. He sat at the hand of the host who gave shelter and food to the King's representatives. He seemed to talk longer with others when you were nearby, in conversation with the son of a prominent nobleman. Or a lowly shepherd. Or a man on your crew.

He has the stealth of a squirrel and the modesty of a peacock, you thought.

One summer morning, you leaned over the plane table, your eye in a squint, and stood quickly when the object in your sight went black. There was Wyl with a raspberry between his fingertips and a small metal bowl filled with more.

Thank you, but I'll wait to eat them. Stained fingers, stained map, you said.

You're tame enough to feed by hand, said he.

You stood bold before his charming smile and the pride he'd mustered. Such a thing he'd never said to you. Wyl looked at the map in progress and noticed the triangles that branched across the parchment.

Where are we? asked he.

You pointed to an open space yet to be drawn.

This land is flat with little to see. Your work must be difficult.

I have my ways.

What would help you?

Elevation, perhaps. I've had dreams of a tower.

Then you'll have this tower, said Wyl.

So it was. You gave him drawings of the tower in your dreams. Wyl found the woodcutters and smiths to make its pieces. He found stouthearted men to test its design, which did not fail, and hired them to tend to its care.

Innocent Wyl. He could not hide his adoration. You resisted your tender feelings. Was it love? Perhaps. When you were children, you attempted to keep the boundary fixed. Much your mother's doing. Bow to him, Aoife, he is the prince. Be friendly, not familiar. Be gracious. Be obedient. Be careful. | yes, be that with his dark brother Raef as well |

You liked Wyl. His disposition was sanguine. He seemed more interested in pleasure than power. Grudges didn't suit him. When you were young, when a girl wasn't permitted to say aloud she found a boy comely, you thought he was just that. As you grew older, you found him handsome. An exceptional example. He, for whatever reason, found you pretty. No boy orbits a girl as he did unless an attraction, a physical attraction, exists.

When you first saw the tower, you toed the great beams at its base. You tugged the ropes that tethered the tower to the ground for safety. You tapped the metal bolts that locked the heartwood beams into place. Then, the best part of all, you didn't have to climb the sides like a ladder but could walk the staircase you had envisioned. A spiral led up to the top.

You took your maiden ascent alone, with a crowd below, Ciaran and your crew, Wyl and his brother Raef. It was summer again. All was green and gold. All was alive. You had stood higher before, in the hill country, but this was different. When you leaned over the side, that caused much shouting on the ground. You saw straight down, your shadow a small dark splotch in the grass. So this is what the swallow sees on the wing, you thought. And as if by invitation, a blue swallow appeared above your head. It hovered before your eyes, plunged toward the earth, and darted away with a green head and long legs crushed between its beak. You called Wyl to join you.

The tower is wondrous. I could kiss you, you said.

Yes, you could, said he.

So literal, Wyl.

Then I'll wait until you mean what you say.

You felt a sting. For the first time, a joke on him barbed you back. You watched him stare afar and wondered why he went to such lengths to please you. Perhaps there is more to this boy I once knew, you thought. You linked your arm with his and leaned into him, both swaying groundless.

YOU THE MAPMAKER TRAVELED THREE LONG YEARS AND CHARTED A fraction of the kingdom. The King wished for faster results, but he knew you and your crew gave him more than he had expected. He himself walked some of the maps on his own and encountered no missed marks or wrong turns. Despite your wish to work through that fourth winter as well, the King summoned you home for a long respite. You had earned it and, you knew, others had insisted.

How strange it was to return home, a woman of twenty. You had been away for so long. The first step over the threshold, and you fell under a familiar spell. You slept in your girlhood bed, under your father's roof and your mother's care, above neglected cobwebs, things that go bump in the night, and maps to hidden worlds.

At each daybreak, you sat on a stool long after you'd slipped on your boots. You remembered where you were again. Your mother always thought you were a lazy riser. You were listening to see if he was gone. You listened for signs of your inconsistently indulgent father with a mean streak. No, he never whipped you with a switch or belt. No, you saw him do that to Ciaran. He'd slap you across the mouth, the face. Unpredictable. You were slapped for saying you didn't like runny eggs. Another time for telling your mother you didn't wish to wear a particular frock to a banquet. You weren't a bratty child. You didn't much complain. What did your mother do? It's for your own good. Serves you right, stop that crying, what a lucky child you are to have that food, that dress.

Home again, you wished to see friends, but all had married and moved throughout the kingdom. Your brother Ciaran was far off and weeks away from a visit. Prince Wyl had been sent to another kingdom for a courtly purpose. Then he suddenly returned to his castle rooms unannounced. You availed yourself of his royal requests. Wyl had become a collector of dubious maps. He wanted your expert opinion, but you avoided him otherwise. You knew your place. He had forgotten his.

One sunny morning, you ventured to the forest in a dark green hooded cloak and brown boots lined with fur. You found a favorite boulder, not yet warmed by the sun, and sat with your back against it to see what might come. The winter was not yet so harsh, the animals not yet too thin. Winter is a dream time, you thought. All that is imagined to be lost returns when we wake up. You looked to the sky with closed lids and open ears.

There came a sudden scuffle of hooves and wheezy breath. You rolled your eyes to watch the deer leap over the boulder, over your head, and stumble into the trees. There was blood on your hands. You kept to your seat when you heard the noise of running footsteps and harsh gasps. You turned only your gaze to see who it could be. You watched Wyl and his brother Raef vie for a lead as they raced ahead. The two brothers resembled each other at rest as much as in motion. The similarity ended there.

Through no fault of his own, Raef was born after Wyl. He didn't receive the same attention, esteem, or respect. By nature or neglect, he was also not as charming or amiable. He seemed desperate to prove himself. In the forest, at least, he could compete with his brother on equal terms.

You peeked through the brush and met the glint of a blade. Wyl grabbed the antlers of the great stag. You clasped your mouth. Raef drew a dagger against the stag's throat. Three arrows jutted from his body. You saw a thick scar on his shoulder. You had seen the ancient creature many times since your childhood. You had drawn him on your maps.

There was some chase left in the old man, said Raef.

Though it was not his season, you said.

The young men startled at your approach. You knelt at the stag's side.

It's the season for boars, you said.

So it is, but we found none today, said Wyl.

She believes she has surely seen them, hiding as she was, said Raef.

You narrowed your eyes at the younger prince. He smiled as he wiped the dagger in his shadow on the beast's fur. You pushed to your heels, wrapped deep into your cloak, and left without a reply. Soon Wyl's footsteps fell in rhythm with yours. He tried to explain the reason for the hunt, the choice of quarry. You had little use for the older brother's defense of the younger.

Be careful of your brother, Wyl. I know this wasn't your doing, you said.

I wanted to hunt today as well, said he.

Raef hunts what secretly reminds him of himself.

He isn't so swift and strong.

That's not what I meant.

Say what you mean, then.

He is cold and weak.

Wyl took hold of your cloak and halted your steps.

What am I? asked he.

A man of good intention, nature, and cheer.

What are you?

A mapmaker, and a subject.

He took your hands and smeared the blood. He found no wound but touched something carnal and raw between the two of you.

What could be, if it were, would come to a dark end, you said. | spoke it into being then, didn't you? |

Aoife, even you can't see that far in the distance, said he.

You turned your head when you heard Raef call out. His bloody hands hovered at his sides. Wyl waved to him, and Raef stood in wait. Wyl took your stained hand and pressed it to his chest. Your palm filled with the heat of the chase, his shirt, your will. All of it pulled away from your grasp as he left to join his brother.

THE KING ORDERED YOU TO THE NORTHERN BORDER WHERE THE land met a wide river. You were told to map as far as you could see on the opposite bank. It was said there was a kingdom on the other shore, but little was known about the people. The King had sent messengers to deliver peaceful invitations, but the watchmen who received the notes only nodded, and no replies came. In his wisdom, the King thought it best to leave the unknown people to their own. For now, he only wanted to know where their fortifications were in relation to his.

You dreamed of a sturdy vessel with a perch to see afar. Wyl found boatbuilders to bend and seal it, bow to stern. The boat still firmly ashore, you traced the dry joints, shook the solid anchors, and climbed the lofty perch. Wyl stood back with crossed arms and tousled chestnut hair. You knew he'd come to see the launch of another good deed done. He would see you away once again, perhaps for the last time.

The night before the maiden voyage, you and Wyl scaled the perch's narrow rungs and sat with legs afloat in the air. You both were in plain sight but in private space. He hadn't spoken again of the announcement he had given you when he arrived. Wyl was intended for another. A matter of alliance rather than the heart. The promise would be sealed the spring after the next.

Ask and you'll have it, said he.

As ever, as always, you said.

Ask, Aoife, whatever it may be.

Can you forgive and forget what I'm about to do?

Then for the first time you kissed him, full under a new moon.

Uncalled-for. What were you thinking? You weren't. You owed him nothing, but his gift was an excuse for the impulse. You had no illusions that he would, or could, choose you over his intended.

Tell the truth.

You desired him. His features pleased you, the rest of him as much. In moments when your concentration lapsed, you caught yourself thinking of him. What he said to you at the plane table. How he moved with square-shouldered confidence. The way he held himself on a horse.

The next morning, you climbed to the highest point on the new boat. You waved good-bye to the boatbuilders, most of your land crew, and Wyl. You felt a rip in your chest as they walked away from the kingdom's shore. Wyl turned to look back once more. Even deep wounds heal, you thought. No matter the cause.

You journeyed out into the seam between winter and spring.

You peered beyond the bare trees for hints of secret forts. It had been said that the other bank had none. So it was that nothing was encountered but animal rustles and rumps, no person or dwelling, for several months. By late summer your hair had turned from bronze to gold. Your curiosity about what lay beyond the river bends turned to daydreams.

When you could resist the mystery no longer, you asked the crew to take the boat to land. They stood in their places with wide, wondering eyes, looking past the bank and into the forest. Birds chirped, clouds moved, water lapped. Then an oarsman cried, Ashore, ashore, men and my lady! Men ashore!

Five young men in blue coats approached the bank and stood in a line. The third raised his hand slowly with his palm toward you, high above his head. You looked down from the perch, and the crew looked at each other. The crew raised their hands, then the other four men gestured in turn. The third man stepped near the boat. You could hear faint voices. Your crew captain shouted and waved his hand to call you down.

You studied the five men in your descent. Blue coats, white belts, flaxen leggings, tanned shoes. Hair long at the crown, swept back, cropped at the skull. Not one seemed to carry a sword, dagger, spear, or club. The third man met your eyes when you stood in front of him and nodded.

Come, said the man in your language.

They refuse to take one of us men, said the captain.

No harm, said the man.

My lady, I advise you to stay. I told them we would leave, said the captain.

You smiled at the captain, who looked unafraid but unnerved. This was an invitation you couldn't resist. You accepted the man's hand as you leapt ashore. He gestured a rectangle. The captain explained they wanted to see the maps, which he didn't want to release. You asked him to gather a selection of drafts. He complied. You noticed the crew had twitches and fidgets. You urged them not to worry and above all to be calm.

Three of the young men in blue stayed near the bank. You walked beside the third man, who gave no name or title but seemed to be their leader. The last man fell in step at the leader's side. They spoke with rich voices in a language you'd never heard. You noticed they were younger than you, barely out of boyhood. You wondered what kind of kingdom would post sentries without weapons. Fools or innocents, you thought.

The two men appeared to utter good-byes. The leader's companion began to run ahead through the trees. The leader stood still and faced you. Your body tensed. You clutched the maps. When your eyes met, the young man told you there was no danger but explained nothing. He put his hand on his chest and breathed deeply. He lifted his brows, tapped his chest, and breathed again. You smiled and returned the gesture. When you laughed, he laughed, too. You both continued on the long, mysterious walk.

The direction you traveled led you to a large rock. Its placement had to be deliberate, a marker of some kind. He touched it as you walked past.

Then in the distance, a subtle glow rose from the ground and met the sunlight. Your footing felt a shift. You looked down. The forest floor had merged into a road paved with gold. At your toes was the wisdom of the bees, a pattern of honeycomb the length and width of the path. The leader kept his pace, which you tried to keep until you could stand it no longer. You tugged his sleeve and begged him to slow down. He replied with a smile meant for a child.

You and the young man followed a straight road. On either side of it, paths turned off left and right. The houses were sturdy and square, with clay brick walls painted in muted colors and pitched roofs layered thick with thatch. All faced the heat of the sun and had garden entrances, some with herbs and flowers, some with small trees and shrubs. Now and then the land lay open and green, sometimes with a fence, sometimes without, where children and animals ran and leapt. There were sounds of work and play, voices speaking and voices singing. People who noticed you waved and smiled. Step after step fell to gold.

Too soon, you came to the center of the hidden village. Graceful trees shaded glare from the road. You noticed a mechanism the likes of which you'd never seen. A great wheel decorated with inlays of metals and gold reflected chance glints of light. At its back, more wheels of all sizes with notched edges lay quiet against each other. Nearby was a well with a peaked silver roof and solid stone surround.

The leader escorted you into a house longer than any of the others. It had large windows draped in gauzy linen and floors paved with stone. He seated you in a high-backed chair with soft cushions and gestured that you should stay.

He took a mug from a nearby table and went outside. You watched him offer his finger to a little boy who climbed a small arch of steps built into the well's side. They peered over the edge together as the leader pulled the bucket's rope. He let the child dip the mug and rub a cloth on its side. The little boy accepted help down the steps and followed the leader back to the building. The child paused at the doorway.

You waved to the boy, who returned the gesture with a smile and a phrase spoken in melody, like a bird's song. Then he was gone. Your eyes suddenly filled with tears. Your throat tightened. The leader moved a bowl of fruit, nuts, and hard cheese to a table next to you and placed the mug in your hand. You clasped his fingers. It was a bold gesture. Spontaneous. You did not touch strange men. He let you hold as long as you wished, knelt at your side as you did. Not a word passed between you.

Three people entered the room from an interior door. You released the young man's hand and stood before them. There was a man and a woman, much older than you, wearing linen clothes with beautiful designs at the cuffs and necks and hair streaked with white and silver. The woman wore a headband and the man wore a wristband made of the same blue cloth as the leader's tunic. The third was a woman near your age, who wore a blue skirt, fitted green blouse, and gold pendant at her neck.

Welcome to our settlement. How could we give you more comfort? asked the young woman in your native language.

You found yourself unable to speak, so you bowed first, then shook your head.

Your guardian will wait outside until we've ended our talk.

You nodded.

The three pulled chairs away from a nearby table and circled you. The young woman gave their names. You managed to say your own. The young woman explained that she was fluent in your language and was there to help the other two, who could speak only phrases. The older man and woman were elders who came to the house to understand the reason for your visit.

You told the truth. You said you had been sent by your king to map the riverbanks and mark any fortifications. The three nodded.

The man asked to see your charts. The three peered from different angles at what he held. The woman asked who had drawn them, and you said it was you. The three nodded. You realized that the young woman spoke your language with no accent, as if she herself were from your kingdom.

You learned that these people had lived in their settlement for hundreds of years and meant no harm to anyone. Their ways were different, unusual to many, and it was best that encounters were made like hers, by chance, without malice. Their ways were older than your kingdom, than any known to recent memory. They wished to have their peace, and their peace they would gladly share. You assured them that you, your crew, and your king had no ill intent. The three sat in silence.

What do you think? asked the man.

She tells the truth as she knows it, said the woman.

They were silent again, until—

What do you feel? asked the woman.

She will protect us, said the man.

And endure grave dangers, said the young woman.

What dangers? you asked.

You shall see. Heed the voice inside, Aoife. Heed it without fail, said the young woman.

You opened your mouth to respond but could form no words. Instead, you stared at the young woman's pendant. You could discern a design of geometric shapes. Circle, triangle, square. The young woman followed your gaze with a lazy shift of her own. Then she looked at you as if she peered through your flesh. She spoke her native language. The man left the room and returned with an object.

You travel much. We are sworn to protect and guide anyone who carries this amulet, said the young woman.

You opened a delicate wooden box with dovetailed edges. Inside was a silver piece the size of a coin. It carried the same design as her gold pendant. What great care they take to the small things, you thought. What attention. You thanked your hosts for several moments.

When you were ready to leave, the young guardian appeared at the door. The three, in turn, took your hand and held it tightly. They wished you well and sent you away with a small bundle of food. Not much time had passed. You could tell by the arc of the sun. However, you felt as if you'd been there for ages.

You followed the guardian through the settlement and back into the forest.

As you reached the large rock you'd passed before, a voice called your name. The young woman who had translated your words rushed toward you. There was something else she wished to give. She told you to listen with your heart, not your mind. She said the known and hidden worlds weren't what they seemed. Like a map, they could fold. The shortest distance between two points was not always a line. Among all that was seen and unseen, there were links, the points, and gaps, the distance between.

Take care to notice the trunks of trees, said she.

Her fingertips touched the hollow of your throat.

Remember what I tell you, said she. See and say clearly in your mind where you wish to go. The words will show the way, if you follow the form in which they appear. The journey could be long in walking or brief in step, and you might be given no choice.

Then she told you the incantation in your native tongue.

| wind howl and whisper, water ebb and flow— |

Yes.

You remember it still. There are some things you will not force yourself to write, not entirely. Subtle forces answer the call, whether the speaker is friend or foe. There is no discrimination of the one who utters. Directions will be shown. The gaps will open to admit all, but you won't reveal the way.

The young woman and your guardian touched the rock. You

did, too, for good measure. She left with a smile. He led you again with one. You felt too overwhelmed to speak. It was just as well he didn't use the same language. You repeated to yourself what the young woman had said. Her nonsense puzzled and fascinated you. A childlike curiosity stirred within.

When the guardian returned you to the river, you stood in front of him for a long moment. Nearby, your crew and four young men in blue kept watch on one another. You saw the captain approach, handed him your items, and asked him to step away.

Who made the gold road? you asked the guardian.

He spoke a word you didn't understand. Then said he, Small man. The young man pointed to his head and toes, flexed his arms and chest, and hovered a flattened hand at his waist.

A dwarf? you asked.

He shrugged. You matched his gaze and, without pause, tossed your arms around his neck. He wrapped his arms around you in response. In that instant, you realized you had known Wyl all your life, had touched his hands, had linked with his arms, had once kissed his lips, but had never, ever held him that close. You felt the young man rip away. The captain wrenched the young man's arm behind his back.

Stop! Don't hurt him, Captain! you said.

The guardian turned in the hold and released himself with a fluid movement that was not violent. The ease surprised you all. The captain charged him in bluster. The young man blinked against the other's stare.

My lady, we must wait, said the captain.

Why? you asked.

An oarsman and the cook are missing. They went into the forest, said the captain.

Why? you asked.

I told them to trail you, said he.

You shook your head. Your guardian signaled he and his

companions would leave. As the five of them slipped into the trees, you waved good-bye. You refused to return to your kingdom's bank to summon guards. There was no threat. You and your King's men slept on the foreign shore.

In the morning, two young men in blue coats returned the crew members. The oarsman and cook arrived unharmed and bright-eyed. You knew what they had seen. You felt a protective impulse for the people of the settlement. You knew what the men would tell if not sworn to silence.

WITH HEARTS CROSSED AND OATHS SPOKEN, THE OARSMAN AND THE cook promised to hold their tongues. Neither their fellows nor their liege would learn of what they had seen beyond the riverbank. To quiet curiosity, you spoke at the evening's shared supper. You told the crew of a peaceful settlement, the people's kindness, and their wish to be left alone. You explained what you saw because you couldn't describe how you felt.

You thought the enchantment would wane for yourself and the two crewmen. But in the weeks before winter sent you home again, you three sometimes glanced at each other, not in warning but in wonder, as if to say, Yes, I did, I saw it, too.

The cold came early, all the colder over water. You released your crew with the intent to finish the work when spring returned. The men of the river stayed behind. The rest traveled back to the castle. The cook seemed unusually burdened, as if the sack he carried was filled with heavy, hidden stores. You stole a private moment with him to remind him of his oath.

On the day of your expedition review, you weren't surprised to see several others in attendance. You had stood at full tables before, the King, your father and various advisers, Ciaran, Wyl and Raef, even the Queen. You had sent occasional letters about your progress, yet specific questions were common at these meetings. There was also much study of the map drafts. The review was as ordinary as any other, except for your report about your visit on the opposite bank. You told no lies yet told no more than necessary. You were careful with your words, careful to raise no eyebrows. The group appeared content with your efforts and relieved that their neighbors posed no threat.

You set to your work of drawing final copies of the new maps but had little peace outside of the task. You suffered your mother's redoubled coaxing to end your travels and settle upon an eligible nobleman. Admit it. A gracious family at times gave you and your crew shelter within and near their manor. The thought crossed your mind that you might meet a tolerable man during a stay. If you did, you could involve your father in the proper maneuverings. This assumed you wished to leave your work. Even on the worst days, the wet cold, hot dry, with your neck thick and tight as a rigging rope, you did not tire of it. You wished to do nothing else. Be nowhere else. Mere thought of the dreary alternatives made you glad for your blisters and calluses.

You relied on your father's hollow torn resistance. He knew well of the King's approval. You do me proud, Aoife, and strengthen us in His Majesty's favor, said he to you once. The uncommon praise struck you like a painless blow. Your father knew his responsibility, but he deflected tradition and your mother's insistence that time was short. The day will come when she will marry and not make a boring wife, said he.

Ciaran was not yet married. For him to do so would be of no consequence, except for what all assumed he could someday propagate and was sure to inherit. He would continue in your father's footsteps. You, however, knew the repercussions of your mother's great expectations and your father's patriarchal duty.

For a while, you were valuable on your terms. You were as

useful as your brother. An exception to the rule. You imagined you were secretly admired for a cunning slip from the way things were and outwardly disdained for the betrayal of role and function.

The women's *tsk-tsk-tsks* that must have trailed your mother as you freely roamed the kingdom's yet uncharted wilds. The burn she must have felt at the banquets you missed. Ciaran missed them, too, as matches were made. Each passing year, your womb empty, your life full.

You had more immediate troubles tearing you in opposite directions. There was your ungratified rut for Wyl, and his for you, and the futility you'd brought on yourselves. He was still promised to a princess. You remained the object of his attention. He was not yours to indulge or keep. You wished you had not kissed him that once. Nevertheless, you entertained the notion of making an even worse mistake.

There, too, were thoughts of the settlement and its people. Never had you felt such an immediate peace in a strange place. You thought of the dear little boy whose greeting brought you to tears. You, who strained not to shed them. The elders and young woman who met with you seemed untouched by suspicion yet were clear that you must have caution. An affection had passed between you and the young guardian. You felt a desire to return, an irrational longing to stay.

Then came the summons.

You paused when you recognized Raef's seal in the wax. You thought his formality undue, even with your shared coldness. You two had had private conversations about matters of state before, petty issues connected to your work, but this request was worrisome. He didn't write the purpose of your meeting, but somehow you knew.

You arrived at the appointed chamber on time. Raef was already seated but stood when you entered. He eased down again, cocked his eyebrow, and dropped his bent elbows heavily on the table. Raef asked you to tell again what you had seen on the other bank. You leaned forward on folded arms and repeated your report. He reached into a pouch, set down an object under splayed fingers, and flourished his arm to his side.

One perfect honeycomb cell lay between you. One piece of the gold road.

What were you told, Raef? you asked.

A fantastic tale you must know, said he.

We'll see, you said.

So it's story time for you, said he.

Raef shouted, Enter. The cook stepped into the chamber. He bowed to each of you. Raef instructed the man to tell what he had seen. The cook told his tale, a far richer one than you had spun yourself. He told of gold roads and jewelry, of grazing meadows and fertile arables, of a tremendous mill and large smithy. He told of the kindness he was shown when he was found in the forest, and the bed where he spent his night. Through this, you kept your gaze on the cook's lowered eyes. Raef watched you with a smirk.

The cook's story became like a dream. He sat in the garden outside the house where he had slept. A little girl came up to him with a quiet smile. He greeted her with a hello. She held a ball between her palms and asked to play. The cook didn't know if this was acceptable, so he told her to go away. She placed the toy in his hands and opened her arms to receive it. They spent some time in the game. Because she had asked, he told her why he was in her settlement. When she tired, she sat on the grass across from him. The cook remarked that she wore a pretty pendant. I have it because of what I know, said she. So the cook asked what that might be. The little girl, who could have been no more than three years of age, began to tell him of a family who lived far and wide all over the world and whose members guarded a red dragon and its treasure. Every person in this family was special, and all had different gifts. She wore the pendant because of hers. The cook asked what gift she possessed. I understand you, said she. Then she kissed him on the cheek and kicked her ball down the gold road.

You faced Raef, who almost seemed moved by the cook's words. You said that much of what the cook had reported, you had not seen for yourself. You were confused by his account of the little girl's visit. The people's language wasn't your own. How could he speak with her if that was the case? You asked him to describe the pendant, although you didn't say why. The cook said the child's was gold and round, with a design he couldn't clearly see. You thought of the interpreter with her pendant. As for the little girl's tale, you said each of you had heard stories of dragons and treasures as children. No doubt she had as well, and embellished the telling to suit herself. You thought her imaginative but not truthful.

After a measure of quiet, Raef handed the gold block to the cook and dismissed him. The man clutched the cell between his hands and looked at you.

My lady, Prince Raef questioned us all. I'm sorry, said he.

I'm sorry. It was my doing that we went ashore at all, you said.

The cook bowed and left you and the younger prince alone.

What did you do to him? you asked.

In a fair exchange, improved his station. He won't die a cook. He's a steward now, said Raef.

THE TIME CAME FOR WYL TO COMPLETE HIS FEAT. HIS WISDOM TEETH had emerged in full. For reasons unknown, that sign, not age, determined when the task was to be done.

The people of the kingdom chose the endeavor. Peculiar, but that, too, was how it had always been. The feat was intended to test the firstborn prince's strength, bravery, and perseverance. They often decided upon a solitary hunt. The man and his bow out in the forest. The prize was the carcass, then a ritual feast. If the prince was out of favor, the people chose a difficult animal to track and kill | so it was said, you heard tales from old villagers | or required three bodies instead of one. For a beloved prince, the quarry could be as simple as a rabbit or a dove. There were rewards for good favor.

Once the task was accomplished, the young man was declared fit to be King, although many years might pass before he was crowned.

Wyl rarely spoke of the feat other than to wonder what he must hunt. He assumed, rightly so, that his task would be easy. The people had great affection for him. They could require that he catch a salmon as the spawning hordes returned. One good leap, said Wyl, and I'd catch it with my bare hands.

Where were you when he said that? Surely you sat with him in a familiar location, the courtyard, the map chamber. Yet within you, he braced himself against the current. He grabbed that giant rosy hook-faced fish out of the water and held it in the air. He was naked from the waist up. His soaked pants molded to every contour from hip to leg.

Aoife, blink, said he.

You closed your eyes to see him more clearly. Sigh. Then you stared at his hands. There he was right in front of you, as distant as the image of him that emerged but didn't exist. Your blood ran hot with lust. You suspected yourself depraved.

Once you spied a crewman through the trees. Bathing. He stood in the middle of a shallow stream. He had a metal cup. He bent and poured and rubbed himself. It was a pleasant morning. When he was clean, he wiped the water away from the hair on his body, then pressed a palm over his genitals several times. He was in profile to you. He took hold of himself with some degree of tenderness and gave his body lingering attention. Although you had seen a man's body, you had never seen it respond as it did. You were shocked to find yourself flushed. The sight made you heavy and light-headed. Hardly seemed ladylike. Then the medium by which a man's seed finds its way out joined the flow of the water. He never knew you were there. He acted no differently toward you, nor you to him. There had been an animal purity about him. He was alive and healthy and in a circumstance that didn't require containment.

Your response was not shame or horror. It should have been. All subtleties and directives of childhood demanded such either-or. No, you felt curious. Did what went through his head and hands go through yours? Of course, you knew that instant, of course. The denial of it made a woman's body an object of submission to the man's expected desire, to her own trained resistance.

You desired Wyl, but other men appealed to you. You were not blind. Now and again, the comely or witty son of a nobleman. During your travels to map the kingdom, without fail there was often a crewman or two near your age, strong and kind. Nothing could come of it, though. You worked and ate together. You slept among them every night but always alone. They and you kept a distance between each other although their bodies were at times so close. You relied on their respect, and they understood the boundaries. To the degree possible, you were one of them. You asked nothing of them you wouldn't do yourself. The illusion that you belonged there had to be maintained.

Indulgence was not to be yours. The crew had options. You didn't care that the crew was not wholly chaste. They had animal urges. You were observant of the discrepancy. There were, as they were called, the used women who for whatever reason allowed themselves to be filled. They were chasms where pleasure disappeared. You knew. You heard the satisfied snores. You heard the men speak of what had been done with whom, to whom, and how. What the women received was a mystery, and you could not ask. Silent, you thought of the good women anxious in virtue, their bodies designed to take in and give as much as the used women yet with greater constraints.

You were philosophical, but not as much as you wish to think. You were young. Healthy. Curious. If they could enjoy that, why couldn't you?

Why not Wyl? Sometimes the sight of him made you mindless. | that grin, that glance | He had fine balanced features and a long lithe body that moved with animal grace. He was beautiful. This could not be denied. On more occasions than you have fingers, you saw women freeze in midmotion, forget to curtsy, and stare at him. They were struck dumb. Other girls and women giggled and looked askance in his presence. He wasn't blind. He noticed, but he thought all princes were treated that way. He thought the women were overcome by his royal bearing. So literal, Wyl, you said when he told you.

After the daydream of Wyl catching the fish, you knew you had to avoid him. You didn't want to feel as you did, but you did. What overtook the beasts of the forest lived in you, too. Your nature contained it, and you had not yet released it. There were risks worse than gossip. If you failed at this, you had no desire for the outcome. The infant inevitable. You wanted what would be allowed Wyl. The pleasure and the power to walk away.

You imagined an escape, but where would you go? You left your father's house for the fields and forests. To leave the kingdom's sprawl to close yourself off in a house with servants and a husband? Unacceptable. To a place all your own? Unlikely, if not impossible. Unless you left to serve another, far, far away.

HOW WORD SPREAD OF THE SETTLEMENT ON THE OTHER BANK, YOU had no idea. The cook | no, now the steward |, unburdened by his confession to Raef, may well have told one person, and another and another. Raef himself, tritely drunk in the company of boisterous fellows, might well have told the tale. Perhaps embellished it. Perhaps got an idea in his head. No one would ever know who revealed this fact.

What occurred was the traditional poll of the subjects to determine what feat beloved Prince Wyl would undertake. You were away when you learned what they had chosen for him. A messenger with news from the King first announced it to the crew.

Then Wyl arrived at the site you were mapping. He demanded a private meeting. You had to obey. Such was his power. The chamber door closed. The guard outside coughed. Wyl paced. The decision troubled him. He expected what generations had done before. A hunt, the lifting of tremendous weights, a night alone and unarmed in the forest.

Instead, he was given the feat of a quest to return with proof of a dragon.

He wanted you to tell him what you'd seen in the settlement across the bank with every possible detail. You didn't want to. It was a place where you returned, if only in mind, during quiet moments. You wondered what it would be like to live there. You questioned whether your memory was true, if you had in fact felt such peace and welcome. Regardless, you were protective of the settlement, although you did not understand why. You didn't wish to betray their quiet.

I said all I had to say before the King and the Council. Why does it matter? you asked.

I want to know if there's evidence of this dragon.

None but a story, you said.

And of the riches in the village?

It's all under one's feet and before one's eyes. That is real.

The people say they've chosen me, said Wyl.

For what?

A new era of prosperity, more than enough for all.

Raef, you thought, the cunning and cowardly. If Wyl found a dragon hoard, he knew the people would get no more benefit than a generous banquet. As a prince, he'd enjoy the riches on top of his inherited wealth. If Wyl failed, you would not be surprised if Raef commissioned a journey of his own. If Wyl died, Raef might have to quest himself, but if he survived, he would one day be King.

You watched Wyl sit on a cushioned bench. His back widened as he leaned forward. You placed both hands below his shoulders. Comfort for him, contact for you.

They say I'm a good, brave, and worthy prince and only a man such as this can attain these boons, said he.

In that instant, no, Aoife, you didn't think the full thought. The glimmer came and went. You felt a shiver at your core and smiled wide with no idea why you were smiling. It was only a nameless, formless possibility at that moment. Then you said:

Wyl, you are a good, brave, worthy prince.

He asked if you believed so. You did. You did. Your hands moved into the curled chestnut scruff at his neck. He sighed a creature's content.

Now here. Your heart tears.

I'm afraid, Aoife.

You didn't deserve his honesty even though you had earned it. His vulnerability was what brought him to you. He trusted you. He desired but also loved you. You wanted what no ordinary woman could have and he was able to give. Influence, intercession. Your life existed as it did because of him. He never once took advantage or liberties. He wanted to. You could tell in his eyes what he wanted. Good, decent, charming Wyl.

What did you do? You didn't console him. No, you pressed your breasts to his back and wrapped your arms around his neck. You let him untwine you and lead you to sit on his thighs. You let him hold you. | why had this taken so long? | You wanted to grab him by the throat and kiss him until he couldn't breathe. | would you know how to do that? | Instead, you sat with his flesh bone heart under your palm. His mouth was on your temple until asked he:

Tell me. You would know. Is there a map to where the dragon lives?

Of course not, you said.

WYL'S PHYSICAL STATURE SUGGESTED POWER, ACTION, AND CONFIdence, but he was guileless, almost innocent. He was a man who meant no harm. | do you love him now, too long later, too late? | You believed his decency was his saving grace. You feared it was also a weakness. He had hardly traveled outside of his kingdom. You had less so, only across the river, only for a day, night, and morning.

On impulse, you gave Wyl the amulet. You told him anyone who held it was promised safety. When he asked from where it came, you claimed it was an old gift. When he asked where he should begin his journey, you suggested he start east. You could say no more because you knew nothing else. You didn't send him to the people across the river. You wouldn't risk their seclusion. As it was, you felt your actions violated an unspoken promise.

You said he would likely have to ask directly about the dragon that guarded a great hoard. He'd learn soon enough, wouldn't he, if the dragon was a lie.

Wyl had no choice but to quest. The King understood it was wise to go with what the people had chosen. That was their tradition, the power they were allowed to wield. Honor it. His younger brother's zeal was manic and infectious. Raef took great delight in the danger his brother would face, although he didn't acknowledge any peril. Big brother, find the treasure and make us rich! said he at a crowded dinner one evening. You wondered what had gotten into him.

So the King agreed to send his favorite son on a quest to find a dragon. What a farce, you thought. Yet there it was.

You kissed Wyl good-bye in private. A kiss that threatened to wear through woven cloth and leather. You had such a good excuse, didn't you? The next morning, you watched him leave surrounded by a cheering crowd.

You returned to your work. You still thought to avail yourself elsewhere once Wyl married. You were of a rare breed, a highly skilled prize. Another kingdom might be bold enough to risk you. Despite your feminine face and shape, you pondered whether you could live as a man. You dressed and carried yourself like one as it was. Until then, you considered training apprentices. You could not ponder the obvious alternative.

Then one morning, you awoke without a doubt of what you'd do that day. You dressed, ate breakfast, packed a satchel with necessities, readied a horse, and rode east.

You wanted to find the truth of the dragon for yourself. If it didn't exist, you would have a grand adventure and determine where a skilled mapmaker might chart a new part of the world.

Some might think you meant only to find Wyl. Much had been made of the fact that there was no reliable map to where he was headed. One might presume you a guide. Others would have another opinion. You knew what talk would be of you and Wyl. There were speculative witnesses about you two. There was no hiding what Wyl had done for you. The tower, the boat. Some might have assumed you repaid him with more than loyal service. You didn't care much. The assumption served in your favor. Was it not amorous that you would chase after your presumed lover?

The dragon was your reason, you told yourself. Wyl was your excuse. Deep down, you acknowledged the possibility that you would somehow find him. Nothing would be familiar. No one would know you. All rules could be broken.

YOU HAD DEVELOPED SELF-RELIANCE DURING THOSE MAPMAKING years. You didn't expect the crew to tend your every need or demand. If you could lift, untie, secure, kill, gather, fetch, or handle it, you did. They offered their help but didn't insist. They respected, even admired, your tenacity.

In spite of this, you worried how you would take care of yourself on the journey. You realized you would be without the protection of the crew. Although they left you alone, you were never wholly unguarded. You secretly resented this, although it gave you comfort. You knew they concerned themselves about you, a woman alone in the company of men. They had their instructions from the King, no doubt, no doubt from others. You surmised punishments awaited them if harm or insult befell you. On the roads, you never led. In the open, when a camp was necessary, you slept surrounded. A woman can suffer greater pains than death.

The clothing you wore was meant to obscure. This you had chosen on your own to avoid undue attention. You had a cloak made with shoulders padded thick and wide. You had mannish boots on your feet for all the trudging you did. More often than not, you slipped into shirts and leggings. A prudent costume.

On the morning you left, you had your own money earned in service to the King. You mounted your strong, reliable horse. You gathered your wits and off you went to see whether a little girl had told the truth about a dragon and a hoard.

You had nothing to lose except your life.

On the journey, the connection you had to that life, and its alternatives, began to disintegrate. You had no inclination to become what every woman you knew became. A wife, mother, domestic. You didn't begrudge them their roles if they were freely chosen. Yet who can choose freely when the options are few? Yes, you supposed you could have become a matronly scholar. That wasn't barred to you. That might well be how you would have found some tolerance with your life, had circumstances been different. Had Ciaran not given a name to the drawing you made naturally. Had your father not put you in the proximity of maps drawn to organize and capture the world. Had Wyl not taken you seriously when you said what you wanted to learn. Had the King not given you a chance and found you worthy to serve. Had Heydar not accepted you as his apprentice.

Now, tell the truth. You were not so different from other women. Your life depended on the favor of men. Your freedom was an illusion that you dared to dream.

ONLY DAYS AFTER THE START OF YOUR JOURNEY, YOU STOPPED FOR A meal in a village at a busy post. It was one stop among several along a main trade route. You and another traveler sat down across from each other at a large table. Bowls of hearty stew steamed below the nods of your heads. You noticed salt in a small bowl with a tiny wooden spoon. You didn't reach over. Instead, you asked that the salt be passed. You also pointed. It was possible you wouldn't know the other's language. The seasoning came to your hand. You said, Thank you, and the person replied, in your tongue in a strange accent, You're welcome.

Another glance, and you knew. You both wore men's clothing but neither filled such skin. She had a large bag next to her, a satchel covered in dozens of pockets with buckles for closures. She asked if you were traveling far. Yes, you said. You assumed it was customary not to say too much and that your response was enough. However, she began to speak.

One carries more than a load on the roads, said the traveler.

Then she told you a tale. She knew nothing of your quest. There was no indication from your clothing, bearing, or words. Yet these are the words she said to you.

An old woman once told me a story.

Once, there was a tribe of seers who lived deep in the forest of a great kingdom. It was rumored that they possessed writings about the whereabouts of the scarlet dragon and its secrets. Although many tried to get answers, the tribe refused to share with anyone.

The tribe was stricken by a terrible illness, and all died save one. She was a girl when her parents died, and because she was so accustomed to living in the forest, she never left. She rarely entered the village except to barter. She lived in her family's tidy hut all alone except for the animals who kept her company. During the day, she worked the land with her father's tools. At night, she sorted and sewed by candlelight next to the small mirror her mother once prized.

Now, it is said that the young prince hunted wild boars in that forest and came to know this orphan. As unlike as they were, they became fast friends. He made sure she was never hungry or cold, while she made sure that he always left her company with a jolly heart.

Their joy was not to last, as all joy cannot. The prince grew to be a strong young man. Soon he would leave for his quest. That was when the visions began. The orphan's dreams were filled with his blood, running thick from cuts drawn by the dragon's claws. She told him of these dreams, and he laughed. He was a valiant prince. He was destined to rule his land. If he died, it would be the will of that which was much greater than he.

On the eve of his departure, the orphan found the prince standing in an open field below a brilliant blue sky. He pointed toward the east, where the sun rises. I must confront the dragon, he said. She asked him why he had to go. Surely, she said, he could rule his kingdom without a dragon scale to place above his throne. But this was not their way.

Night fell as quietly as the strands of her newly shorn hair. She prepared for a long journey, hemming tattered garments into the morning light.

Yes, this orphan followed the prince for several months, never far from him. He never knew of her presence. And finally, one day, he came upon the dragon. He was locked in dreadful battle with the beast, trying to get a scale from its body, when the dragon knocked the weapons from his hands. Its enormous claw poised in the air.

A sharp blinding flash of light pierced its eyes. It reared back and closed its cold lids. In a glance, the prince saw his friend holding a beam of light in her hand. Without another thought, he grabbed his sword, sliced through the beast's breast, and grabbed a fallen scale. Together, they ran into the forest.

He thanked her for the act that saved his life. She showed him the mirror that had focused the power of the sun. When they returned to the kingdom, he told a tale of mortal battle. He did not speak of his friend.

She was among the crowd who very soon saw him crowned. Even as King, he arrived at her door to enjoy her company. They remained good and secret friends. The orphan seer cherished his visits, for she loved him truly.

Very soon after that, the young King fell ill. The sickness was painful and grave. Everyone worried for his survival. When word reached other kingdoms of his health, strife entered the land. Many wished to claim what the King called his own.

This was not to be, the people cried. He fought the dragon and returned with his proof. His success deemed him worthy to lead. Someone is to blame.

And in his delirium on his deathbed, the young King confessed the truth. He had received help to obtain the scale. He named her name.

Armed men sought the orphan seer, captured her, and took her before the court. They demanded the truth from her, which she told. All gasped in horror.

He was meant to die there, a great nobleman said.

How do you know? she asked.

Because young vibrant men do not fall deathly ill at random. This was ordained. You interfered with his destiny, and our kingdom's.

She said the journey itself was very dangerous. There were bandits and rogues and all manner of Nature's risks. He could have died then, but did not.

A man walked through the hall to her side. She recognized him at once, those beady eyes and strange robes. He was the Wood Wizard.

I know the future and the past, he said. Where they go is my land. It is my business to watch, and, on occasion, interfere. Tell us, woman, why did you save him?

Because I love him, she said.

And great nobles, why did you risk his life with the quest?

Because that is how it has always been.

The Wood Wizard pulled a small pouch from his robes. He asked what had she given to protect the King. Of course, she had given nothing but her wits and concern. Then the wizard asked if she knew what the kingdom had given to ensure his safe journey.

The orphan seer looked at those who judged and blamed her. She did not know.

The wizard tilted the bag and out poured gold coins, more than could possibly fit in the pouch. He caught several coins and sniffed them between his fingers.

Every life has its price, he said. I will leave this for them to spare yours, for your act was done out of love and not duty.

So the orphan seer left with the wizard. When the young King died, never knowing of her deep love, her mother's mirror shattered. The kingdom fell to greedy foes. She herself was far, far away in a new life.

You were unnerved. The story carried an echo. Perhaps of warning. You managed an appreciative smile for her gifted telling.

I enjoy the old tales. Don't you? asked she.

Most entertaining, you said.

She grasped the clothing on either side of her chest and moved her torso. You knew that discomfort. You, too, adjusted the cloth that bound your breasts when the spiral wrap twisted. Then she pulled each buckle tight on the pack. She hoisted it on her shoulder and seemed balanced in spite of its size.

Safe travels, friend, said she.

It would not occur to you until much later that the braided cord and placket on her tunic were a certain shade of blue.

YOU JOURNEYED FARTHER, STILL ALONG THE TRADE ROUTES. YOU waved at fellow travelers. You marveled at the wares at the larger trading posts. There was no point in buying or exchanging any goods, but you did look. Traders offered you weapons, jewelry, and spices. Two or three attempted to sell you red flat objects with the texture of a soft horn. Dragon scales, they claimed. You laughed. Indeed. When your horse was stolen, you didn't try to acquire a new one. You continued onward on foot.

You inquired about Wyl here and there. You described him, but not his quest. It was not so difficult to find at least one person who marginally spoke your language.

Sometimes you could determine whether someone's help was sincere. You didn't always reply the same way if asked questions. Your intent was to follow Wyl. At times, you lied to do it. Sometimes you claimed he had a debt to pay, sometimes you owed one.

Once, you encountered a young girl who greeted you for no apparent reason. She twisted a blue hair ribbon around her finger.

How odd that she knew your native tongue and was unusually helpful. She refused your offer of a coin. Others had insisted, for no better information than a suggestion to look below the sun and under the moon.

As wide a world as it is, you did manage to trail him. Remember, Wyl was likable. He didn't engender suspicion or fear. He might have been generous with his fellows at times. Cautiously, you hoped. Wealth like that wouldn't go unnoticed.

One day you received a clue that he had been seen. The one who wears a coin at his throat? said someone when you asked after him. A coin? you thought. The amulet was the size of a coin. He must have decided to display it for protection.

Then you got lost, or so it seemed. The road disappeared. It ended in the middle of nowhere. You remembered the incantation the young interpreter had told you. The wind quieted, and you could hear water. You walked toward the trickle and followed the flow for many miles. You were utterly alone, lost in the world.

Of those days and nights you remember little, as if you had dreamed them. The animals were familiar, although at times you saw a creature you had never seen before. Most of the trees and plants were similar to what you'd known but somehow not. You trapped game or caught fish. You gathered fruit, bird-pecked, worm-nibbled.

You used the incantation to guide you. Animals and insects caught your eye, and you followed them. Sometimes you misread what revealed itself. You were still learning how to use the power of those words. Once, you felt led to a small hut. Inside, the space was neat and spotless. On a table there was a large wooden bowl filled with dried peas, and a metal pot with a heavy lid. You filled a quarter of the pot with peas. You gathered wood and built a fire in the hearth. You fetched water, then cooked the stolen food. You returned everything as it was, clean. You left a piece of silver for what you had taken.

You made a point of observing the land. You watched the movement of stars, the peel of the moon. You who had lived by maps were without direction in an unknown location. No one knew where you were, if you were alive or dead. Although you thought you should be afraid, you weren't. You felt no concern beyond what you would eat or where you could sleep. There was a peace to the unmooring.

A part of you chanted. I escaped. I escaped!

Then one afternoon, unseen forces brought the two of you back together. You don't know how or why. So much cannot be explained. You almost didn't recognize him, or he, you. He had grown a beard, roughly groomed. His hair was long, with a blunt trim.

Wyl! you shouted.

You ran through ferns and fallen leaves. You watched his expression shift from suspicion to recognition. You jumped on him like a spider and wrapped him within your limbs like prey. You cannot remember whether you kissed him. | why does that still seem to matter? |

There was a task to do. You couldn't linger. Wyl expected the quest to be easier, and you sensed it wouldn't be. You wondered why the young woman had given you the incantation. You weren't certain how it worked, but you'd used the words. It led you to safety more than once, going through instead of around trees. There are links and gaps, said the young interpreter. Notice the trunks of trees. Yes, you would go into their hollows instead of around them. You thought about when you used the incantation. Did you need it for food or shelter? What was happening? You often received what you needed, but how would you find a dragon and hoard?

It was an accident, a test. A mental focus.

Where is the dragon? you thought.

You imagined the creature as best you could. You repeated the incantation quietly inside. Before, you had said it aloud, but then you were alone. You thought Wyl might think you mad. If he didn't, you sensed the words had powers best not exploited. You had been entrusted with them. No matter what you felt for Wyl, you were never thoroughly unguarded. It wasn't that you felt he'd take advantage. You thought it possible he'd share it with someone who would. Someone nefarious like Raef. Or Raef himself. You two were there because of him anyway.

Wyl trusted you because of your work. You were a mapmaker. You had studied a navigable world in miniature, hadn't you? But you followed more than land. You looked to the skies, the stars, the movement of birds.

You were near a glade. You saw a swallow dash over the ground and disappear in the forest. Such a bird preferred open spaces. You were curious. You entered where it had, took several steps, stood still. You heard a buzz at your ear, then looked ahead as a small bright speck whizzed into the gaping hole in a dead tree. Its petrified trunk straddled the ground, hollow through and through. You approached it, then stopped. You called Wyl to follow. Another winged hum, a bee, flew into the hollow, the link.

As you walked into the hole, you entered a gap. You stepped through to the other side. You crossed into the realm. There, the air was light and conductive. Although it wasn't a cold day, the air had an autumn crispness. Had there been an animal to stroke, its fur would have snapped and stood on end. All was vibrant.

The surroundings looked as you might expect given the geography. The trees, the plants, the light. Yet it was different, somehow even more beautiful and alive.

You walked not so long, as long as it takes a good fire to boil a pot of water. The trees edged what you had expected to be another glade, but it wasn't. Beyond the narrow strip of sod was the foot of a mountain. You repeated the incantation in your mind. There was another swallow, a dart at your left, then out of sight. You and Wyl walked in that direction, around the mountain's base. The area smelled of metal, slightly of smoke.

You saw the wide welcoming entrance to a cave. Wyl wished to enter, so you did. The anticipated darkness yielded more to light. The great cavern was filled with objects made of gold, silver, and copper and decorated with jewels, stones, and designs. Vessels, pots, cups, cauldrons, daggers, swords, shields, helmets, rings, necklaces, buckles, bracelets. It was a hoard you couldn't have dreamed or imagined. You both were beyond words among such riches.

You noticed another entrance within. It was a glowing space framed in wood carved in a repetitive pattern. The horizontal timber was inlaid with overlapping circles of gold and silver. The union between them was amethyst. You stared long at the design's simple beauty.

Beyond the threshold was a step. Beyond that step, another. A spiral staircase had been chiseled into the mountain's body. The corridor was a coil of soft light. Whoever had built the place covered the walls and ceiling with reflective metals, crystals, and jewels. You stepped through light hopeful as dawn, calming as candle glow. The space defied reason.

Neither of you complained of the climb. Neither wondered how long it would take or what you might find. You had not seen the size of the mountain, its height or breadth. You had no sense of its enormity or which dimension the staircase builder had chosen to follow.

The air became cooler. A breeze glided past. The light intensified. You squinted. Then there was sky, solid smooth blue. Your head and shoulders pushed into its depth. You emerged on the mountaintop. It was flat in parts, craggy in others. There was a copse of trees, some in fruit, some in bloom. You explored the landscape. Wyl went in one direction, you in the other. You reached the edge first.

What did you see?

You aren't certain.

Sometimes you remember a vast forest fed by the curve of a river. You recall a distant ocean, gentle as sleep, blue green blue green. There, too, was a desert, a broad seamless yellow. And still you ponder a valley that breathed in colors, a lap of flowers, an embrace of blooms. Impossible, all of it. It was one, or nothing. Wasn't it?

Wyl joined you at your side. He smoothed his hand against your head, neck, ended at your back. Neither of you spoke, but your eyes conveyed awe. You stood with him at the top of the spiral, where the world turned from the rupture from which it had sprung.

He led you to an indentation in the rock. The space was lined with moss and straw. The cozy nest of a giant bird, it seemed. Wyl lifted his arm. He held a clear elliptical object with a jagged top and rounded edges. A diagonal crack reached to its center.

A dragon's scale, said he.

You shook your head.

This is its lair.

Your head swung like a plumb. No no, no no.

You were suddenly starving. You picked fruit from the trees. Fruit that you knew grew in different seasons and climates, all ripe at once. You filled a pouch at your hip. You ate a perfect fig as small as your thumb. You remember that. It was the only raw one you had ever eaten.

When you descended and emerged from the cavern, night had come. Still, the wood-framed stair entrance glowed. You were dreaming, you decided. Only a dream. Yet it continued as you drank from a spring near the foot of the mountain, ate the fruit with Wyl under a light-splintered sky, and fell asleep in each other's arms on a cushion of ferns.

You dreamed more that you awoke and found him with the hoard. He cut the space in front of him to shreds with a sword. His movements were graceful, arousing, but not playful.

This is no mere dragon's hoard. It's the store of a great army, said Wyl.

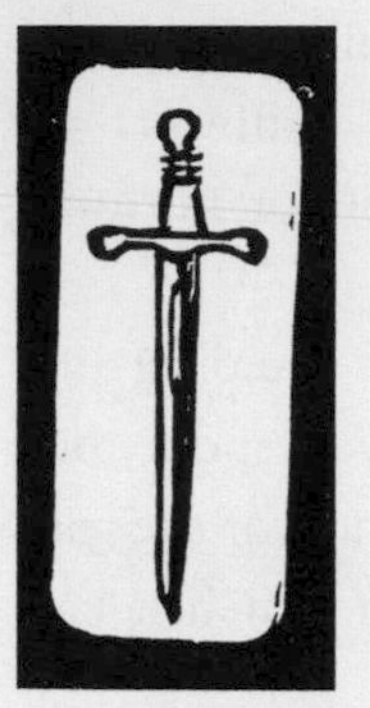

He speculated that the wealth and weaponry were unlike any they could have imagined. He handed the sword to you. It was beautiful, with a balance even you could feel.

There are far more items for domestic use and adornments, you said.

The rest of the weapons must be in use. In hand.

No, perhaps not.

Likely so.

So literal, Wyl.

Good that I am. I must warn my father and our people.

You knew you couldn't reason with him. Not in the state he'd created for himself. He hadn't seen what you had in the settlement. He had not felt what you had. A deep peace that belied this evidence.

A day and a night cycled. The dragon didn't appear, not as you expected. Neither of you knew the habits of such a beast. Where it might go, for how long. You decided to leave. Wyl believed he had his proof. He wanted to take one of the fine daggers but chose not to in the end. The spontaneous thought came that Raef would not have been as honest as his brother.

You were not blameless, however. You wanted to take something, a bracelet or a chalice, but you resisted the gold's lure. A childish part of you wondered whether dragons took tallies of their possessions and sought their stolen treasures. If there were dragons, of course.

The task complete, you departed. Before you left, you turned back to look. What you saw perhaps was not a cloud.

A red fleeting shape.

You left accompanied by a man who was not your relative or husband, your captor or guard.

There you were alone with Wyl. You were more alone than you had ever been or would be again. Your lives before seemed distant, unreal, the rhythm of it jarring. Buttons, buckles, beltings. Walk again in those shoes on that soft forest floor under dappled light. Watch the man stripped of his title, his horse, his responsibilities, his future. Watch him move steadily, sure-footed. Feel that emptiness, the awareness of nothing but the ghost of your name and the pulsebreath of your body.

And his body. Wyl in the flesh.

Oh, you were caught in a timeless place where you both would always be young and firm. Infirmity, impossible.

You weren't ashamed that you found him beautiful and virile. That first time, you had no shame because there was nothing familiar about your life then to be so. Once it was done, it could not be undone. You had. You did.

One morning you woke up without him near your side. You found him and for a moment watched as he bathed in a stream, oblivious. You moved away from the shrubs to the narrow path that deer had trampled to the water. Wyl, lean, strong, bare. What was so long hidden plainly revealed. He glanced toward you. He sensed your stare. | woman, what happened to the impulse to turn your head? | Because you didn't look away and he didn't seek cover, he approached you. You could not believe how fast his blood rose. The air on your skin a caress. His skin on yours a shock. You wanted to bite him, so you did. His neck exposed, a taut tendon. When your forces joined, you laughed. Yes, you laughed, until the human in you became bestial again. Until Wyl's weight released you full to the ground. Until he lay flat at your side, attempted composure, and gave way to a mirthful howl.

You understood each other much better when you weren't speaking.

The twins were conceived in this primal state, when you slept, ate, and moved like animals through forests of staggering beauty.

You were not naïve but you were foolish. Mindless. Seeds need fertile ground. That is all. You thought the vomiting came because you crept ever closer to home.

You told Wyl. He didn't seem surprised. He wasn't angry. He took the announcement as an inevitability, but his response was not predictable. There was no suggestion to find someone to purge your womb. If so, you know you would have faked surprise and horror, then relented with feigned resignation. Of course, this is best, you would have said. There was no offer to place you in a remote part of the kingdom where you and his offspring would live your days in hidden comfort. As for that consideration, Wyl knew better. You were not one to be kept.

No. Wyl proposed. You protested. He was betrothed already. To break the agreement could be disastrous for the alliance with the kingdom of his bride. You gave every political reason you could conjure, each one a consequence Wyl was willing to face. You said you had not intended to become pregnant and didn't expect to marry him.

Now. Tell the truth.

You never said you didn't want to marry him or bear his children. Remember what happened. You told him of the life within. His expression was empty, then he smiled.

You will honor me with a son, said Wyl.

Not a child, no. A son. He spoke out of hope, not preternatural knowledge. You carried this hope. You carried an unborn prince. He touched your belly, and you looked into his eyes. Wyl was happy. You felt powerful, that you could affect him in this way.

Now name it. You wouldn't then.

You also felt guilty.

You, Aoife | who had anything, everything, you ever wanted from him | felt guilty for the life he'd given you because you had given him nothing in return. There was no other favor, gift, or tribute you could give to set the balance right. You had shared your body because you desired his. That was not payment. What came of the union might be.

So, you accepted. Where was your courage? You knew the word No. Instead, you rationalized that Wyl would not restrict you as another husband would. Perhaps you might continue, and eventually complete, the mapping of the kingdom. You might become a tutor for those who wished to learn the craft. Pupils from far and wide. Young men belligerent at first. The indecency done to them to have to study under you. The bad feelings wouldn't last long. You would follow Heydar the mapmaker's example. Fairness, encouragement, guidance. Perhaps, by some turn of fortune, one of the students would be a girl. You would help her. You would help her see the wider world.

Decision made, future set. Still, no peace settled within. You couldn't stop yourself from what you began to do. You knew the act was brutal. Cruel. Desperate. Nevertheless, you beat your abdomen enough to bruise. The excuse for all of this would be gone if the act succeeded. You wondered how something so loosely sown could so tenaciously root. You considered there was a flaw in your being because you felt no warmth toward that which was coming. Wyl did. His sleep-heavy hand pressed sore muscles and guarded what he'd wrought.

Then you returned to the facts of your previous lives still intact. You had been away for a year. That seemed impossible, but that was what they claimed. When you entered your old room in your father's house, all was as you'd left it. No one looked much older, other than the servants' children.

Arrangements began for a celebration of Wyl's successful quest. Before the event, he called your families together. As he wished, he announced you were to marry. Your body did not yet betray the impetus. You saw Mother overjoyed. Father elated. Ciaran confused. Raef dumbfounded. The King and the Queen mute.

This is no royal match! What blood might mix? said the Queen.

You overheard her speak to her ladies-in-waiting. The forced intimacy, the assumed trust. Your fate once married.

The shocking declaration of your betrothal postponed everyone's curiosity about the quest. That did not endure for long. You and Wyl were called to meet with the Council. They wished to hear of the quest before the story was given to the people. The subjects knew Wyl was alive and well, but the custom was they would also see and hear proof of his feat.

Charming Wyl, what a tale he told. The Council hardly breathed as they listened. Such adventure and danger, most of which he had seen but had not experienced. Brave, cautious Wyl, who aided those in need, who used his wits, fists, or weapons all in good time.

You didn't challenge his story. You had no way to confirm or discredit what he had encountered before you'd found him in the forest. He didn't mention the spiral stair or mountaintop view. Neither did you.

Then the disagreement began.

He said he had seen a great hoard filled with the makings of war. There surely was a kingdom nearby with the power and men to fight a long battle, if provoked or inspired to do so. Wyl accounted the spoils. He described the craftsmanship of the weapons. He expressed his awe. He insinuated his dread.

Then you spoke of what lay among the swords and shields, the evidence of peace. Surely these were a people of remarkable skill and quiet times. What you discovered was beautiful beyond brief description. That which was functional | a pot, a cup | appeared strong and durable. They were lovely to regard, comfortable to hold. What was decorative | a buckle, a bracelet | seemed done with exceptional emphasis on beauty.

Did you see the dragon? asked Raef.

Oh, it exists, said Wyl.

From a pocket, he withdrew the prize he had found on the mountaintop. His proof. The object covered his palm and fingers.

A scale from its body, said Wyl.

Murmurs and gasps escaped the Council. You watched them lean forward and in to one another. You had touched what he held. It was a strange flattened thing that felt like a thick fingernail. Or the surface of a horn. You had never seen anything like it.

Did you see it, my brother? asked Raef.

I believe I did. A brief sighting of an enormous haunch and curving tail. Then large wings beat into flight.

Did you see it, Aoife, my soon-to-be sister? asked Raef.

I don't know. The land was strange, with queer movements of light.

Is my brother a liar? asked Raef.

We saw differently. That's all, you said.

You didn't reveal the shadow you'd seen the morning you'd left its realm. Before you followed Wyl into the margin of the trees, you looked back at the valley and mountain. Darkness fell from above like a passing cloud. You expected to see the outline of the white's inverse on the ground. Instead, a shape took form and circled on itself three times, lithe, serpentine, winged. You turned your face skyward to a hint of what you thought you saw. There was only a wafting reddish cloud. The edges were blurred. Its shape was speculative, interpretable. Show yourself, you wanted to shout. You said not a word, not then, not later.

Now you do. Now you can't contain the words.

The Council determined that Wyl had fulfilled the people's chosen feat. Soon enough, a few months later, you would learn Wyl unknowingly obtained curious evidence to corroborate what Prince Raef had seen for himself in the settlement. The beloved welcoming settlement on which he had imposed a visit while you were both away.

So, the next day, in the great hall, the people pressed together like sheep to hear Prince Wyl tell his dragon tale. The story was almost identical to what he'd told the Council. They cheered when he displayed the peculiar scale. You watched a small man spatter himself with ink as he scrawled notes. Later, Wyl's feat would be transcribed into the official chronicle.

Wyl's raised arms bade silence. As planned, he announced your wedding. He reached his hand to you. The heat of embarrassment filled you as the people muttered. Polite applause created its own modest din. He noticed and reddened. He knew they had known of the marriage promised to another. A princess. Even you understood, as well as shared, their confusion.

Wyl continued. He touted the fine service of your father on behalf of his own, the firm loyalty and sound counsel given to the King. For generations, your family had served with honor. The implication. You were good solid stock.

Furthermore, said Wyl, the woman at my hand journeyed at my side. I couldn't have chosen a more valorous, patient, and beautiful wife.

He drew your fingers to his lips and kissed them with affection. The people saw this. As you and Wyl dropped your arms, they clapped and cheered. Hail! Hail! Wyl, beloved prince, smiled and repeated the gesture. However, that time, unseen, his tongue moved against your knuckle. You had a dissonant response. Your viscera received. Your mind recoiled.

You found yourself back under your father's roof until the wedding. Your parents didn't know you felt confined. Certainly, at first, they had no idea of the confinement yet to come.

You had never felt so restless. Long walks in the forest kept you strong and occupied. There was no work to be done, no copying to complete. You realized you missed the company of your crew. At the start and end of each day, there was your mother.

Oh, this marriage will settle you nicely, Aoife. Enough of the men's business. Do as you were meant to now, said she.

To some degree, you did. You yielded to your mother's insistence. You acquiesced to repeat the past. You worked haphazard stitches on some linens. This tradition was the least sufferable. But there was no silence in the effort. Finally, captive listener, you sat as she spewed the woman knowledge for which before you'd had no time or need. Domestic details, daily, monthly, yearly. How to manage servants, guests, children, a husband. That was her hoard, poured out to you. You had no need or want of it.

You had not spent so much concentrated time in her company since you were a child. Then, as now, you were given instructions. She didn't know, in fact had not asked, what you had seen on your journey. The time alone with no demands, no expectations, you were yourself, not her daughter or the King's mapmaker. Aoife, traveler. But had she asked, that wasn't what you would have said. You would have told her so little. How could she understand?

You returned as a shame to her. Vanished! Worried me sick!

Then the announcement you were to marry Wyl. Elation! Oh, happy day!

You endured fittings in silk. She knew, as the seamstress had to pluck the stitches and expand the seams, she knew your secret. Why the limited pageantry. Why Wyl insisted you get your wish for little fanfare.

You stood mute and thought of the southwest border near the sea that you had not yet drawn. There would be less terrain to cover when you arrived. That land Wyl had given up in his exchange for you instead of another king's daughter. How arbitrary, the movement of borders and the acquisition of property. Yet there it was. Wyl assured his father this was no disaster. You were valuable because of your contact with those across the river. You came from a good loyal family.

YOUR FIRST WEDDING DAY. YOU REMEMBER BEING COLD. YOUR BREASTS crested over the bodice. You could not breathe. Despite the week's purgatives, your body fattened and threatened to rupture every stitch.

Wyl wore a dashing long coat. It was dark blue, almost black, embroidered with yellow leaves and trimmed in ermine along every edge. He also wore a simple crown. Gold, of course. He looked happy and handsome, unbearably both.

You exchanged rings and vows. You smiled as the line of guests wished you and your husband well. The feast could have fed a village for a day but stuffed a wedding party for a night. Wyl led you in the traditional dance of which you hardly knew the steps. You managed. Your dress seam gave way at the hip and midback. For the rest of the evening, you kept your right hand pressed below the waist and the veil bunched at your spine.

Each of you bade farewell to the large group who enjoyed endless food and drink. Then you went to the chambers prepared on the castle's second level. Someone had built a fire and tended it well. You heard a latch drop. Wyl stepped away from the door. He looked at you muted in the light of candles and fire. What shall come of this? you thought.

You tried to fill your lungs full and could not. Another seam ripped. A fury spread beyond your skin. You pulled the veil from your head. You kicked your slippers across the room. You grasped the bodice of your gown and ripped it away. Ripped the entire frock from your body. Naked, you were. There had been no room left for undergarments.

Wyl threw his coat on the ample bed. He had stared at you in that way before. This time, he misunderstood your actions.

What talk there will be among the servants. It's true. I cannot wait, said he.

His hands | warm, a mercy | cupped your cheek, a breast.

You glared at him with a passion not for consummation. You gathered the torn gown and threw it into the hearth. You took an iron and stoked the fire until you were certain every fiber would turn to ash.

So literal, Wyl, you said.

You knew your wifely duty. You lifted the bright crown from his chestnut hair, set it aside, and worked his buckle loose.

You enjoyed every moment in spite of yourself.

TELL THE TRUTH.

You wished you had been taught plant lore. That knowledge power you needed but didn't know who to safely ask. When you walked alone in the forest, leaves seemed to reach out. You chewed them and made teas. They tasted of bitter freedom but failed to give release. You no longer hit yourself because of the pain it caused you. No matter the method, you are not the only woman who ever has done or ever will do what you intended. What would have been lost would have seemed routine. Men take so little notice of the spill of women's blood.

Women concerned themselves, though. You noticed how other women reacted when they learned of another losing a child. Miscarriage, stillbirth, any manner of death. They clutched their chests and bellies. Their hands and lips fluttered uncertain as moths. The anguish they felt with the mother. The sincerity of the pain. You would not understand this for many years, until Wei.

The life inside engorged.

You were perplexed by the women who came up to your swollen body. Remove your hands, you wanted to say. Don't touch me. What a blessing, said they. What a blessing? No, you were an animal, you thought, a heatless bitch, ewe, cow, doe. You carry one of your own kind. The conception is nothing. That happens whether chosen or not. It is the persistence of life. One is begotten. One begets.

Beasts easily make more of themselves. Almost effortless.

You felt like a beast, but you weren't simply one. Once you accepted the pregnancy was yours to bear, you did become vigilant. They were to grow. You were to tend them. But you were mystified by other women's joyfulness at your condition. You remembered overhearing, as a girl, their talk of how a young woman would hear a coo one day that would turn her soft and make her want a baby. Such a thing had never happened to you.

In their presence, you felt flawed. Not with guilt but curiosity. You wondered if women lied to each other. So little was allowed them. A home, the people in it. Through generations, out of necessity, complicity transmogrified into desire. Separate the act, the biology, that inevitability. Consider the will, the awareness, that consequence. Where did the true power lie?

Surely you didn't feel as you were supposed to feel. The terrible ambivalence. The dread. Surely you would grow to love the children. Oh, no, you did not wish this to happen, but there it was. A result of your beastliness. You acted with non-sense. If you would have stopped to think, you would not have done what you did. But Wyl was so beautiful.

Somehow, you thought it might be possible, after the birth, to return to mapmaking with the company of a nursemaid. You spoke this aloud to your husband one night.

Are you earnest? Am I to join you? asked Wyl.

You did before.

That was before. You are soon to be a mother, no longer a maiden. Besides, we have what we both wanted now, don't we?

His response, composed, almost mirthful, was clear. For a moment, you thought perhaps Wyl would acquiesce in time. Certainly he wouldn't take that from you for good. He rolled you toward his muscular body. You stiffened under your soft flesh.

Your mapmaking days were numbered, whether you married me or another. A man wants his wife at home where she's safe, said he.

I see, you said.

This is your place now, said Wyl, but it was your mother's voice you heard.

Stay in your place. Take your place. Know your place.

But, Mother, what if my place is not here?

You were once slapped for saying that. Your father's tined hand caught your cheek and raked your mouth bloody.

Boundaries drawn, invisible. The line in the bed you shared with Wyl. One's sphere of influence. The domain of woman, the domain of man. Where a nobleman's holding began and another ended. The kingdom's edge. Your place in the world shrank tight as the skin of your belly. You felt breaths away from bursting. You thought of the freedom you had known, soon to be denied.

Tell the deeper truth.

That was all a ruse, a lie. Your skillful mastery was immaterial. You were only as free as the King had allowed you to be. You made maps for him. Any displeasure or disfavor, that would have been the end. He made an exception but that didn't change the rules. What a fool, to believe yourself beyond such constraints.

For weeks you lay confined with the reasons why you would never be so indulged again.

THOSE WHO COUNTED THE DAYS BETWEEN YOUR UNION AND THE births might have thought you more ewe cow doe than woman. None said a word. Wyl married you after all.

You were unprepared. Never had you cared for an infant or small child. Once, twice, by accident or necessity, you may have held one. Ciaran was older by seven years. There was a dead child before and after you. Spared of sibling supervision, you spent time among other children as a playmate rather than a caretaker. You understood the basics. Mouth to breast, wet hungry cold, swaddle to shift to shirts and dresses. The women claimed a mother knew what to do when the time came.

You had overheard tales of labor full of pain and blood. What you imagined was difficult. What you experienced was violent. Agony. You felt terror when your body took over itself. A mounting relentless rhythm of contractions. No amount of will could stop it once it began. You could have ripped a man in half with your bare hands. You remembered a cow that had bellowed through an awkward birth, her calf a breech. And there you were screaming on a bed covered with straw in unreasonable summer heat. No better than a beast.

Dawn became noon became night.

Then there was the girl. When you heard the midwife declare her to be, an unexpected apology rushed to the back of your tongue. I'm sorry, Wyl. You swallowed the sounds. The sudden anger of your first thought upon hearing of your first daughter's birth stuck in your throat.

An apprentice took the girl, but the pain returned. You both screamed in unison as her brother was born. A prince, a prince, the midwife's herald.

The vessels closed. The two membranes were expelled. The midwife and apprentice peered over the gore. They brought the twins swaddled tight in linen, eyes open. You regarded their smallness. You felt a twinge of pity. So helpless, you thought. So the obligation begins.

With relief, you thought then you were not a monster. Your

instinct wasn't to abandon them. Not at the moment. Not when they mewled like kittens and your breasts weighed heavy in their waiting function.

You were given the option of a wet nurse. She would attend the necessity of their nourishment. You might also preserve your shape. Too late, you thought, when you saw your belly and wondered how it would ever tighten again. Wyl, even before the twins arrived, had no complaints about how your chest had changed.

Wyl did appear to love the children. Even the girl. He would go into the room you shared with a nursemaid and the twins. The place lingered with the smells of vinegar and rosemary. He unswaddled them in turn. The nursemaid was aghast. He held their hands and feet in his palms. He talked to them, about what, you do not know, because he whispered.

Already there are secrets among you, you said.

He smiled, no malice, no hint of conspiracy. Strangely, he didn't hold them, not for any longer than it took to remove them from their crib to your bed. Always gentle, always, but he did not hold them. You didn't think to ask why. Babies, after all, as you witnessed, were women's work.

You soon grew bored with the castle and courtyard. Once your strength returned, you would leave the twins in the nursemaid's care and go into the forest to be alone. You stole moments away from what you had brought upon yourself. You were restless, exhausted, but resigned to their care. The beastly mother returned to her children when her teats began to leak. You would walk in just as their crying became wails.

What a good mother you are. You know when they need you, said the nursemaid.

The Queen saw them on the day of their birth and rarely again in your presence.

Your mother couldn't seem to keep herself away and visited almost daily.

Oh, they will settle you nicely, Aoife. Enough of the men's business and the company of common people. Do as you are meant to now.

You did as you were meant to do, as your mother might well have perceived it. Bared your breasts for the twins, at times for Wyl. He desired you but you lacked it for him. The intensity never returned. You assumed the disinterest was because the twins required constant use of your body. Perhaps you'd made a mistake not taking a wet nurse. However tired you were, your mind could still think. You had no carnal thoughts at all. With enough effort, Wyl could stir sensation without actual pleasure.

YOU BEGAN TO DAYDREAM MORE OFTEN OF THE SETTLEMENT AND HOW peaceful you felt there. You knew nothing of how they lived or how the people related to each other, but you sensed it. You thought of the young man who had led you in and out of the forest and settlement. You'd never met someone like him. He gave you immediate comfort. You weren't afraid of him after he encouraged you to breathe on the way there. He treated you with kindness. You felt it. It perplexed you how you and the cook and Burl the oarsman could all have similar reactions, almost as if you'd been under a spell. You'd learn it was no enchantment.

The events of your experience in the settlement weren't as important as the emotions you had about them. You wanted to live someplace where you could breathe and be. How could you possibly know the Guardians offered this and more? You wouldn't speak of the settlement to Wyl or anyone. Its memory was a refuge. You walked among their roads, stared at the Wheels in the settlement center, waved at the people, content in the quiet.

The daydreams surprised you. You were a woman of action, not reverie. They gave you comfort, however, because in the day-to-day you felt uneasy. You sensed danger.

WYL MENTIONED THERE HAD BEEN MOVEMENT ON THE RIVER TOWARD the settlement's presumed port. You knew as well as he did that a trade road connected to the river on the other side. Activity likely happened all the time without anyone watching. You realized there must be men stationed along your kingdom's bank who hadn't been there before. You asked Wyl why there was such attention on the border.

Raef visited the village when I was on my quest.

How do you know?

He told me.

And?

He found them suspicious.

Of course he did, you thought. You said no more. You knew Raef had some fodder under him after what Wyl said about the hoard.

Then you were called to a secret Council meeting. So were the steward, the oarsman, Raef, and four other men.

Your father presided in his role as the King's most trusted adviser. He said that there was curious activity across the river as of late. The Council wished to speak again to those who'd been to the other side.

First, the steward told the same tale as he had to you and Raef so many seasons before. He handed his piece of the gold road to your father, who passed it among the members.

Burl the oarsman faced the Council next. He clearly didn't wish to be there, although he didn't appear nervous. He answered with polite Yes, sire, No, sire, to the Council's queries. All other responses were terse. Burl kept to the facts. He was asked if he had a last statement, and he did.

I felt as if I'd been to a place where I belonged. That is the manner of their peace, said he.

Then you learned of Raef's visit. He had asked the kingdom's best miller, smith, woodcutter, and farmer to join him. No envoy of guards, no officials of the King, except for himself. The Council asked what they had seen.

The miller said the people used water, not yoked animals, to turn their mills. Beyond the settlement was a tall structure bridging a clear rapid stream. Outside, a giant spoked wheel with paddles dipped into the water. Its movement powered a shaft and gears inside the building. Connected to the mechanism were the millstones which rubbed together to grind the grain. A large bin dropped grain to the stones, and a chute under that led the ground meal to waiting baskets. The miller surmised they produced more grain than the settlement's people could eat.

The smith spoke of a tremendous forge built of stone farther down the stream. He listed the well-crafted tools hung on pegs and lying on tables. There was a blazing fire kept alive with the split logs piled nearby. The smiths were teaching young people that day, two of them girls. In a storage structure there were pieces to be mended or melted and chunks and ingots of metal yet unused.

The woodcutter described a forest with trees larger than he had ever seen. He and his fellow visitors weren't shown vast empty spaces where the wood had been cleared. Sparse areas had been planted with saplings. Where trees were felled, care seemed taken to disturb few others. He mentioned the store of heartwood timbers and firewood.

The farmer told of the black soil that smelled sweet and

crumbled with ease. The vegetable crops were prosperous, the orchards well tended, the grain fields full. The oxen grazed nearby, the sheep and goats not far. Even within the settlement, fruits, herbs, and vetches grew near the dwellings.

The men all agreed that they had been treated most graciously.

Raef addressed the Council. He affirmed what the four men said they had seen and how they'd been hosted. He stated that while the miller, the smith, the woodcutter, and the farmer visited with others of their respective trades, he visited within the settlement. Through the course of the day, Raef noted they possessed cloth, furs, leather, and jewelry as fine as any he'd ever seen. The people adorned themselves with these items. They claimed to make and grow most of what they had, and traded on occasion. The elder hosts, a man and a woman, said their people wished to live in harmony with each other and with that which surrounded them. Raef said he found their wealth and behavior odd. They were a rich people, although he couldn't discern who owned it all. No one would confess or confirm.

Then you spoke. In all the reigns of your people's kings, never once had there been a confrontation with those across the river. You took them at their word that they wanted peace. You noted they carried no weapons, not even the Guardians on the border.

You risked a conjecture of your own.

You said your long-ago visit to them resulted in knowledge of a dragon's treasure. The people chose its discovery as your husband's quest. You chose to follow to learn for yourself. What Wyl and you saw confirmed that a hoard existed. However, not one among you knew what the treasure suggested or represented. It was so far away that it would be impractical and difficult to move its stores. For all each of you knew, it might be the spoils of a lost civilization or the repository of a great one. Regardless, you thought it reasonable to leave the stores alone.

My brother showed me the amulet he carried on his quest.

How interesting its image was the same as the one on the lovely interpreter's pendant. This symbol must give mysterious entry, said Raef.

How can you be sure? you asked.

There is no other explanation, said he.

You could think of several but said nothing. You wanted to ask the obvious but held your tongue. Was there intent to strike the settlement? You knew the answer somehow. You received it when you watched Raef's eyes narrow.

We know of their treasure now. They will want to protect—or move—it, said Raef.

He looked at his father when he spoke. The King tapped his fingers together. The Council muttered among themselves. Your father asked Wyl his opinion. Wyl said that he noticed a similar design on the amulet and some of the hoard's objects. This, to him, meant there was an undeniable connection. However curious that may be, it was not necessarily cause for alarm.

Well, then, we shall wait and see, said the King.

Raef's expression collapsed into an angry pout. He looked at his father and brother, then at you.

You dared to look at him. You expected to meet him with disdain. A jolt flashed through your limbs. The darkness in his eyes you understood. You felt what he felt in that moment, although you couldn't name it. The recognition frightened you. You closed your lids against it. When you looked at him again, he sneered and walked away. You turned to watch the other men, unnerved.

You liked the King, to tell the truth. For a man of his position, he was a pragmatic, decent fellow. You recalled what he had said when you thanked him, years before, when he ordained your apprenticeship. His reply: This is a boon for the kingdom. It is practical to train you, unusual as it may be. That you may enjoy it is a stroke of luck.

Wyl remained on the Council's dais while Raef kept his

distance. No one urged the younger prince to join the conversation.

You understood quite well, even then, that the event was rooted in something other than concern for the kingdom's safety. There was, of course, mere greed for the riches seen and assumed. You sensed another greed, and it was Raef's alone. He was constantly ignored or set aside in Wyl's favor and opinion. Wyl was the firstborn son, in line for the throne. What else need be said? The younger prince vied for attention, for recognition, and received little. You had no affection for Raef. His meanness disturbed you. But nevertheless, you had some pity for him.

You knew that you and Burl felt protective of the people you'd met. When the steward told his story, you realized his interest was self-preservation. He wanted to protect himself, and to him, telling the story of what he had seen was a cooperative act. He wished to appease those in power. The steward had little, but even that was too much to lose.

WYL TOLD YOU SOME OF WHAT HE AND HIS BROTHER HAD SAID PRIvately. This was how you knew Raef intended to push for confrontation. Perhaps an invasion. There were comments about what Wyl had given up of the kingdom for you, now less territory, fewer resources. Raef understood that more land meant more wealth. That meant more men granted favor to tend, till, tax the land, more men beholden to him. It was a twisted logic, you thought. It wasn't danger but greed and neglect that fueled Raef, his influence stirring Wyl.

You pointed out with stark plainness that a river separated the kingdom from the distant settlement. If he feared unrest, place guards along the bank. No reason to cross. It was a natural barrier, wide at parts. But Raef twisted him, twisted his goodness. He told Wyl he had children, an heir. He would have the domain over many children. Protect us, Wyl. Tell Father to protect us.

When you could see that Wyl was losing his discernment, that his goodness was about to be turned, you decided to warn the Guardians. You regretted the circumstances, but not the reason, for crossing the river again.

You knew you must travel by yourself. You required a direct route, safe shelter, and kindly hosts. You entered the castle archives, where your life's work was kept under guard. Beneath candlelight, you reviewed the maps. You had drawn memory traces of your travels on the parchments, where you'd been fed honey cakes and savory pies and told wondrous tales. You sketched an alternate path, where no one would know how to follow.

Of course, first, you offered to serve as an envoy. Under cover comfort, in pillow talks, you suggested this to Wyl. It was reasonable to meet with them. They had an excellent interpreter. He stroked your hair, your hands. Don't worry yourself, said he.

Then you thought to tell a ruse. Tell Wyl you had a childhood friend who lived away. She, too, had babies. You would so like to visit her. You'll miss him. You don't know how long you will be gone. Not long. You'll take your nursemaid. But you couldn't bring yourself to do it. This wasn't easy to arrange. This was like planning an escape. A cart, a driver, a good horse. Maps to direct the way. Then what would you do when you reached the border?

You decided to go alone. Then you changed your mind and decided to take the twins. They were still small, breast-fed. You weren't certain they'd accept strange milk. You couldn't justify the risk they would go hungry.

Since they were newborns, the girl and the boy traveled well in the pouches you stitched to a cloak's back. A trotting horse bounced them to silence. In the forest, you would leave them sleeping in a shelter under a bush. You hid them as any wild mother would hide her young. For hours you would sit, sometimes blank, sometimes in thought. Sometimes a child again watching a spider build its web. How did it know to do that? When the twins were awake, you let them roll around naked on a clean cloth. When they soiled, you rinsed them in a stream and held them at arm's length to feel the water's full flow.

You were attentive to their creature needs. Still you knew you didn't love them, not as a mother should. Duty is not love. You had the strange thought it was your responsibility to bear them but not to raise them. The latter was not necessary, in fact. A nursemaid could take over their full care once they no longer required your body for nourishment. Your mother had been tended by a nursemaid from infancy through childhood. I hardly remember my mother, said your mother. Her mother, so often cautious and quiet, would babble and sing to herself when strained. Then she would be sent away on respites. Your mother was told that she and her siblings were nerve-wracking handfuls and their mother had to leave to rest.

You knew your disappearance would worry Wyl and everyone else. You intended to be as quick as possible. There seemed no other way. Unfortunate that you couldn't be direct. You believed Raef, even Wyl, would have found a way to stop you from going. Pathetic that you had to resort to lies and manipulation, but there it was. The world seemed built on lies and manipulation.

One autumn morning, you kissed Wyl awake in his bed. The twins were in their pouches on your back. He sat up, spun you around, and spoke to his babbling children. Then, as you had before, you left for the day with saddlebags filled with food. You rode like a shadow, a gray figure on a gray horse, steady as mist, fleeting as a phantom.

On the first night, you stayed with an old woman. You had met her years earlier when you were somehow turned around in the forest and lost your way. She found you, took you in. You were not lost this time. Again, she fed you, and told you a rhyme different from one she shared before. In her strange accent, said she:

What is for dinner, my woman, my wife?
Tender stew of the stag you slew
With bread and ale and honey cakes
What of the wider world, my man, my mate?
Peace abides where all reside
Which leads to the pleasures of life

What is for dinner, my woman, my wife?
Hearty stew of the beans I grew
While our new babe turned on its stalk
What of the wider world, my man, my mate?
Unrest in the distant west
Far from the cry of our young boy

What is for dinner, my woman, my wife?
Thick stew of the sweet lamb we knew
The one our child begged to be spared
What of the wider world, my man, my mate?
Some discord with the threat of swords
Not near your round belly or bed

What is for dinner, my woman, my wife?
Plain stew of large birds that once flew
Until arrowed through by our son
What of the wider world, my man, my mate?
The drum of war strikes no man numb
Though our frozen unborn are late

What is for dinner, my woman, my wife?
Tender stew of our son so true

Who would not be fed to others
What of the wider world, my man, my mate?
The ground is red, new peace is found
Warm my blood again, now with love

A dark quiet followed her words. You thought of the traveler you had met on the quest, the tale she'd told of the orphan seer and the prince. You couldn't deny the presence of a warning.

The next morning, the old woman prepared breakfast while you nursed the twins. Her back was turned. She adjusted her shawl. It was made of thin-spun blue wool. Blue, again and again.

Tell me, where's the hollow tree near your hut? I didn't bring my map to find it, you said.

You remembered no tree. You guessed she would understand. Hoped. You hoped there was a way out near the river.

A sturdy one stands like a man with wide legs where the sun doesn't cross. She pointed north.

Alive or dead? Hollowing, or hollow through? you asked.

She faced you with a smile in her eyes. He leafs, so he lives, but appears aflame as he dies for winter. I will take you there, but the horse must stay. She cannot pass.

You trusted your steed to her care. She refused payment. She led you to the tree and wished you a safe journey. When she walked from your sight, you whispered the incantation. A mouse ran across your toes and into the gap. You followed with the twins on your back.

In moments, you were miles away. You reached the kingdom's river border. You found Burl the oarsman. As he took you and your children over the water, you told him your secret purpose. As he helped you from the little boat on the opposite shore, he asked if he might escort you on land. His eyes were wet with more than the sting of the cold. You held the knots of his knuckles in your hands.

I must go alone, and no one can know, you said.

May I, my lady, ask for a simple story on your return? asked Burl.

Such a small reward for your confidence, you said.

Gold spent is gone. A tale can be told again, said he.

You and Burl looked up the bank and saw the line of five in blue coats. You and Burl raised your arms in greeting. The five returned the gesture. The third approached, not the same young man whom you had met before. You explained in plain language why you stood on that ground. You couldn't tell if he understood your words as he watched your eyes. He told Burl to stay, sent a man ahead, and instructed the rest to keep the bank.

Come, friend, said the guardian.

You walked the same path as before. At the large rock, you watched him touch the impression in its surface. You did the same.

When you reached the honeycomb road, the same young interpreter stood in wait. Behind you, the gold glow rose with hearth smoke. Again, you walked past the dwellings and noticed many people outside in the morning sun in all manner of activity. You entered the center of the settlement, where children balanced and leapt on the tree-limb shadows.

The strange mechanism made of wheels released a sharp ping. The children rushed to surround it. Music played. You could not believe your ears. It's the sound of bells. No, icicles. No. The twinkle of stars, you thought. The smallest children circled around the Wheels and turned wide eyes toward the top. Some twittered to each other. Some clutched their hands at their chests. Most of them sang the melody beginning to end. Then, in a rush of chimes, the great round wheel at its front finished its cycle and up popped a swan, crafted in copper. The children cheered.

Splendid swan! said the Interpreter. She touched the heads of the children within her reach.

Does this happen every day? you asked.

The music, yes. A smith places a new creature each morning. We never know what it'll be.

Why is it here?

For the children's pleasure.

You felt dozens of questions tangle in your throat. Instead of speaking, you followed the Interpreter to a guest room in the building where you had the first visit. You smelled pine. There was a clay vase filled with evergreen sprigs and dried flowers on a low table. Next to it was a wide bed on the floor. No crib was in the room. A young man and a young woman arrived with food and drink. They also took the twins. The children had been fussy most of the day. Each sighed as they lay their tiny heads on the young people's shoulders.

The Interpreter escorted you to the same place where you'd met the elders during your first visit. Inside were nine people. Five women, four men. Two were the ones you had met before. You told them all you could. The tale of the former cook, the quest, the hoard, the scale, what Raef wished to instigate. You believed the people of the settlement meant no harm. You wanted to warn them of the misunderstanding. The danger.

They asked questions. Why do you believe this may occur? What do you think they hope to gain? What if you are mistaken? What if you are not? What might do they possess?

You answered as truthfully as you were able. They thanked you for bringing the matter to their attention. They weren't surprised that you had gone to find the truth about the dragon and its treasure. Such curiosity is reasonable, said an elder woman. They all nodded. One man winked, one eye, then the other. You hadn't seen the creature, but you sensed it. The shadow of doubt was not quite so long.

You were invited to share a meal that evening with the Interpreter and a family. You went to your room to feed the hungry twins. The young woman who watched them left. The Interpreter offered you rest in a deep bath. You were curious, and dirty, and accepted. She left to give word to those who tended the bath. As you finished nursing the babies, the young man you had met earlier returned. He spoke your language in fractures but made it clear he was there to watch the twins. You felt an impulse to protest. A man, alone, with infants? Then your son squawked brightly at the sight of him. The young guardian lifted the boy to his shoulder and sat next to your daughter. He smiled at you. You smiled in return, comforted. You wondered how you could so easily trust them.

The Interpreter led you to the bath. No shallow tub on the ground in the house where you were to sleep. No, this was in a separate dwelling. Outside, someone tended a fire under a huge cauldron that had a pipe connected to it. The pipe entered a wall. Inside, a huge copper trough, beautifully decorated. You were shown how to use the clever knobs that started and blocked the water's flow. The tub filled. You stretched the length of your body with room past your toes. The luxury. You had not felt that since you were a little child.

Memory merged with the steam. You recalled your mother washing your hair as you sat curled in a Z. You were three, four. Milk and egg and your mother's squat fingers running through your hair. The fire ahead. Mother loved to wash and brush your hair. She was gentle. You were her daughter then.

There in the bath, you were alone. A small fire blazed nearby. Large candles burned and sweetened the steamed air. Bottles of thick liquids were at your hand. You marveled at the object that absorbed water and felt soft on your skin. Later, you would ask and be told it was a sea sponge. No one hurried you. No one called or knocked. You lingered until the water began to chill. Linen cloths for drying were stacked within arm's reach. You rubbed the water from your hair and skin. For a long while, you sat naked before the fire. A moment in your own skin. Then, from the clean garments left on a chair, you chose a fresh green wool dress. You left the shirt and leggings you'd worn for two days and nights.

You returned to the guest room rejuvenated. The young man sat on the ground with the twins on a thick blanket. They played with soft toys. You sat on the bed and wondered how much room a person needed to call her own. A space wide enough for your thoughts, you thought, with a few feet to spare past outstretched fingers and toes.

The mirror on the table drew your attention. Your mirrors were made of polished bronze and copper. This one was a flat black oval. Obsidian. You beheld yourself in that dark reflection as if you had seen the image before. A shadow, a dream, a memory. You didn't know. You whispered, as if you knew what it meant, the darkness in the light.

The meal with the family was simple but delicious. Fish, bread, greens, apples. They asked questions about your kingdom and customs. The Interpreter translated for the adults and the older boy, but not for the girl, who remained quiet. She looked at you with calm violet eyes. The same color as the Interpreter's.

We don't look alike except for our eyes, said the girl.

She spoke your language. You realized at that moment she was the child who had told your cook the tale of the dragon and hoard.

There is a reason why, said the girl.

What is it? you asked.

I'm a Voice just like she.

The girl danced a doll across her knees. She explained that they were different from most others. The Interpreter lived with them to teach her special lessons. They could understand things other people didn't. Words and feelings. Sometimes secrets and stories.

Such as the dragon? you asked.

Her name is Egnis, said she.

The next words were in her mother tongue. You asked what was spoken.

She wanted to know why the ones born away never know that, said the Interpreter.

Why, then?

It is forgotten or disbelieved.

You shared the story the former cook claimed the girl had told him. You chose not to mention the coiled shadow and the winged cloud you saw near the mountain. Between thoughts, you remembered a storyteller at a festival when you were small. A dragon puppet with a long tail. The desire to believe in such a mythic creature was equal to the fear that it might exist.

The Interpreter said the girl's tale was accurate. One so young couldn't convey the subtleties, however. That required a deeper mind. She spoke to the family, who then nodded in response. They took your hands and kissed your cheeks. The older child, who didn't resemble his parents at all, and the little girl were led to bed.

So you settled on cushions near the young woman with violet eyes. The Interpreter, a Voice. You were brought your children, who suckled, then slept. She told you the myths of how the world and its witnesses came into being. Egnis the Red Dragon. Ingot the Gold Dwarf. Incant the White Wisp. Azul the Orphan, whom they'd saved.

It's quite simple, Aoife, said the Voice. The Three cared for Azul, our people came from Azul, and now we care for them. We are linked to Egnis, she who first saw the world. We protect her from forces that wish to rob, exploit, or destroy. The hoard you saw? That's a store of gifts made by the hands of many generations meant for renewal but not for use. Despite its appearance, that's not the treasure she holds and we, the Guardians, attend.

She told you the Voices are mysteries, a gift from Egnis as much as Azul. Her people believed that they tapped into the well of All That Is. As if Nature willed it, they seemed to be born when they were needed. They could speak any language of human tongues. All had highly sensitive feelings. Each had a gift for healing, some stronger than others. Nearly all of them were girls. A rare boy might be born a Voice, but his gifts were weak in comparison.

She expressed concern for the ones born away to families without knowledge of their Guardian blood. Now and then their young people moved to seek different lives in the world. Usually they returned, but sometimes they didn't. Within a few generations, the descendants of those who had left had no knowledge of their origins. Voices born in these circumstances would have no one to guide them. The children would be thought incorrigible and strange at best, deranged, perhaps evil, at worst. Patience and careful training was in order. That was why an adult Voice helped a family with their remarkable child. The Interpreter understood what the girl would endure.

Part of you felt you were in the midst of madness. Part of you knew better.

You went to bed. The twins slept all night next to you. For a moment when you awoke, you were confused about where you were. That was the first night in many you'd slept well, deeply.

You decided to leave early. You nursed the children and ate a breakfast of porridge, nuts, and fruit. Someone prepared a package of food for you. She or he couldn't have known the meal was what you had prepared for your childhood expeditions. Hard cheese, soft bread.

The Interpreter, rather the Voice, arrived to send you off. She kissed the twins cozy in the pouches. You took a drink from the well. The great Wheels, unwound, were silent. You wished you could hear the music.

The breeze changed. You heard human voices blended together. You walked to find the sound. The Voice followed. What is that?

You saw a little house surrounded by people of all ages, men and women, children, a circle of them, all singing. The door was closed but the windows were not shuttered. Beautiful enchanted sound.

What is happening? you asked.

A child is to be born. This is a song of welcome.

You burst into tears. A rupture of awe, the beauty too much to hold in your body. The Voice gently touched your shoulder. You stopped crying as quickly as you had started. You asked how to return to the river.

She told your guardian to lead you a different way. At the large rock in the forest, he touched the groove. He turned in a direction perpendicular to the path that led to the river. You came upon a hut built within a small glade. The door had a blue circle painted on its surface. An old woman greeted you at the threshold. The young man spoke to her. She beckoned you inside.

She took a poker and tapped a stone that lay beyond the hearth's fire. A chiseled design on the stone was the same as that on the Voice's amulet and on the one given to you. Circle, triangle, square.

Safe, said she. She struck the symbol and pointed at herself.

Many, said she. She lifted the poker and swept an arc in front of her, back and forth. She looked beyond the curve.

Follow, said she. She placed the poker's tip at one angle of the carved triangle. From that point, she scratched a line into the dirt floor. On the ground she drew the symbol enclosed in the shape of a hut. She stabbed the drawn triangle and scraped a thick line through one of its angles.

You pondered her simple words and gestures. You thought of kind old women you'd found all alone, deep in the woods. Not all were like she. Some were. Certainly those who wore that color blue.

Thank you, you said. On impulse, you took the woman's hands and kissed her cheek. You sensed what you had learned was more valuable than gold.

Burl was at the bank when you arrived. His trustworthiness had been tested again. He rowed you back to the kingdom's shore. You told him of your meeting with the elders, the evening meal, and the coming child's welcome song. He looked at you with wonderment. As you disembarked, Burl said he'd been questioned the night before by men representing the King. He had returned home after he'd left you, to avoid suspicion. He claimed not to have seen you.

In fact, you'd given little mind to what awaited you when you reached the castle. You thought to linger in the forest by the bank to decide what to say. Instead, you used the incantation again and crossed the miles as if they were feet. You claimed your horse from the old woman. | her hearth bore the symbol | You made your return home. Such a long distance in so brief a time. Once everyone learned where you had gone, you imagined some would wonder how you managed a journey with no sleep.

NO POINT TO LIE. NO POINT TO SAY YOU'D BEEN LOST. WHO WOULD BElieve it? You had mapped the lands yourself. You admitted what you'd done, certain in the rightness of your effort. The settlement now knew the threat that loomed.

The parade of the aghast began.

First, Wyl. He was furious but more so relieved. He appeared to care less about what you had done than about the fact that you'd taken the twins. He grabbed the children from you with his own hands and marched to his chamber.

They are mine, you know. My issue—and my heir! said he.

Next, your mother, livid. What possessed you? You had us worried sick! Your place is here with these children. What business is this of yours? No, your father didn't listen to me all those years ago. Let you do as you pleased. And this is the result!

Then Ciaran. He controlled his anger. He admonished you for your disregard for protocol. In the years that had passed, he had garnered respect and power among the nobles. He was a fair man who honored the rules. He was also your brother, and that was why his ire was tempered by curiosity. He knew you wouldn't do such a thing unless there was a good reason. No, no one would call you impulsive except for Wyl, for certain reasons.

You told your older brother how lovely it was in the settlement. The people were kind and gracious. You couldn't explain why you felt so peaceful there, but you did. Some of the people you spoke to claimed they did protect a dragon and its hoard. You had seen the latter for yourself. It was unimaginable but real nonetheless.

Then. Yes. You realized Raef's deepest motive.

The settlement and its perceived threat were one matter. The possible entry to the realm of the hoard was another. Raef believed Wyl and you had seen this great treasure store. You felt a sinister chill through your body, as if you'd learned of a murderous plan.

You looked your brother in the eye.

Raef and his loyal brutes will try to find it. It's meant to be known, but also meant to be hidden, you said.

Do you believe the beast exists? asked Ciaran.

Yes. I do now, you said.

He was quiet. Ciaran's skepticism was reasonable and expected. He liked tallies and tangible proof. You assured him that you had seen a place of astounding beauty. You saw what couldn't be explained. What you saw defied sense, no matter the tales you and he had heard as children.

Wyl now claims to have seen the dragon, said your brother.

I cannot confirm or refute that, you said.

In the coming days, that's not the main concern. There are real and present issues to address, said Ciaran.

He looked old beyond his years in that moment.

Your father never made an appearance. You saw him in passing but he made no acknowledgment that he had seen you. You shared a bond of shame. His of you and the trouble you caused him. Yours of yourself, for no clear reason why.

WYL CAME TO YOUR BED THE NIGHT OF YOUR RETURN. WHAT OTHER appeasement could you have given him then? You passed several nights like that. A time of suspense. There were meetings, many meetings. Some to which you were invited. The rest into which you stormed.

Why are you here again?

Yes, yes, we've heard this before.

Can you not control your own daughter?

We have a matter of security. This is not your place.

Drivel. Insanity. Raef at the center of it.

No one listened to you when you said the hoard was not a war chest. Your thoughts and opinions were ignored. They had no sway, although you believed words had power. You wondered, if there were no words, could battle be? How would one plan a siege or strategy without them? What kind of war could happen in the midst of silence?

The King fell ill, then dead.

Who knows the cause? Who knows the truth? Such things have happened to other sons and fathers.

The Queen, in grief, watched her favorite son crowned as King. Your husband.

Unlike his dispassionate father, Wyl was more easily persuaded. Council advisers warned against waiting. Raef reminded him of the wealth and weapons they had both seen. You tried to argue with Wyl. You tried to find allies. Desperate, you turned to the widowed Queen with hopes she could still reach the gentle side of her son.

No use. The Queen had made up her mind.

Think of the children, said the Queen.

Whose children? you asked.

The kingdom's children. It is our duty to protect them.

They're in no danger, Your Majesty.

Then why would my sons lie?

Intractable. Hopeless. You and Wyl had seen the dragon's lair. Both claimed to see different sights of the same thing. You and Raef had been to the settlement. Again, one place, two witnesses.

As a mother, who would you choose to believe? Who would you choose to protect?

Yet there again was the horrible flaw. You, too, were a mother, yet you were unsure whether you could have such a blind allegiance to a child. Would you know if your child lied? Not the tiny lies. I finished my peas. I didn't break the cup. The bigger lies, even the ones unspoken, the lies children might tell to themselves. But this matter of Raef and Wyl was one most mothers would never confront, wasn't it?

THE MIDDLE OF THE NIGHT. FOR EFFECT, OF COURSE. THERE WERE MANY ways to do what was to be done. But Raef was unsettled. You were still uncertain whether Wyl knew the entire plan.

Two men dragged you through the castle. A guard was next to you during a ride in a cart. For all you know, they rode you around the castle several times, then went to a nearby house. You were locked inside.

They did let you keep the children. They were not yet weaned. A woman you didn't know was sent to tend to their care and to some extent your own. She cleaned the chamber pots. She bathed the twins. There were bars on the windows. A tremendous bobbin and latch on the door. The noise of its mechanism like a giant foot-step.

Raef arrived the next morning. He ordered you to make a map to the hoard.

What if I refuse?

I'll kill one of them. The girl.

Of course, you thought. Never mind the child was his niece. Raef's own blood through his brother. He thought he played upon your mother horror. At the moment, perhaps he did. You felt your body move without thoughtful volition. Your back to the twins. Your body between them and Raef.

How will you know I've given you an accurate map? you asked.

I have my ways, said he.

Do you?

I know you take pride in your work's precision. You wouldn't risk your reputation.

I'm glad to know of my esteem.

Raef glared at you.

Remember as well that my brother traveled the route. He will see the chart when it's complete and decide what to do with you, said he.

Of course, you could have refused to make the map. Had you been merely asked, you would have declined. Now you were trapped. To refuse meant imprisonment or death. Within, the answer emerged. You chose the unknown without knowing why.

Make a list of what you require for this task, said Raef.

You asked for your drawing tools. You also requested maps of the whole known world. The works of charlatans and fools, the works of genius. Some you knew were no more than conjecture. None you had drawn yourself.

You required translated tomes on great travels from the castle library. The authors needed to be ones with keen eyes who described creatures and plants. Also, you needed illustrated references on birds and beasts, flowers and trees. The natural world was one, but all was not the same.

As you studied and compared, you thought of the old mapmaker. One of your first tests had been the most important.

Take these maps and merge them into one, Heydar had said.

You glanced at them, unsure where to begin.

Adept, what point do they have in common? you asked.

He pressed his fingertip to a mark on each chart.

And, Adept, what is the orientation? What is the scale? Shall I draw distance only? Must I account for the world's curve?

These considerations you had learned before your place in the apprentice's seat was held by hope. You were grateful to Ciaran, who had slipped materials from the castle's archive for you to study.

I throw out most of my pupils straightaway. They don't understand the basic concepts. This is not simple geometry! said he.

No, Adept, it's not, you said.

Work, Apprentice. Let me see what you can do.

He smiled, a feral yet friendly one.

Now, as a prisoner, you reviewed the old maps. You considered that some boundaries had changed. With time, land altered. Nature moved rivers and shores. Man cleared new paths and built places to live. You had to approximate. It was the best you could do with knowledge of geography, flora, and fauna.

You thought of the expectations. They would want the towns and villages where they could rest, eat, and make merry along the way. They would need that which didn't move easily. Hills, mountains, lakes. You knew you would give what they wanted and what they couldn't see.

The drafting began.

During this time, the twins weaned themselves. You had been feeding them the milk of fear. It could not have been nourishing. You were replaced by a goat and soft foods. They liked the textures.

They grew as all babies did. The girl had her likes. The boy had his. They were very much their own little beings.

Wyl went to you. He couldn't stay away because, you believed, he didn't honestly think what you had done was wrong. But it was all too late. He informed you that the confrontation had begun. Confrontation. The word was meant to tame the truth. You shook your head. You hoped the Guardians had considered your words earnest.

This is for our own good, said he.

Is it, Wyl?

The woman suddenly entered after an outing with the twins. One in each arm. When they saw Wyl, their arms flung out. They smiled. They knew their father. He greeted them. The woman put them on the floor. They pulled themselves up and hung on his legs. The boy bounced at his knees. The girl patted his thigh. Their open affection surprised you. The woman left with clothing to wash.

You continued.

There are fathers who will never do again what you're doing right now. Men who will never return home. Why?

Your place is not to question, said he.

You knew what he meant. The implication was that you were unable to comprehend the complexity of the wider world.

Then what is it?

Swords have been brought back from the battle. I've seen them. They resemble what was in the hoard. This is right action, said he.

He kissed his children. You could tell in his eyes he wanted to touch you. He didn't. He kept his arms at his side. It was a complicated moment. You never thought Wyl was capable of what he had helped to set in motion. What he, as King, had ordered.

Raef came in to see your progress. His presence was intended to frighten you. To some degree, it did. He seemed volatile and moody. Unstable. His eyes were blank and glistening. You wondered if he would slit your throat right in front of the children. But he did not. He looked at what you had done since his last visit. He said nothing of what would come of you after you were finished. You didn't ask. He patted the twins on the head like dogs, then left.

You feared for your life. However, in your most secret moments in the darkness of night, you didn't fear death. Perhaps it would be preferable to what you imagined. Confinement of many forms.

You pondered escape. Who wouldn't? There was no way to dig under the foundation of the walls. There was no way to take the bars from the windows. You couldn't stack furniture to climb through the roof. Even if you could have, the house was tended by two guards at all hours. You knew they both stood at the door when the woman went in and out. Prisoners are safe on the inside. One doesn't know the lay of the land outside. You thought perhaps of running through the door, knocking down the woman, the babies. The surprise might be enough to startle the guards so that you may run. You thought it might be worth the risk of death.

There were the twins to consider, and not consider. Your primal tenderness made you protective of them. You didn't want to see them in harm's way. The desire you had for the life you'd had before didn't let you ponder taking them with you. Wyl and tradition would never allow it anyway. They were his. His son, the prince, would be King.

You had no idea what awaited you once the map was complete. Wyl had defied custom to marry you. There was no way he could be so outrageous again. You expected death and hoped for exile.

One day, you idled. You glanced at the spider that lived between the legs of the table. Its egg sac would split wide and spill soon. The quill's nib left overlapped circles on a scrap. You inked the shapes. You remembered such a sketch from your childhood. The circles were marked deer, squirrels, birds, bees, ants. It was a conjunction, and a conjecture, of shared space. As a girl, you saw the places where they met. As an adult, you saw the same places as voids. The intersections as keyholes, punctures, gaps.

The incantation, the response of Nature, your crouch into hollow trees. You arrived closer to your destinations than was chronologically or geographically possible. You didn't claim to understand what occurred, only accepted that it did.

At first, when you reached the dragon's realm, you thought you had traveled far enough. The location seemed a tremendous distance from the kingdom. Yet in your journey you had used the incantation. You went where you were led. You experienced the gap between the seen and the unseen. Simply because you couldn't explain it didn't mean it wasn't there.

Wyl thought the amulet gave him access to the realm. Protection was what it offered, you realized. Those he met along the roads didn't lie when he asked for direction. They pointed his way, but no one explained how to get there. He might have wandered for ages or died if you hadn't brought you both through. His path had converged with yours. You led the rest of the way. Perhaps it was possible to stumble upon a gap. You had doubts by the time you sat in that hut under guard.

By then, you knew you were mapping a lie.

Yes, the sun rose and set in the same locations. The stars changed their predictable places. You had not met an ocean, though the wind carried its salt. You had not crossed a desert, but suspected one was near. Somehow, you had noticed the flyways of migrating birds, left to right of the rising sun.

A literal map would lead to the destination but would not assure entry.

The bobbin and latch clattered. The door opened, its frame full, for an instant, of a shape that had once pleased you. For a moment, you forgot and smiled at Wyl your lover. Then you remembered Wyl your husband. He had arrived to visit again as you were finishing the task. He caressed his children's cheeks | they resembled him | and sent them out with the woman.

He told you the settlement had been vacated. The residents were dead or in exile. The King's men, his men, had taken control.

Well that they did, because the smithy and its materials revealed their strength. Quantities of iron, tin, and copper were found. A store of metals enough to make swords for an army, although there were no mines nearby, said he.

They don't make swords. They make cauldrons, you said. | you saw them, those cauldrons |

Then he spoke of expansion, the need for more. The population was growing. There was trouble in the fields in much of the kingdom. Crop failures, fungus. You wondered when those matters had become dire. The information was new to you. You questioned its source and validity.

Is this part of the justification now? you asked.

Would you see our people suffer?

You laughed. I traversed miles of this kingdom and saw pockets of plenty in the midst of want. Year after year, the same. How is now any different? you said.

I've been assured it is, said he.

You had not the strength or recent facts to argue.

What's to come of me, Wyl? I'm rumored a traitor to the kingdom. I have been forced, under intimidation, to create this map. And I know I can no longer be your wife.

He dropped his head. When he looked up, tears glazed his eyes. You realized he hadn't admitted the truth to himself.

I don't know what to do. There's pressure to make a decision soon, said he.

There is talk of execution, isn't there? you said.

I will not agree to that. You're the mother of my children, no matter the circumstances.

That leaves imprisonment or exile.

Wyl remained silent.

At least promise you won't allow Raef to harm the twins. Don't punish me with them. They are innocent, you said.

He seemed shocked. You knew then he had no idea what threats had been spoken or the depths of his brother's darkness. You wondered what power was truly his at all.

YOU FINISHED THE MAP. YOU PLACED A LARGE *X* WHERE ENTRY TO THE realm might be. You drew a swallow in the lower space between the lines. The bird was the second-to-last creature you had seen before you walked through the hollow. This notation was typical for you. The map was populated with animals here and there. It was your signature. You marked all of your maps with the presence of beasts.

The latch moved up. The bobbin came down. She is done, said the woman to the guards. The knock beat against the inside of the door. Yes, that is backward. You remember this strange order.

The guards let the woman out. She had taken the map. Proof. What if you went mad and destroyed it, had to begin again? If allowed to. The swallow was barely dry. You watched the sunlight sear through the doorway and cast a trapezoid of light on the floor.

The woman left the twins behind. They played with wooden blocks. A hard wood that could take the sharp edges of cutting teeth. You said their names. They looked at you. You smiled, and they smiled. Sweet little creatures. You will not leave me. I will leave you. Nature reversed, you thought. You took them suddenly to your breast, sunken and milkless. You held them, that innocence, that helplessness. It was the girl who cried out first to be let go. She sat on the floor with the small of her back against the spread of your leg. The boy pressed his toes into your right thigh. He beat his tiny hand against your chest, ma-ma, ma-ma. You didn't remember your mother teaching you shapes. Ciaran, he was present for that. You placed the boy facing his twin and held up the blocks, slightly gnawed, and told them, Circle, triangle, square.

Tell the truth.

In the moment, you thought you could love them. If you had more time.

Ciaran came first. That was how you knew the end was near. You sat across from each other at the table. He looked around. He glanced at the barred window. The pallets where you all slept. The chamber pot. The bundle of dirty clothes. On a shelf, long and high, the maps rolled tight. Your ink, quills, compass, straightedges in a box on the table, latched but not locked.

He told you the fighting had spread. In other lands, hidden in plain sight, there were more settlements like the one across the river. The people were often not prepared to defend themselves. It had become senseless, said Ciaran.

This was senseless from the start, you said.

We acted on good account. The decision wasn't made in haste. We deliberated. We cannot be blamed for unforeseen results, said he.

I told you they were no threat. Why didn't you believe me?

Your counsel was based primarily on impressions, not facts.

I can say the same of yours as well. But what's done is done.

Ciaran embraced you with awkward tenderness. He struggled with affection even at that moment.

Keep your courage, my bold sister, said he. Ciaran paused at the open door. Don't expect to see Father.

You hoped, but without good reason and in spite of all that occurred. You knew your father was ashamed that you had defied the dead King's authority. He had been proud of you as long as you did your liege's bidding. He'd approved of you as long as you obeyed and kept quiet. You remembered the way he had looked at you when you stood before the Council and implored caution. It was the slap's shadow. You tasted blood in your mouth, although he didn't touch you. As well, you had no doubt what he had advised the King | your husband | to do. Your father didn't raise a sword, but his actions were in every blow. How you wished to understand the reason for his violence.

Your offense was telling the truth as you saw it.

And you never saw your father again.

Your mother. Your mother a stream, a stream of words, the rocks of why?

The flow. You married a prince. Wealth beyond dreams was yours. The children. Didn't you think of the children? I knew no good would come of your running wild in the woods and the studying. Your father wouldn't listen to me and rein you in. Now look at what you've done to me. What do you know of the ways of the world? All you did was draw pictures of land. Your father so disappointed and shamed, before the King, before his fellow noblemen! Had you kept your mouth shut, you would be Queen. Queen!

You stopped hearing words. The sound reminded you of a panicked cow you'd once heard calling for her calf. You had seen the corpse. A wolf likely found it when it strayed. The poor beast didn't know her baby was dead. As you walked away, you heard the noise rise to a wail, a roar, and howl of madness.

It was done. You didn't bother to defend yourself. Perhaps you were dead but somehow still breathing. You were a criminal, though you had not defiled, stolen, or murdered a thing. Your mother couldn't understand the circumstances. You couldn't believe the quiet in yourself at that moment. You were broken. Untethered. No one wanted you. They wanted a memory of you.

Aoife.

You looked at her.

What will happen to my grandchildren?

I suspect Wyl shall take them.

Silence, beloved silence. Then:

Be grateful they are so young. They will not remember you.

I will remember you, Mother.

The words slipped out, off your tongue, a ripple.

She began to cry. You were numb. She went to you and put your head to her chest. You didn't resist. There had been times the gesture had brought you comfort. Not that day.

You were in the hut but saw a different wall. A stone wall. You heard the sound of Ciaran being beaten on the other side. The rage. Don't you ever make your mother cry. You screamed against your mother's hand. Leave him alone. Leave him alone. As if somehow that memory explained this moment.

Then spring, on her lap. The flower chain you made around her neck. Her soft fingers on your cheek. She's laughing. You're laughing.

That was the last thought in your head as she pressed her hand to your crown and said, My daughter. Then she left. No sunlight through the doorway. Darkness had come.

THE DAY OF YOUR EXILE, YOU STOOD ACROSS FROM WYL.

Your hands were tied behind your back. The moment hardly seemed real. Within two turns through all seasons, you had crossed a river, met a reclusive people, learned of a dragon, journeyed far away, found its hoard, sated desire, married, birthed twins, warned the people of danger, and brought disaster.

Yes. This can be reduced to its parts. The whole somehow included standing bound in front of your husband. You were no traitor in word or deed unless you betrayed that which was unspoken. You wanted to hate Wyl but you couldn't. He was still the good-natured boy you knew whose center had been twisted.

A bell. Yes, there was a bell on the table that he shook and it sang. The twins, a year old, walked in, almost on their own. Their nursemaid led them in as they wobbled. The girl looked up and noticed you. A squeal, a bleat, then she walked on unsteady feet. The boy followed. Your body urged to reach out for them and seized at your back. They pulled on your skirt and teetered as if a-sail.

Wyl picked them up and held them before you. You kissed each of them on the forehead and cheeks. You said nothing, not even their names. Your tongue filled your mouth with a carrion weight. Then their faces were a blur. The nursemaid took them from their father. A rhythm of familiarity between them. This exchange had been done before. You turned to watch them leave. Was it the girl or the boy? Ah, a lapse here. Which one of them raised its hand above the nursemaid's head and said bye-bye?

You were alone with him.

When we leave this room, before witnesses I will read a decree that you are to be exiled, said he.

Why?

You betrayed the kingdom.

Some may think so, but I didn't betray myself.

He bowed his head.

How could you, Aoife, when I gave you all I could, including my heart? said he. Without anger. In tears.

You were too stunned to reply. Wyl clutched your waist. He kissed you on the mouth. A cool press, as if you were a corpse. A part of you revived and returned the kiss with a passion that vanished as fast as it came. | you had warned him, with blood on your hands |

The decree was announced. You were on your knees with two guards at your side. It was a public spectacle. You remember much shouting. The rope came loose from your wrists. You were wrestled upright on a horse. No part of you was left untouched. Push shove grab. The manhandling was worse than when you were kidnapped and brought to the house. Then, a gag in your mouth. Your hands were bound in front. You held the reins.

Later, one of the two guards said you would be taken to the border and released. Which border? Land, river, or sea? You thought of Burl and his safety. You suspected something was wrong.

The armed guard escort was for your family's sake, perhaps Wyl's. They saw you leave alive. Strange courtesies are done at times.

You knew neither of these men. Young. Proud in their saddles. Their weapons' sheaths jaunty and bright. They were under orders. Under orders. You pondered the thought. Can one suffocate that way, as if under covers? You giggled. It was involuntary. A trickle of madness. The ice beginning to crack. One looked back at you. You felt your horse quiver and buck. Flies. It didn't like flies at all. So you three rode along. One decided to tie a rope around your neck as you went to relieve yourself. Better than being watched.

Then it was night. There was no nobleman's home waiting for your arrival. You would sleep outdoors. You had done so before countless times but had never felt so unsafe. You thought of all the men who had been on your crew. Decent and respectful to you, at

least in your presence. One of the guards produced metal shackles and tied you by one leg to a tree. They ate. There was a jug of ale, strong by the smell of it. One and the other one, you called them. The one eased into his drink. Neither was drunk. There wasn't enough between them for that.

The one moved his hand across your head after he handed you dinner. Cheese, bread, tough dried meat. You willed yourself not to react. His intent was to disturb. You kept your eyes down but your ears up. It grew dark. You didn't wish to sleep. The moon was split in half and leached light through the treetops. You drifted off somehow.

You felt the sensation of a finger easing a wisp of hair behind your ear. You weren't awake. You were caught in a past life. | violence can be tender | You almost said Wyl's name. You opened your eyes and gasped. The one crouched near you like an animal. You thought him beastly, but his human agency made him more dangerous. You sat up. He said nothing. He moved his eyes from yours to your leg, exposed to the thigh. | where your son and daughter had stood | You were an exotic creature leashed in the darkness.

Again, with your body in one time and place, your mind leapt to another. You, six, Ciaran, thirteen, at the close of a spring festival. Chained at the neck in a cage that gave no room for movement, a golden beast with a nimbus of silken fur. A creature with dark moons under its eyes as if it cried itself to sleep every night. Ciaran held your hand. This is the grandfather of cats. He's called a lion. You wept and pled for its release.

Where would it go? asked Ciaran. It doesn't belong here.

Your mind returned to your body. You watched the one stare at your thigh. He knelt. His fingers touched the ground. You knew then there are fates worse than death. He placed his hand on your leg. Suddenly you could speak.

Why?

Because I can, said he. He pushed you down at the chest.

The tethered leg pulled taut at the rope. No farther could you go. You tried to kick with the other, but he pressed his shin to hold it still. He held a dagger above your left breast. The glint numbed you. His other hand fumbled below his waist, then touched the flesh where your thighs met. His fingers rushed full entry into the hidden space between your legs. You screamed and struggled and hoped to die first.

Then his weight was gone. He was on his feet. A man next to him. The other one. There was an argument you understood by tone and feeling, not in the words. A jostle back and forth. Then you heard, No matter. We have our orders, said the one. The other one didn't move. He didn't speak to you, but he looked in your direction.

You awoke the next morning with a scab on your finger. You weren't certain but you thought you might have cut it on the small dagger that had been pointed at you. There it was in the dirt in the place where the one had been. You accepted the danger. You put it in a pocket of your skirt. Your arm felt sticky. There was more blood. The one had cut you. Nicked your breast and gashed your left upper arm. You ripped off a sleeve to bind the wound. No pain. You were too shocked.

You asked the other one to let you be untied as you mounted the horse. He complied. But he tied your hands once you were astride. You rode. You were the blade in the pocket. You became the blade. You drank little, although you were thirsty. Fewer reasons to get off the horse.

The third day and third night. The one was off behind a tree. The other one near you. You returned with the rope around your neck. You lifted your hands for him to bind. Odd what the body's will does on its own when it becomes used to bondage. He removed the loop at your throat.

He looked directly into your eyes and whispered, Run.

THE GLADE YOU FOUND FELT TOO OPEN. YOU WALKED THE MARGIN until you heard a trickle. A stream. You knelt and drank and drank. You cried for every reason why, then stood up. No one knew where you were or if you were dead or alive. You thought you must go to the Guardians' settlement. You also had to eat. You still had the dagger. No rope for a snare, though. Perhaps some wild fruit. | summer, your twenty-fifth year, a third of your life | You found an unlikely row of peach trees, which led to a hut with one blue shutter.

You had nothing. No coins, no jewels, nothing of value. You didn't wish to steal, but you were so hungry. You smelled food.

Inside, a pot was over a fire. The beans were nearly cooked, good enough. Only morsels, enough until you had the strength to hunt.

Eat, child, said a voice.

A woman older than you'd ever seen walked through the door, nimble as a girl. She placed a basket on the table and pulled a stool next to you.

She asked no questions. She cleaned and dressed the wound. You were given a basin and a cloth to wash yourself. She put you to bed. You wore a large linen gown the color of lilac, the smell of lavender.

I'm lost, you said.

The world is full of people missing by choice or circumstance. Rest now.

I'm an exile.

A nod, as if she understood a deeper matter. Yes, this has happened before.

You awoke to the smell of cooked egg. The old woman smiled and invited you to eat. You did. She made a pouch of food, salve, and bandages. She gave you a loose clean dress with fine embroidery at the cuffs.

Then she crouched at the mouth of the hearth and pointed to the dirt floor. You recognized the design there, one you'd seen far away from that place.

Her finger was parallel with the point of the triangle.

Continue that way, said she.

So you did. The dress felt light on your shoulders, heavy at the hem.

YOU FOUND BURL. HE DIDN'T RECOGNIZE YOU AT FIRST. THE SIMPLE clothes you wore became an unexpected disguise. He had heard of your exile. Word had not yet spread through the kingdom of your possible escape. Perhaps the one and the other one agreed to say you were dead.

He led you across the river at night under a waxing moon. You both walked along the bank until you found the familiar spot. No one was there. Burl let the boat go adrift.

I will not return there. There is bidding I cannot abide, said he.

You both decided to search in daylight. You slept under shrubs protected by trees.

The next morning, you found the large rock with the worn groove in the forest. For a moment, you leaned against it. Solid. Fixed. Solace. You led Burl to the settlement. There were gouges in the earth where the gold road had been. Men who wore emblems of your kingdom roamed about. You crept with caution. Many of the houses were destroyed. All that you entered had been ransacked. You approached the settlement center. There was a hole where the well had been, with debris piled within. The great musical Wheels were gone. Some of the gears lay scattered in the dirt. There were no rotted bodies in view. You couldn't see but somehow felt blood on the ground.

Burl burst into quiet inconsolable tears.

Why? Why? said he, as if the rubble or you could answer.

He found a child's toy boat and placed it in his pouch.

Once Burl calmed himself, you led him into the forest to find the old woman's hut. It was deserted. You sensed it was vacant because she was away and would return again when it was safe. You knew your journey must continue. You sat upon a stool near the hearth and saw the symbol that pointed to haven. You fingered the hem of your dress. There were objects in the fold. You gnawed at the stitches and withdrew a gold coin.

You and Burl crept back to the settlement. You found clothing and sacks to carry what you needed. Burl found a sharp knife, which he wrapped in a cloth. With no idea where to go, you hoped for safe refuge and spoke the incantation. A rabbit appeared from the brush, then hopped back a step. You took its direction.

For miles and miles, between link to link, through gap to gap, you and Burl were alone. He was the first true friend you'd had in many years. He told you he wanted to leave the kingdom because he didn't wish to live and die an oarsman. He had become one because it was the most tolerable job he'd found as a man of his station. He believed there was something else he could do if he was given the chance to try. He hoped to discover what it was in another land. You understood.

Eventually, far, far from your kingdom, you found a Guardian settlement. You knew this because the people wore the familiar blue and spoke the musical language. The roads, however, appeared newly paved with stone. You both greeted the first people you encountered. Someone brought a boy to meet you. His eyes looked as if they couldn't decide what color to be and settled on dark. He spoke your language and led you to the settlement center. He was the first male Voice you'd met.

You learned they had been affected by the war but not destroyed. There was no account for why. Many other settlements had been less fortunate.

For several days you rested, and considered a permanent stay. You were offered refuge. You felt comfortable and safe, but you didn't sense you were meant to remain there. Burl claimed his new home.

On the morning you left, Burl wore new clothes with a blue cloth belt. He said he was grateful for what you'd done for him. He felt a sense of expansion and peace he'd never known. He looked years younger than he had when you'd first met him. You told him he looked happy.

I am, and I hope you will be, too, said he.

Burl embraced you and kissed your cheek.

Winter entered its turn in the cycle. You defied common sense. Your journey continued. How you managed to travel so long through that winter was not so much a mystery as it was a meandering, hut to hut, gap to gap. You seemed to wander without boundaries. Sometimes you found yourself far-flung to strange places you wanted to believe were dreams. In and out of hollows and huts, you moved through. Old women gave you shelter and tasks to do with your hands when you entered a land where the weather was too bleak. You became better at sewing, nimble at spinning. They didn't speak of the reason for their solitude in those hidden places. You didn't ask. You intuited their purpose. Each was fluent in the language of her time and place, yet transcendent in that each had spent part of her life among the Guardians. This you would learn in fact later. They understood the need to protect you. When it was time to leave, you left a coin in payment if the old woman would accept it.

You noticed sparse green shoots, brave harbingers in half-light. Spring was near.

The forest's edge met a flat plain. You looked out across an expanse of land intimidating in its openness. You had so long traveled under the cover of trees. Squirrels often served as guides in the branches.

With no idea which way to go, you spoke the incantation. In the distance, a low noise rumbled. Wild horses in full gallop passed over the land in a great herd. Their bodies were thick and powerful.

You followed one with your eyes. It had a streak of white in its brown mane. It gave a jaunty leap that made you laugh. How long had it been since you'd laughed? As if it knew, it leapt again with a flamboyant toss of the head. Then it muscled into a run to pass the others. There was no man astride this beast. No boundaries to where it wished to go. No demand for its return to a stable for the night.

The wild herd kicked holes in the earth. You followed the

hoofprints. You were somewhat fearful of the distance. You saw nothing but blue sky and gold earth. The land had been burnished in its sleep. You carried a light bundle on your back with food and a bladder of water. The sun approached the end of its arc.

By twilight, it was very cold. You came to a small cluster of trees. It was as if they hadn't been told to move. Or had refused. You walked toward the center. Perhaps the wind would not be as strong. There in the dimness was a crouched furry back. Shouldn't it be asleep? you thought as the bear turned to reveal the front of a man. You gasped.

An encounter with a bear would have frightened you less. You began to move away. He walked toward you. He held up his hand. Slowly, with gentleness. He smiled.

He was an old man. A huge man. He gestured for you to approach. Your body didn't tell you to run. You followed him. He moved like the beast whose skin he wore. At his thigh, a dead hare swung to and fro. He held it by the ears. He led you to a little dugout in the earth surrounded by enormous stones. You wondered where they had come from. Thick branches lay across the top as a roof.

Nearby, there was an open fire. He gestured for you to sit and gave you a hollowed wood knot filled with water. He set to skin and gut the hare with a knife so sharp there was no effort in his work. You watched him skewer the animal over the fire. You shivered. He noticed. He gave you a musty wool blanket that smelled of animal dank. However, you were warm. He took off his tight red cap and scratched his brilliant white hair, which muted to silver then gray to the tip of his beard. The old man sat with contentment. When the hare was cooked, he gave you a knife to carve some meat. You brought the thigh to your mouth. He made a noise. A grunt. You looked at him. He clasped his hands and bowed at the three-legged beast. He stared at you as if to say, Now you. So you did, too.

After you both ate, he took the remains away. You heard him

scratch around, although you couldn't see him. He returned. You yawned, and he smiled. He gestured to the pit in the earth. A wild-smelling place. Not foul. Untamed. Still, your body didn't tell you to run. You entered, then turned around to peer out at the mute glow of the fire. He spoke to you then, a deep distinct human row of syllables. Later, you would learn what he had said. Sleep, lost child. His sounds were what you repeated to yourself as you allowed yourself to rest.

The next morning, he was gone. The fire was dead. A leather bag filled with shelled nuts was at the entrance. You left him your last gold coin on top of the folded wool blankets that protected you that night.

What you intended to find or see, you had no idea. How would you know where your new home was to be?

You had arrived at the thaw.

You stood with your back to the old man's solitary den and spoke the incantation. Water droplets spattered the ground. An ice storm had come in the night to re-create the world in crystal. A bright sun and temperate breeze had come to melt it away.

A great stag slipped through the trees. Its magnificent antlers glimmered in many points. Icicles had formed on the tips. They dripped slowly. You found him so beautiful, so familiar, that you followed him. With no foliage, only frostbitten buds and branches, you were able to see him with ease. You walked a short distance. He marked his territory and stamped his feet. Somehow, you both knew you were to part ways.

With mere steps forward, you entered the settlement through an unusual space. There was no well-worn path.

A woman found you. You wanted to speak. Help. But you didn't and you didn't have to. She saw a strange woman alone at daybreak and no real harm could come of that.

The woman told another to find aid. Those who passed you did not stare. They saw you with absolute clarity. They gestured with fingertips joined, raising hands to a bowed head, touched at the brow. They all did this. | we do it still |

As you walked through the broad, busy settlement, you began to melt like the ice on the stag's antlers. That had not happened before in any other place. That was how you knew you'd found your new home. There would be no leaving in the state you'd fallen into. Your body moved as if your limbs were connected loosely. For a moment, you couldn't remember your name. So long had it been since you'd had to tell or hear it.

They had a guesthouse. You'd learn they all did. That was where you were sheltered as a visitor who would never leave. You were given food and drink.

Someone wrapped you in a covering that smelled of borage. Your shoes were replaced with warm slippers. | beautiful, embroidered in striking colors with a pattern of plants and creatures | They embraced you with their way. The quiet. The woman who found you sat an intimate yet respectful distance in front of you. A calm smile on her face. Piercing blue eyes with a slight slant at the corners. Broad nose. Hair like a crow's shiny tail.

A woman near your age entered the room.

Hello, you said.

Welcome. I am called Aza. What is your name? asked she. Her eyes were violet.

You wailed in reply. Aza took your hand. You have no memory of what you told her. Perhaps you said nothing. She might have learned your story through the mysterious means some Voices possessed.

Still, you must have said something. Aza gave a piece of your story to the woman who aided you with permission to share what she knew. They were told directly who you were. This was their way. Facts, no judgment. Your name was Aoife, who had journeyed long from the kingdom that had provoked the war.

Yes, provoked. Started wasn't accurate. You would learn they claimed responsibility for participating. As they see it, there is no fight if one side refuses to do so. You say the alternative is slaughter, although that's what happened.

Aza stayed at your side and translated your words.

You were taken to a woman who knew of healing plants, and were given teas to clear your cold.

I have no means to pay, you said.

How could I turn away a sick child? asked the gentle old woman.

You were fitted for new shoes with sturdy soles and soft covers.

I have no means to pay, you said.

Your feet cannot wait until you do, said the fatherly shoemaker.

You were led to a small room in a warm house with a neat bed covered in soft linen, a painted chest open and waiting, and a table with a brush, comb, and mirror.

I have no means to pay, you said.

You are the one from that kingdom, said the young woman.

I am.

Is it true you were forced to leave?

Yes.

Sleep now. You're safe.

You slept and slept. A horrible noise startled you. A dream, you thought, until you realized you were roused. You ran outside, afraid, but no one was rushed or alarmed. Someone noticed you. He touched his chest and breathed. He sat you down on a bench and gestured for you to stay. Aza came quickly.

What is that terrible screaming? you asked.

Someone is returning from the war.

The wind shifted. The sounds grew faint. You decided not to ask yet what she had meant. You learned you had been asleep for three days and nights. You were tended in your twilight state but not awakened.

THEN YOU WERE AMONG THEM. THE GUARDIANS. THEY TOOK YOU IN like a foundling child and allowed you to stay. You were asked if you wanted to remain. As if you had a choice. That is incorrect. You could have returned to your home kingdom, but why? You would have had to lie every day of the rest of your life about your origins, your circumstances, your name. Bear in mind, what life would you have had? You had a rare useful skill put to serve kingdoms and conquest. You could have done that for another land. No matter the distance, however, you knew the whereabouts of a woman mapmaker were sure to be found. Even one in disguise.

You recall little about the first months other than the physical actions done. You did fall apart. The loosening limbs was only a start. The details of your grief were too deep in memory then, too muddled with exhaustion. You exerted energy acclimating to the new home, rather than contending with what had led you here. You lived among them, grateful for the peace, grateful that someone gave you food on days you could barely manage to go outside. You were quiet when you wanted to be, found company when that suited you. You were alone, far from where you were born, but you weren't lonely.

On days when you were dark and confused, and there were many, no one told you or gave you the feeling that you should feel differently. The people of your settlement knew the facts of your life before. Where you had come from. That you had been a mapmaker. That you warned the distant Guardian settlement of what the kingdom might do. That you had been married. That you had been exiled from your land. You didn't mention the twins. You didn't say your husband was also the King.

If people wondered what had happened, they could have asked, but no one did. Instead, you were asked what could be done to bring you comfort. You were told if you ever wished to speak, there were many among them who would listen without judgment and in confidence. There were rituals to release and cleanse. You were told there was a ceremony to give yourself a new name if you wished. One of your choosing. The name Aoife was the only vestige of your life before that you were certain you wanted to keep.

The shock subsided. You were asked to help with at least one chore each day. Card wool. Tend crops. Cut wood. Knead dough. You had to be taught these skills. It was good for you. You were often outdoors and busy with a constructive task.

You were like a child. You were clumsy, prone to distraction and easy tears. They were so patient. Everyone. At times, your frustration made you scowl and flail your limbs. They remained still until you were ready to begin again. If it became clear you weren't suited to a task, they expressed no judgment. You were given a chance elsewhere. There was always something else to be done.

You communicated as best you could. You made an effort to learn their language quickly. They immersed you in its musical sounds. Even the children with their sweet avian voices helped you.

ALL THAT YOU HAD HAD BEEN WRENCHED AWAY, YET YOU WERE STILL yourself. Your tendency to observe and study what surrounded you hadn't changed. The first year with the Guardians was spent in pain as much as wonder.

The settlement was on the margin between a deep forest and an expansive plain.

You roamed the forest and the river that rushed through. In your stillness, you saw hares, roe deer, aurochs, boars, hedgehogs, herons, owls, bears, foxes, ermines, and, only once, a pack of wolves. Birch and pine thrived in the rugged earth. Oaks and maples greeted you with splayed branches. You touched these cousins of ones you had known. The shade in high sun gave respite from the heat. That first full fall, you delighted in the bright cheerful scent of spent needles under your feet. When the snow came, you turned to a stand of firs for strength. They bore the cold white weight on their shoulders until the sun and wind gave relief. They endured. So could you. Spring did not unfold or emerge. It screamed a chorus of verdant tongues all at once.

The plain lay wide and full. Wind twisted the blades and blossoms against the light. Flocks of birds whirled to weave earth with sky. The beauty threatened to drown you but instead made you drunk. Summer waved in green and gold, flickered with wildflowers. The grass muted to sand as the cold arrived. Under the snow, it rested in a brown light sleep. It roused when the melt stole its cover. The blinding white thwarted your admiration of the wild horses. Their tracks vanished at the horizon. Poppies sustained the note of spring, red beyond reason.

Unlike the other Guardian settlements you had seen, this one wasn't hidden among the trees. It coiled into the open near a small lake and close to a river. The center contained a well and the Wheels. The road started in the east, curled toward the sun's curve, and moved around where the sun didn't rise or fall. Straight roads radiated from the center to the far edges of the spiral. You sketched the image in your mind and recognized the pattern. It resembled a wheel, but more so a web. Spiders cast such orbs, but you didn't feel trapped.

Like most of the settlements, it was within walking distance of a

mine. Beyond the roads and buildings were tracts of land rich with grain crops and vegetables. Oxen grazed within view of the soil they turned. Ample pens held goats, sheep, and swine.

In the spaces between the roads were small gardens, little pastures, tiny orchards, and many buildings of all sizes. Some dwellings were equipped with the tools of trades. There were some for storage of food and goods. The rest were for housing.

In structure, the buildings were much the same, although all faced the heat of the sun. A rare hut was made of stone. For the rest, thick wood timbers set in the ground served to make the rectangular frame. More timbers were used to erect the pitched roof and brace the walls. Mud mixtures or clay filled the hollows around doors and windows. Some of the houses shared walls, and some stood alone.

Roof material was thatch, clay tiles, or slate. Windows had clever woven screens and heavy shutters that bolted shut. Main entry doors hung on sturdy fanciful hinges. Small narrow doors led to shared covered privies and their stores of ash.

Each house was similar but had its own character. The outside walls were painted or decorated with whatever delighted the dwellers. Inside, the first floors were covered with tiles or stone. Upper floors had smoothed wooden planks. Heavy woven and braided rugs blocked what chills they could. Walls were coated in thin plaster and painted with single colors, simple designs, or elaborate murals. Solid walls sometimes separated space. More often, thick curtains hung from the ceiling and wrapped to offer privacy. The first floor had at least one fire pit with an elliptical low brick wall with small holes at its bottom edge. A copper-capped opening in the roof allowed smoke to escape.

Furniture varied in design but not in function. Rough simple tables, benches, and beds were as common as pieces with fine joints and delicate inlays. High-backed seats gave comfort with soft

cushions. Chests held what required storage. Baskets held what was often used. Pegs kept overclothes and hats at the ready.

When you left the visitors' house, you were given your own curtained space in a home with three other women. | you chose not to live alone | You went into unlocked storage buildings to select your furniture, bedding, and clothes. In one, you found an obsidian mirror that reached the outstretched span of your fingertips. It rested on a base of wooden talons. A carved owl's head hooked its beak over the top to hold it in place. How long it had been since you chose something for yourself.

Around you were all manner of arrangements. There were family groups of parents and children under one roof. Near relatives lived in the house or close by. Shared dwellings were occupied by men, women, or both, of all ages. Some chose small, single huts. Others lived in pairs. The term applied to any two people who agreed to a bonded relationship. Some wore symbolic rings and some did not. You were shocked at your shock at the adult consent without scrutiny, and at the seeming lack of formality.

Most of the members of the settlement bore a basic resemblance to each other. They were strong and solid. Their eyes narrowed at the far edges, and their skin had a warm tone. Many had dark hair and eyes. Although the Guardians as a whole shared the same culture, the groups didn't all look alike. The people of the other two settlements you'd seen looked different in bone structure, features, and coloring. There were also those born away who joined them and had children of their own.

They dressed with great variation except for one detail. Each person wore the Guardian blue. Some part of a garment or adornment had that color. It was their acknowledgment of a greater unity.

Otherwise, the people clothed themselves in what made them comfortable. To your eyes, it seemed some were costumed. Their garments were sewn with elaborate seams and decorated with embroidery and appliqué. Yet most chose basic but finely made tunics, leggings, skirts, blouses, and shifts. Every person could wear jewels or precious metals if he or she wished. You learned that, to the Guardians, gold and the like had no intrinsic value other than beauty. Human perception made it a commodity, easy to trade.

The Guardians organized themselves with shared effort. Every person who was able worked in some way. You observed trades like the ones people had in your life before. There were smiths, carpenters, and wheelwrights. To provide food and drink, there were farmers, hunters, shepherds, bakers, brewers, and millers. To provide clothing and wares, there were weavers, potters, shoemakers, and tailors.

The settlement also had singers, musicians, and storytellers. To make beautiful things, there were jewelry makers, painters, and embroiderers. Midwives, healers, and Voices tended the pregnant, sick, and distressed.

Mundane tasks were not daily chores as you had observed them. Neighbors arranged to help one another with meals and washing. There were cooking spaces in the buildings with the baking hearths. At the river were inventive water pumps, troughs, and wringing cylinders to clean linens. When harvests ripened, extra hands went into the fields and forest.

Within a short walk of any house or work building, there was a nursery for babies and young children. Elders, young people, and warriors served as tenders. If they wished, mothers and fathers could place the children in the tenders' care while they worked.

No one was forced into work based on birth or sex. No one was expected to do the same tasks without change. The Guardians encouraged each other to try new skills and practice what they learned. You observed that it was common for people to work in different trades or service through the years of their lives. They believed each child was endowed with gifts from the start. Adults were expected to nurture the children they knew until the gifts were discovered. That was why children of all ages were so often in places where adults worked. That was why their play received attention. This was insight into who they were to be.

You realized the Guardians saw their work as reciprocity. The person who grew vegetables made it possible for another to prepare them. The sustenance given to others made it possible for them to mend, build, or sing, which served someone else. These were the connections among them that bent and skipped and leapt. The Guardians saw linkages, not lines.

You were perplexed by the open stores. There were buildings stocked with goods of all kinds. There was no exchange, barter, or use of money. No tallies were taken. No accounts kept. You were allowed to choose whatever you wanted. If you missed that day's early beets or milk from sweeter goats, you might be fortunate another day. A wish for something new often meant an exchange at one of the stores. The once-used item left behind, a new one taken in its place. Clothing, jewelry, wares, furniture. It was all available.

People made gifts for one another. Special requests were sometimes made of those who had appreciated skills. The items were treasured, then perhaps one day given to the stores for someone else to enjoy, or kept with one's family.

Your neighbors were not perfect, but they were ideal for you. They exhibited the same emotions as people you knew in your life before. Dark feelings and light ones moved through. What made your neighbors different was their acknowledgment. When troubles arose, they took themselves to quiet places or called upon friends to help. They were willing to find peace and understanding. They were able to nurture those qualities.

The Guardians' cooperation perplexed you, their giving perhaps more. They lived simply but not poorly. In the years you would spend with them, there would be hard times of illness and scarcity. We drew together to ease the suffering. We trusted one another.

Tell the truth.

Their ways were a telling contrast to your life before. Until then, you had been anchored in privilege. Part of you believed that was your lucky fate. You were born better. That made you better. But part of you knew it was a lie. When you traveled as a mapmaker, you saw the lie exposed, although you weren't looking. You detected few differences among others once you looked past their belongings, comforts, and status. Your crew and the conditions in which you often worked and lived kept you humble. | you allowed that | You knew the King and his nobles collected their portions for the coffers and promised little more than protection. Still, you paid homage to hierarchy and to power, the wielding of it, because of what it offered you. Favor was mutable. | Raef, the steward |

Continue. Admit it.

You wanted to find fault in the Guardians. You did not want to believe that all was as it seemed. You felt an elusive unease with their goodwill and welcome. You desired what made you suspicious. The latter was the poison of your past. You had seen little proof that peace within one's self, one's home, and one's world was even possible.

It was. You had to unlearn.

TRUE ENOUGH, YOU NO LONGER WORKED AS A MAPMAKER. THAT WASN'T needed among the Guardians. They had other means of finding their place, orienting themselves. They knew the world was round and felt no fear of falling off the edge. You didn't miss the work as much as you expected. What you loved about being a mapmaker was the freedom to be outside, even though you so often stood still for hours on end. You felt the sun air rain. You liked the precision of the work. The relationship of angles and points. The creation of order and meaning. There, too, were the secret subtleties. You had your own maps of oddities and wonders, favorite cake eaten here, favorite story learned there.

You liked the art of mapmaking. You, like your adopted people, believed function and beauty belonged together. However, your craft wasn't limited to creation of a map necessarily. That was the end result, when in fact the pleasure was deeper, wasn't it? Go beyond the effort, the job you had to do. Yes, you were untethered from the role of a woman, freed from the restraint.

Do not think for a moment you were unaware of the anomaly.

Tell the truth, Aoife.

You had wanted to be free to live as you pleased since you were a small child. You wanted no part of woman's work, not as it was, not as prescribed by the place and time of your birth. No, you were not to have a poor woman's life. You would never have to cook, clean, or wash for yourself or others. Your mother had veiled contempt for those who made her life tidy and easy. They were common, beneath her, but she depended on them for her life as she knew it. Instead, she was born and married into an existence of relative comfort, as you were and might have been.

Your mother covered every strip of fabric she could find with decoration. She was skilled but didn't adore the task. | her work was beautiful | That gave her hands purpose. Otherwise, she bothered after the servants, her children, her husband. As a girl, you thought she smelled of boredom.

You lingered with notice of the days she sat with friends. They gossiped and complained. You wondered whether any of them spoke the darker truths of their lives. The secret things that lurk deep but surface unexpectedly. What is forbidden to do as well as to think. What had been their wishes and aspirations, confined by circumstance?

What had you escaped?

WHEN THE FALLING APART WAS COMPLETE, YOU FELT GRATITUDE BEyond any you had ever experienced. You wanted to give as others had given to you. There were the practical ways as you took your turns with washing, weeding, harvesting, and cooking. | you did grumble at times, like anyone else | You enjoyed the bakery most and dedicated your mornings there.

A young boy found you one day and said his mother had told him you had drawn maps of the world. Wide-eyed, he asked if that was true.

Part of the world, yes. But when I was your age, I drew maps of hidden worlds. What I imagined lay beyond anthills and beehives or deep inside places no one can see, you said.

He said he wanted to learn. You explained the concept to him. He practiced with drawings in damp clay or on the ground. He had to wait to make ones to keep. You learned the Guardians didn't keep writing materials in their stores. Their language was not recorded. None of them could read or write.

You had to make a special request to the Guardians of the trails. They were, in fact, warriors who moved as traders along worn routes and side roads. They returned with goods that couldn't be grown, unearthed, or obtained near the settlement. In turn, they took what was produced or made among your people to exchange with distant others.

Somehow, they returned with good ink and acceptable parchment. You understood the cost of what was given and encouraged the boy to be sparing. To explain scarcity to a child who'd never known it required a visit from Aza.

He was bright and eager. You taught him basic concepts of geometry with a carpenter's compass and straightedge. He came to have little interest in the mathematics but much in the possibility of design. The maps he abandoned. What he learned flourished within him. He would one day paint an intricate pattern on a wall of your daughter's private space as a welcome gift. He remembered your kindness.

You realized you missed the feel of writing and drawing. You missed reading, as rare as that opportunity had been. What you began to do was at first an innocent amusement. You thought, A map is to space as an alphabet is to sound. You began to craft a written form of the language you spoke daily. You told no one, showed no one. There was a childlike thrill in writing what no one could understand.

YOU LEARNED WHAT YOU COULD THROUGH OBSERVATION. AT TIMES you had to ask questions to deepen your understanding. Your friends were willing teachers. Edik was your favorite among them. He was an elder and a Voice. He was the person you asked most about the Guardians' interaction. They were as human as the people of your kingdom, but why did their difference seem so great?

We've chosen another way. Have you been told the tales that guide us? asked he.

You had. Although you didn't believe the myths were of a genuine primordial past, you did admire their care for those who had been abandoned or lost. The Guardians told of a newborn orphan. The child was renewed to life under the care of Egnis the Red Dragon, Ingot the Gold Dwarf, and Incant the White Wisp. Azul grew with the light and dark emotions of their humankind. Yet love prevailed, and all that comes of love. Azul left the realm and returned to the rejecting world to test the strength of this love. They understood that the innate emotions of humans were mutable. Anger didn't have to lead to violence, hate to cruelty, fear to oppression. There was a space for change between what words were said and what deeds were done. After many trials, Azul sought to create places of compassion and harmony. The children of Azul were born. Their peaceful settlements were built throughout the known world. Many old ones still thrived, and new ones were formed as needed.

Edik explained disagreements were not bad. This was to be expected, and this was how people learned to consider other points of view. They didn't believe there was only one right option. They considered what was needed at the moment, what sometimes affirmed the whole rather than a part. No one was completely free from fear, anger, or self-interest. Yet none of that need be the center of power.

A choice is always present, said Edik.

Between thought and deed, there is the space of possibility, he explained. Those born away noticed that those born among often paused or breathed before speaking or acting. That pause was learned. That pause was the possibility, what happens after the thought and before the words spoken or action taken. Sometimes a person did lash out and hurt another. The result was an unfettered reaction or deliberate choice. With practice, one learned to consider what brought pain or peace.

We wish to live in a place where each person feels valued and loved. Whatever gifts each has are respected and brought to bear, said he. The Guardians as a people wished to help one another. They intended that no misunderstanding led to hatred or violence.

He was quiet for several moments. You watched him rest his hands in his lap and look toward the distance.

All begins with the helpless little child, said he. It is a creature in one way, which must have food, water, and shelter. Without the basic needs fulfilled, it will physically die. Then there are the attendant needs to be kept clean, to be taught skills to survive. This can all be done without affection or care. But humans are complex beings. Without words, they know what is done out of obligation, spite, or love. A child is easily broken and easily warped. A child requires little more than a meeting of its animal needs and to feel it is beloved. A child can endure much change and difficulty if she is surrounded by love.

As a Voice, Edik helped those born away understand the ways of their new home. He felt much sadness for many of them. They often carried hidden pain that inflicted itself time and again only within. In extreme, they stole, hoarded, struck, lied, belittled. The actions gave life to what was underneath. They had suffered a great lack. They appeared difficult to love, and they were the ones who needed it most. They wanted the comfort and peace offered to them but mistrusted both. Even the ones who behaved with respect and kindness found life among the Guardians difficult to comprehend and accept at times.

Why do you think that is, Aoife? asked Edik.

Without a pause, you said, Because we've been betrayed.

How so? asked he.

You shook your head. You spoke the truth but couldn't explain why. You had begun to question more deeply the manner of the world to which you'd once belonged, or rather, been born.

Who might I have been had I been born among instead of away? you asked.

Fragments of your life streamed out to him. Shattered nonsense. He listened to the pieces, to what you'd been reduced to. Tears pierced your eyes. Edik opened his arms. You leaned away. Deep within, you wanted nothing else but to be held. He didn't move. You forced your head to his shoulder and wept. He held you until a calm settled throughout your body. When you slipped from his embrace, he smiled with warmth.

Until love and peace are constant, our purpose is not fulfilled, said he.

ALMOST TWO YEARS HAD CYCLED SINCE YOUR ARRIVAL IN THE SETTLEment.

Three years had passed since the war had begun, and at last it was over. The end came almost as abruptly as it began. Violence had reached far beyond the boundaries of the settlement across the river from the kingdom you had left behind. The remote settlement that had accepted you was spared destruction but not loss.

You couldn't conceive why the fighting had spread as it had. You couldn't imagine the shock of the reclusive Guardians suddenly invaded. The warriors of the trails fought to protect Egnis from harm. They endured random acts of violence. Their settlements had never been attacked in this way, not according to any remembered history. Many of them had been betrayed by villages who had been neutral neighbors before. You wondered what the armies of aggressive men thought when they found enough to loot but no evidence of real threat.

Several people of your settlement were relatives of warriors who never came back. Although these warriors had returned for brief visits during the war | gift of the gaps | they were otherwise missing or dead. Hope paled among their friends and family.

You twice saw a warrior knock upon the door of a waiting family. The news brought grief and shrouded bodies. Worse, grief and no body. Worse still, no word.

There were ceremonies for the bereaved. If a body returned, a ritual took place near it before it was cremated. A fire was built in a large iron cauldron for each person and tended by companion warriors until the ritual's end. Anyone could speak or share an offering. Friends and family sat nearby while words were spoken or gifts were given to the fire. Most heartrending were the children, who had received tender care from those who had died. He taught me, he showed me, I loved him because, said they. Some did not speak. They fed the fire with gifts made with their own hands. Dolls, carvings, sculptures, with meaning special to the person and the warrior. When the ceremony ended and the fire died, the family took the ashes to scatter in private.

You attended each of the ceremonies. These warriors you had not known. You were tempted to hide, but you faced the consequences of your actions. Long glances forced your eyes to the ground. They knew who you were.

Once, before you were fluent in their language, Aza said that a group wished to speak with you. They had lost their beloved in the war. She hoped to bring peace to you all. You agreed. Aza prepared you for the meeting. She assured you they didn't wish to persecute. When you sat in the circle among them, all wept. Aza translated as they spoke of their pain and confusion. Their people had lost warriors before but never so many in so short a time. They wanted you to explain what events had taken place before the first attack. They wanted to know why the war had begun. They wished to understand what made those born away so hurtful.

You told of your involvement. Beginning to end. You revealed your husband had been the prince, then King, but that seemed to matter little to them. Your explanations of what had taken place, of your world away, fumbled as excuses which you didn't agree with or believe. No more than they, could you make sense of the cruelty. You told the truth as you knew it. It was all you could give.

A woman who hadn't spoken leapt into a pause of silence. Aza translated.

You didn't kill my spouse, but a shard of your deeds was in the blow, said she.

You rose and knelt next to her.

Yes, it was. I am sorry. I am sorry to you all, you said.

She bowed her head, then embraced you. Together, you cried. You couldn't bear her forgiveness.

YOU AWOKE IN THE MIDDLE OF THE FREEZING NIGHT. NO NOISE HAD startled you. No sounds disturbed your return to sleep. Yet you went to the window and looked down to the road. A lupine shadow carried moonlight on its shoulders. You crept back to bed, stalked the image in your mind like a dream.

The next morning, word passed from one and all that Leit had slipped in through the darkness. He wished for tempered greetings. That is to say, he didn't want to be swarmed. The adults honored this. They waved or bowed their heads with respect, but the children couldn't contain themselves. They ran and leapt toward him. They shouted his name. He accepted their affection and returned it. The first time you saw him, from a close distance, you thought he winced with pain each time he was embraced.

You had heard people speak of him.

He was known as the warrior without a deliberate kill.

He had been away longer than the other warriors. He was dispatched soon after the war had begun. His role was to train those who had never before felt called to take up arms. His gift was discipline. He was adept at self-control. Under his guidance, the angered men | some women | would learn cool restraint and conscious action. Mindless violence and bloodshed offended his nature. No warrior took life lightly.

The people had believed he would return. They couldn't conceive that he would not. They honored him for his bravery, kindness, and composure. None was more skilled to maneuver the perils of the world.

As well, Makha the wolf accompanied him. Her loyal presence gave many comfort. She had been Leit's companion since his voice had changed. He had saved her as an orphaned pup. Some thought her not quite mortal. She was old for a creature of her kind, but her body and mind did not fail her. She protected Leit, kept to his side.

Within days of his arrival, the entire settlement felt brighter, as if a cloud had drifted away.

Leit requested a time of transition. He didn't hide but did not reenter a peaceful life again at once. Although he had a home of his own, he took refuge with an elder warrior and his spouse. If he was seen in those first weeks, he was often entering or leaving the forest with Makha or tending children at a nursery.

The next occasion you saw him, he stood with an infant asleep on his chest. The baby rested against the copper breastplate on which it lay. Leit's eyes were closed and turned to the sun.

YOU WERE CURIOUS ABOUT LEIT. ALTHOUGH YOU SAW HIM WHEN YOU passed nurseries or the smithy, sometimes in the fields, you hadn't found the courage to speak. You wanted to experience for yourself why he evoked such affection and respect. No matter that you were accepted among them, you were still the woman who had caused the war. That made you responsible for his pain, the depth of which you would be horrified to learn.

The daily work you chose had little connection to what you had done in your life before. You found pleasure in making bread. Precise measurements reminded you of what you once marked on a plane. Repetitive kneading brought to mind trudges on monotonous terrain. What you had done before fed no one, but it had satisfied a sort of greed.

Then came a morning when a mother and her twins stopped for a large loaf. The girl and boy were no older than four. You and your fellow bakers had made small dried-cherry buns for the visiting children. You gave the girl and boy their treats. They thanked you and smiled through the crumbs. The mother looked at them as they ate. Her expression was content and filled with love. In that simple moment you thought, I never looked at the twins that way.

You began to watch parents with their children, mothers in particular and their young ones in response. You had told no one of the girl and the boy. Your neighbors knew where you came from, that you had been a mapmaker, and that you had been married. For whatever reason, you couldn't speak of the twins.

Troubled in mind and heart, you found sleep elusive. Some nights, you walked to a location that overlooked the plain. The land was elevated and surrounded by trees. The low plateau had been worn bare by contemplative others drawn by the quiet and the view. Mountains rose in the far distance. On occasion, wild horses raced and grazed in the valley below. There was no escape from the moon.

One late summer night when you arrived at the plateau, you saw a figure sitting in the space. You decided to turn back. Your movement caused a rustle. A low growl froze your blood.

Thank you, said a man's voice. The growl stopped. The figure split into two forms.

I meant no intrusion. I will leave, you said.

You've come for a reason, said he. He didn't stand. He turned his body to slip a shirt over his head.

There's room enough. Sit, said he.

You approached. The moonlight brightened the two forms, a large man and a wolf.

I don't recognize you, said he.

You spoke your name and admitted that you knew who he was. You had seen him in the settlement.

Did you come for silence? asked Leit.

Yes, you said.

Please, may we share it? asked he.

You sat away from him and Makha the wolf. The moon was high and bright, almost full. Cloud shadows drifted on the plain.

The wolf sat next to him with her body pressed against his left side. Her shoulder met the back of his shoulder, her hip at the base of his spine. Her muzzle and throat were brilliant silver, the rest of her coarse fur burnished.

She regarded you with a gaze wild and wise. You remembered the shadow in the road on the night when you had awakened. Surely that had been her. You dared to look her in the eye. Only for a moment. What kind of beast shows such devotion to a man? you thought. As you turned toward the open land, you noticed a stain on Leit's shirt. He wasn't wearing the copper breastplate. You knew then it wasn't ceremonial or official. The thin armor covered a wound.

NEITHER OF YOU PLANNED TO SEE ONE ANOTHER ON THE PLATEAU BUT you encountered each other there often enough. Some nights you spoke. Other nights you agreed to sit in silence.

Of course, in time, the familiarity extended beyond the viewpoint on the plateau. You began to speak together in public places. People noticed. You've made a new friend, Aoife. What a fine man he is, said they.

You knew this to be true. He was not prideful or superior. The regard others had for him could have shaped him so, but did not. He welcomed questions of the Guardians' ways. | our ways | He replied with kindness, a willingness to teach. He spoke of his life before he became a warrior and before the war.

You replied to questions about your place of origin. This inquiry didn't disturb you. As your ability to speak the language improved, you were asked about your former home. Those born away—the exiles, the foundlings—told of customs and beliefs they remembered, in some instances still held.

Leit's questions remained open. In time, you perceived that he was trying to make sense of a greater matter. He wished to understand the war he had witnessed. He wanted to know what had ruptured like an abscess and spread from mind to heart, mind to heart, of a few, then to many.

He didn't delve into your own story. He gave you quiet and space. You said little on your own, limited yourself to facts. Your father was an adviser of high status in the kingdom. Your mother kept a tidy house with organized servants. Ciaran, your brother, was a smart, reliable man who planned to fill your father's role. As a child, you liked to draw maps. You were trained to do so and charted large portions of the land. You married the prince, who became King. You were exiled because you were believed to be a traitor.

Leit spoke of his father and mother. They died before the war. His father died of blood poisoning from a wound that wouldn't heal. Leit was a young warrior on the trails then. His father had a strong body, quiet nature, and focused mind. Leit received those from him. His mother died in a gentle sleep a season before the war. She shared with her son watchful dark eyes, skill with a hammer and anvil, and distaste for disorder. Both his parents expressed love with words, embraces, and acceptance. Leit had been a rough, physical boy with a tender heart. They recognized the warrior in him. They told of ancestors whose path he followed. He received guidance early. He proved to be a boy capable of discipline and restraint, of quick reflexes and mind. His teachers expected great tales to be told of him.

YOU NAVIGATED AROUND EACH OTHER'S PAIN. YOU APPROACHED THE edges but did not enter. His pain was too close. Yours was too deep. The reverse was true as well.

Leit was your friend, and you loved him as such. You hadn't tried to hide the nature of your exile and assumed many in the settlement knew the reason. Whether he had been told, you had no way to know. He didn't ask. Because you loved him, because you knew the pain he hid was linked to yours, you chose to tell him the truth.

When I was a mapmaker, charting a border of the kingdom, you said, I chose to step upon the bank across the river.

You said you were brought to a Guardian settlement and treated with kindness. Never had you felt such peace. You sensed an abiding goodness all around. The calm unnerved but beckoned you. Two men on your crew attempted to find you, and they, too, experienced what you did. You three agreed not to speak of it to anyone, but one did. He confessed to the riches he had seen in the settlement. He told of the little Voice who spoke of the dragon and the hoard. Your people chose a feat for Prince Wyl, a quest to find the dragon. You followed him. You both saw the hoard, but there was disagreement about its purpose. On the journey home, you became lovers at last. After the return, you married him.

Later, you learned Wyl's brother and four other men had gone to the settlement while you and Wyl were away. There were inquiries among those who had visited. Suspicions festered. You traveled to warn the Guardians of a potential attack. You wanted to protect them. When you returned home, you admitted what you'd done. No one heeded your arguments. Everyone was inclined to think the worst and take action. Then the King died. Your husband took the throne and authorized the first blows. You were imprisoned and ordered to draw a map to the hoard. After it was complete, you were exiled, sent away with two armed men. You suspected you were to be killed, but one of the men let you go. You traveled until you stopped at this northern settlement and felt you'd found your home. You were grateful to be accepted, in spite of who you were.

I'm the one who caused the war, you said. I would understand if you didn't wish to speak to me again.

Leit turned his eyes from you to the plain.

What makes you think you have such power? asked he.

You expected no such answer as that.

There are forces far greater and more dangerous than the curiosity to see what's on another side, said he.

But if I hadn't been . . . You couldn't finish the thought.

He rubbed his chest with his palm.

There's not one straight line between cause and effect. Many roads lead to the same place, or not. The choice depends on the travelers. As a mapmaker, you understand, don't you?

Yes, you said.

Makha focused her eyes on you. Never once had you tried to touch her. You were somewhat afraid of the wolf. She stretched her head beyond her crouched forelegs and sniffed the air near your face. She raised her ears, then settled again at Leit's side.

She accepts you, said Leit. He spoke as if the wolf's gesture meant more to him than any word you ever said.

One night at the plateau, he didn't wish to speak. He was in your presence but far away. His eyes glazed. His body seemed heavy, immobile.

You had never touched him other than in the customary ways. As you learned, the Guardians were an affectionate people who greeted and parted with kisses, handshakes, and embraces. Yet that night, your hand reached for the back of his neck.

He flinched but didn't pull away. His dark hair brushed your skin. His flesh was raised but not raw. You tried to read the relief without moving your hand. You turned your mind to each place where your fingers touched. You realized there were permanent welts on his skin. He had been branded.

He remained still.

Please, don't ask me now, said he.

YOU WANT TO REPEAT THE STORY OF HOW YOU CAME TO LOVE HIM. YOU want the tale of the woman who feels passion again, but this serves no purpose other than diversion. Remember, old woman, be sparse with nostalgia.

What emerged between you and Leit was not the bloodthick wildmind rut you had with Wyl. No matter your higher feelings for your first spouse, it was that at its core. Whereas with Leit, you loved the man before you loved his body.

Leit wasn't a man you thought physically beautiful at first. You had a different idea of masculine beauty. Wyl embodied that. The proportioned angles of his face. The length of his limbs in relation to the rest of him. The width of his shoulders. The shapes of his hands. Had you drawn him yourself into being, you could have done no better. He fit you in all the right places.

Leit had a slant to his eyes. He had a suspicious look. He was a big man. Tall. Thick-muscled. His back wide and meaty as an ox. He appeared hewn from stone. Like the blood-born men of their region, he grew his own dense coat of dark hair from his head to his legs.

Yet you came to appreciate the qualities within. These softened his brute shape. You had watched him beat metal to leaf thinness and appreciate the delicate result. His broad arms held little children with warm gentleness. He gave thoughtful counsel when asked for his opinion. To his warrior companions, he was affectionate and devoted.

Both Leit and Wyl were good men. Neither was compelled to do harm on purpose. Wyl was good the way a steed can be good. Reliable, strong, harmless unless provoked. Leit's sense of honor held him at his center. Your first spouse's weakness was of will. He questioned his own. He was easily swayed. Leit was firm in himself.

There was a core to Leit that there wasn't in Wyl. Wyl could be manipulated.

Tell the truth.

You didn't respect Wyl for that reason. You hated Raef for the undue influence he had over his brother, but Wyl allowed it. What you despised about Raef, you possessed as well. You rationalized that you deserved to work with the old mapmaker. You did. You proved your skill. Yet your place in the apprentice's chair came through guile. Subtle and suppressed as it was, you had no right to wield it.

In slow progression, your bond with Leit strengthened. Still, he didn't fully trust you to touch him. Within the settlement, you came to greet and depart as anyone else did. No more, no less. In time, your affection deepened to holding hands and close embraces. | he withdrew at the hint of amorous possibility | The instances happened only within the forest's cover. Neither chose to consciously hide this. Yet the closeness wasn't lost on others. Many could see you had formed a special friendship, although few dared to inquire of its nature.

A WOMAN YOU DIDN'T KNOW WELL, WHO WAS BORN AMONG THEM, APproached you one day. With sincerity, she said she was glad to see Leit and you had become friends. She asked if you wished for more than friendship.

No, you said.

Some wonder whether he'll share a room beyond a bed, said she.

Her direct reply was uncommon. You weren't sure how to respond. You understood the meaning. Leit had had lovers but had never formed a pair with one. You remained quiet.

Have you heard him sing? asked she.

No.

I feel distressed to hear that, said she.

I don't understand, you said.

He can sing so beautifully. Many have missed his voice in the evenings, and in the nurseries. He's not quite the same man he was before the war. I believe part of his voice was lost, said she.

You'd heard speculations about Leit before. To be more precise, you heard concern expressed. Has anyone seen him remove his breastplate? Does there appear to be a scar under his throat? Has he done a witnessing?

They didn't enjoy seeing others in pain. They found no pleasure in pondering another's misery. What they said of Leit was rooted in genuine distress.

Friends spoke to you in private. They said they had sat with him and encouraged him to share what he appeared to hold deep. They admitted they had shared their worries with the elders and Aza. They had seen your affinity for each other. They hoped you could help him, as they seemed unable.

One friend who visited you was a warrior who had long served with Leit. The man wept with deep pain.

We return home knowing there's no fight here. We're supposed to unarm, said he. But Leit wears that breastplate. It's a thin metal I could pierce with one sharp stab. We all understand the symbol. He covers something he wants no one to see. Even if it were physically removed, his armor would remain on.

I agree, but he has shared no more with me than what he said at his return ritual, you said.

What he hides can't be spoken at a ceremony, said he.

How do you know? you asked.

Most of us witnessed deeds we could never have conjured even in our nightmares, said he.

You took his hands in yours. The ache in your palms traveled straight to your heart. You willed yourself to let him cry and allowed yourself to join him.

You had attended the ceremony after Leit's return. What took place wasn't entertainment or a spectacle. After returns from the trails, and the war, the rituals were held upon the warriors' request. The people owed them witness for the service they gave. No one was required to attend, but a large group formed each time. The people were part of a symbolic transference. It was understood that they, too, shared in the warriors' pain. Unless it was released and transformed, the pain would warp the warriors. It would hide inside and could, as it was seen outside of the Guardian settlements, erupt when there was no call for violence.

Each warrior was allowed to be as explicit as he or she wished to be. There was no directive other than to tell the truth as they saw it. Within a huge cauldron, a fire burned. The warriors spoke without interruption. They told of what they had witnessed and done. They told of human beings they had injured or killed. After the warriors were finished, the people asked questions and shared their thoughts. When all was quiet, the warriors gave offerings to the fire.

At the ritual you attended, a man held a tunic covered in dried blood and tossed it into the flames. Another threw in a pouch, another a short sword. Leit burned a length of rope.

The people stood to form a circle around the warriors and the fire. They sang a song of thanks for their sacrifice. We claim their truth as our own, said they. We bear witness to their witness. We take the burden of deeds done in our name. Someday, they sang, peace will reign. Someday, peace will reign.

A subtle brightness returned to the warriors soon after the ceremonies. The rite served its mysterious purpose to a degree. Neighbors commented that the warriors who came back from the war were different from those who had served only on the trails. The warriors' beloveds agreed that a strange vigilance never left them.

When you heard Leit tell his story, you had not yet met him.

You had no point of reference for the man he was before the war. That would be, despite the pain, to the benefit of you both. He would not have to bear the comparison in your eyes. You would not have to bear the memory of a time before the darkness.

As you came to know him, you knew that he held a burden. He carried himself in a crouch and at a distance. You sensed his guard. He could hide it from others but never from his companions and, later, rarely from you. One day, it would drop full away in his daughter's presence, the child who moved through impossible gaps while she stood still.

YOU WATCHED LEIT WITH LOVE AND CAUTION. YOU PLACED YOURSELF near the nursery where he tended children in the afternoon. He held the ones who wanted to be held. He played with the ones who sought a partner in games.

You recognized a pale little girl with light green eyes. A foundling. A lone warrior had returned with her in his arms two years prior. You remembered your first months in the settlement. How unremarkable it was to see an orphaned child welcomed into a neighboring family. The immediate embrace fascinated you. The children were not of the Guardians' bodies or blood, but this didn't matter. They were loved on sight without condition.

It was their way. Few families had more than one child who resembled either parent, or both. If two or three children were with their parents, one or two were often foundlings. This, too, was how the Guardians lived by their myths. Egnis the Red Dragon had saved the newborn orphan Azul. In honor of Azul, the Guardians saved the lost and abandoned.

The pale girl wrapped her arms around Leit's neck. He smiled as she spoke into his ear. He laughed when she leapt away. A young warrior sat on the bench next to him with an infant against his bare chest.

What had seemed unnatural had become normal. You once recoiled at the sight. You had never seen such behavior before. | the twins, a kind young man in blue | It unnerved you less, but still to some degree, to see fathers, grandfathers, and uncles touch the little ones with affection. But the warriors often had no familial ties. No matter. The infants slept against their ursine breasts. The children flittered around their knees. The warriors cared for them as gently as loving mothers.

Edik explained the meaning of their ways.

The warriors' time among the children is to remind them, said he. You, too, were once this small, this helpless. This being remains in you, and all beings were this, are this. When you kill, you kill the part of the person that was and always will be innocent. You deny that person the means to connect again. Helpless and innocent, they require your protection, no matter how cruel or evil their actions appear. This is what is asked of you.

Yes, everyone in every settlement was taught the same. You learned in time. | only now do you understand and believe |

Leit would tell you that the warriors were trained to injure and kill. Yet their greatest duty was to protect all life. All life, even the lives of those presumed to be enemies. There were times, however, that the lesser choice was chosen. The Guardian warriors believed that to take another's life was grievous, and they lamented to do so. But under no circumstances, said he, should any commit the wicked act of killing a child.

AZA SPOKE TO YOU AT LAST. SHE SAID SHE COULD SENSE A DEEP WOUND in Leit. She believed his return ritual had not given him release.

Friends had shared their worry. The elders who had the courage and wisdom to ask about his scar were met with silence. Aza offered her aid, but he had not confided in her. She would not violate the Voices' ethics and search his thoughts. As it was, she sensed he blocked her anyway, trained as he was to mask what was in his mind.

Aza explained that Leit was born among, and he understood that pain ignored or denied is a poison within one's being. He wouldn't be right within himself unless it was acknowledged. His pain reached beyond himself, too. Subtle as it may be, like a vibration along a spider's web, others would feel it.

You told Aza you wouldn't pry. She said you should not. However, if he chose to tell you, he would likely do so through a witnessing. She asked if you had experienced one.

You had. The practice took place in a quiet room or secluded outdoor space. The person who spoke was to receive no judgment from the person or group listening. The person's story was confidential, and no listener was allowed to repeat it. Those born among didn't struggle with these rules as did those born away. They were not prone to gossip.

In the moment, you remembered the housemate who chose you among her witnesses. She resembled many of the Guardians, but she came from a village some miles away. She left behind her life and wandered into the wilderness. She wanted to die. Instead, she stumbled upon an old woman's hut. The woman told her which direction to follow, which led her to the settlement. The people received her without judgment. She was shocked by the kindness and care. Neither could she give to the children or husband she'd left behind. Their need of her had become parasitic and intolerable. They were better off without her. She believed herself sick. No one she knew seemed to feel as she did. | yes, yes | If they had, she would have thought them sick, too. You listened as rage, confusion, disappointment, and despair streamed from her. Then, after she fell silent, her face softened. She said that day was the start of her unburdening. Telling the truth meant losing the protection of lies.

Aza said that if Leit chose to speak, you must listen with every fiber of your being. Listen as you would want to be heard.

What if I cannot bear what I'm told? What if what he says must be known by others? you asked.

You can refuse, if you believe yourself incapable of being a witness for him, said she.

She cautioned that choice had a consequence for him and you. As well, you had to understand that if you witnessed, you entered a sacred trust. You cannot tell another. You could speak only with him about what was said. You may choose to encourage him to tell the elders, if you felt that was important. But your judgment of who must know was but your own.

You told Leit that his friends and Aza had spoken to you. He wasn't surprised. He expected it. They had come to him as well. Their concern was valid.

He said part of his experience was one he didn't wish to reveal. No one born among could comprehend what had happened. He could make no sense of it. What he had seen had begun to alter his thoughts about the Guardians' place in the world.

Our people acknowledge the burden we warriors carry on their behalf, said Leit. We're the vessels of their aggression as much as the executors of their sense of justice and order. This understanding among us has served for many generations. Our storytelling does give relief. We do feel respected, but now, among those who survived the war, we don't feel understood. You were born away, and you can contrast our ways with the ones you knew before. Your experience leaves you less surprised at the violence and cruelty, but no less injured by it.

Even you wouldn't believe what was witnessed during the war, said he. We cannot tell the truth of it all. Our people want to believe our warriors' role is right and good. Our people don't want to know the pain we bear and see. If they understood, truly understood, they could never again call us to sacrifice our lives, the body and the soul, or do what we do to other human beings.

You moved to comfort him. You anticipated the breastplate's flat heat, but you didn't feel it. He swayed away from you.

Don't touch me, said he.

The cold rejection seared against the controlled burn between you. So close, not close enough.

TELL THE TRUTH, OLD WOMAN.

Did you tell him when you did because of what you wanted?

You hardly acknowledged that your love for him had changed. There had been no chase, therefore nothing to fight or flee. There had been no intention from either of you to extend beyond friendship. You had no conscious wish to pair yourself again. Yet you were not yet too old, were still ripe. Had the animal pursuit been all there was, you had no outer resistance against following it. You could have shared a bed with anyone. The Guardians didn't worry over such matters.

He was reluctant to trust you fully, you decided. You had no such reservations about him. You told him more about your life before than you had to any other friend. Make no more of this than it was, though. You spoke little of those you had known. Your family, Wyl, Raef, Heydar, Burl, your crew. Not at all, not yet, of the twins. Instead, you told of the kingdom, its land and people, its customs and standards. You shared a removed, anthropological point of view.

You didn't plan to tell him, the night you did. It hadn't entered your mind as a complete thought. But you sat on the plateau with the wolf between you and the breastplate not. The scar at his throat was a shadow. Then you were telling him of your exile. You spoke of the one and the other one. You told of the night you were awakened by the one and what he had done to you. By chance, the other one stopped him before you received more than a scar on your arm and the taint where he'd entered your body.

He molested me. He meant to rape me, you said.

The Guardians had no singular words to describe what had happened and almost happened to you. You had to say some of it in your native language at first, then you tied words together in your adopted tongue to explain. Silent at last, you shook and cried because of what you'd exhumed. You remembered the animal fear and human horror. You had fought and wanted to fight harder but you had not the strength. You hadn't expected to feel such shame and rage. Because I can, said he. He would have, if he hadn't been stopped. What would have happened to you if he had?

Leit crawled around Makha. He put his back to the nearest tree and held his arms open. You curled against him. You welcomed the comfort.

Tell the truth.

His response gratified you. You were not proud you felt that way.

I feel sad and angry for you, Aoife, said he. You're not the only woman born away who has come to us with this story. You're safe now. You're with me, with us, and you are safe. Go to Aza, and she'll help you come to peace.

Neither of you spoke for a long while.

Then said he, That doesn't happen here. That doesn't happen here yet.

Days later, he said he wanted you to be his witness.

You agreed.

He told you the story of his scar. When he was done, your heart and mind could not contain what he'd said. You had to let it out. You secreted yourself away and wrote down his words. | you were told never to tell | They are here. His pain lives, although your beloved is dead.

This is what he spoke of the child, the tree, the wound, and the wolf.

| of evil incarnate |

We kept them at bay.

Our people didn't know how close they were. An easy three-day walk from our settlement.

The closest village—a people who had always been an ally—gave us away to the men who came to invade and plunder. Our Voice was brave and moved through the village as a peddler, all the while listening to the adults speak. They were promised a portion of the bounty seized. What they did not fear, as it turns out, they envied. They knew of our mine, land, and livestock. The foreign men would sate their desires through our near neighbors' complicity.

Our warriors entered the forest armed and ready. We didn't want to kill but we were determined to stop the spreading violence. We knew what losses our people had suffered.

Our restraint—and it was restraint—wore thin. My warriors had spoken of their urge to kill. I reminded them of their oaths, as they reminded me. The men who assaulted us were crazed with exhaustion and hatred. Our restraint infuriated them all the more.

We battled through the morning, spattered with blood, vomit, piss, and shit. Our own, that of the other men.

This you know. You've heard this before. These tales we tell about our deeds.

We gathered our injured and dead. Both sides. They lost heart, lost too many men. I don't know.

Then I saw the child.

She peeked around a tree, then was gone. Our Voice—oh, our Voice, who sang to our bleeding and dying, trying to heal them—she said to leave the child alone. I pleaded with her to help me find her to see if she needed to be led home or taken as a foundling.

Our Voice relented and searched, but the child eluded us. She thought the girl had gone back to her family. I argued we were too far from the village. She reminded me there were many people hiding in the forest who had fled the village soon after the foreign men arrived and the fighting began. I believed there was just cause for my concern.

Our Voice wasn't uncaring. She was grief-stricken and overwhelmed and wanted to save the warriors who had a chance. I did, too, but after all the bloodshed, sick with the knowledge that I had killed on purpose, I wanted to save someone.

You knew, didn't you, I was known as the warrior without a deliberate kill.

Her rescue, I thought, could atone.

I said I would stay behind until the last of my warriors were on the way home. I kept watch for the girl.

I saw her again. She sat against a tree. She was four, five years old. She wore no blouse and she carried an infant. I watched her attempt to nurse the limp baby boy. He was naked and dirty. He cried weakly. I knew he was dying. I called to her and waved. I approached her with calm and a sweet tone in my voice, although she understood not a word I said. She stood on thin legs—she was so thin—and ran with the baby in her arms.

I pursued her. I know now I was delirious, lost in my own way, because I abandoned my warriors when they still needed my attention.

I tracked her and didn't sleep, to keep an eye on her. In the night, the baby boy died. She carried his stiff body and shook him. I'm not sure she understood.

I tried to gain her trust. I reached my hand to her from a distance, and I left her food in the open and where she could see me.

I could have captured her. She was weak and small. She could not outrun me. But I didn't want to take her by force. She was enough afraid.

I lost awareness of what was around me—and her. Some of those rough bloodied foreign men remained in the forest. Lost, far from their homes. Angry men who perceived defeat and failure in their fight.

You must know, Aoife, not all foundlings are lost and abandoned. We take into our care children who bruise and bleed from all parts of their bodies, who are sick with neglect, who survive horrors they did not cause. Explain to me a human being who can do this to a child. Explain to me how anyone can again do what was done to them.

So—

There were three of them.

They captured us—the girl, the dead boy, and me.

I understood not a word they said. They debated what to do with us, I could tell, debated long.

Makha, yes, I failed to mention Makha. She accompanied me everywhere, watchful, loyal companion that she is. She understood to stay away from the human battles. Her teeth and stealth were no match for blades. But she would not leave the closeness of my side, or the sight of me.

I knew she watched as the men subdued us. One grabbed the girl and the dead boy she refused to drop. Her brother, no doubt. Two wrestled me to the ground and bound my arms behind my back. I knew this danger was worse than any I had ever faced.

They bound my hands and ankles and tied me to a tree. They took the baby from the girl and threw him to the ground. She screamed and wept. She was tied to a large tree several feet away. The rope coiled around her chest. In my delirium I wondered where they found the ropes. Why they let us live.

It was night. There was a cooking fire. A hare torn apart among them. A squirrel, too. I was starved, thirsty, sore. One of them tossed a shred of meat near enough that I could bend to the ground and take it. I tried to breathe. My training all came to one breath and the next. This moment. This moment. They had no drink but they were drunk. The man who seemed to lead, the cruelest of them, but also the most calm, flashed his sword at me. Pricked my skin enough to bleed. He spoke and they all laughed. The girl looked at her brother, who was lost in the dark.

Then this man, who made me bleed, approached the little girl. He knelt in front of her. He spoke in a tone that froze me as I became hot with a terrible fury. I cried out and he laughed. I had told him to stop, which he didn't heed, no matter my words. One of his companions drew his sword at me at a threatening distance.

What provoked what happened next, I cannot say. I don't know. I cannot fathom. Why?

I remember he looked at me. Looked me square in the eyes. They were dark and they glistened. They were strangely vacant, then strangely full of elation.

The man robbed the girl of her clothing. He wrenched her legs apart. He desecrated that child before my eyes. What was the word you said in your language? Rape? Rape of a child. I screamed and she screamed screamed screamed screamed. I strained against the rope, my chest raw with thrashing, screaming to let her go.

The sword sliced me open and Makha howled as the blade swept through. My wound her wound. Blood from my throat to my groin.

The rage. I had never felt such rage. I wanted to kill them all, especially the fiend. What being does that? The other men did nothing to stop him. Not a word or gesture. They allowed it.

Yet worse. Worse. I wanted him to kill the girl. I wanted to kill her because I could not imagine how she could survive this horror.

I wanted her dead. I wanted a child dead. I might have killed her myself with my own hand, given the chance, if the fiend had not stabbed her again and again with such force that he had to pull the sword from the tree. I saw the tree sway and felt its roots moan under my feet. It wailed and I cried and I welcomed the wicked mercy.

My legs were wet with my own blood. Makha howled again—that time with warning—and the men looked at each other with fear. She was near enough to attack. Had I called her, she would have risked her life for mine.

I couldn't decide whether I wished to live or die, so I breathed and willed my blood to clot to give me moments to decide, or to prepare to die at their hands.

My wolf lay in the brush. I sensed her. She watched me.

Someone cut the child free and pulled her body and the baby's into the forest. They fell into thick exhausted sleep. I reached into the well of myself. It was so empty. I never knew such emptiness.

Come morning, I was still alive. My body hurt. Flies crawled on my open flesh. The men arose. They seemed surprised, then angry, that I had survived the night. The fiend and one of the men went into the forest, while the third kept guard. They returned with a hare snared on a rope. The fiend laid a piece of raw meat within reach. I bent to take it—my body primal in its response to survive—and I took it in my teeth. I raised myself to chew as a man and swallowed a loose morsel, then saw what was hidden under the flesh. The orb of evidence stared at me.

The fiend laughed and laughed and laughed. I gagged and tried to stand, and he kicked me in the jaw. I fell to the ground. They untied me and—still conscious, though barely so—I was thrown into a crevice where soil had eroded from the roots of a tree. They covered me with dirt and rocks.

They buried me alive. A narrow stagger of stones must have given me enough room to breathe.

The next moment I remember, Makha licked my face. She dug her teeth into my arm enough to hurt. She forced me from the hole. I lay on the ground as she licked my body. The wound was sore and alive. Alive, yes, because I saw the white maggots in her silver muzzle.

She bit into my hair and forced me to crawl to water. I drank. I vomited. I drank. I went unconscious. She hunted for me but I could not, would not, eat. She disappeared, only to return with a honeycomb in her mouth. She crushed it with her jaws. The honey oozed on my skin and into the wound. She smeared it with her nose. I screamed with pain and she whimpered in reply.

She wept with me under the moon. She forced me into that dim light and slept against my side. Some nights, I didn't know whether I was man or wolf, alive or dead.

She fed me honey, dressed me in honey. We did not speak, not what we humans call speech, but she communicated beyond words in a way I always understood.

You must live, she told me.

Why? I asked her.

That is your reason to decide, she said, but I love you and want to save you as you saved me.

I could eat, then sit, then stand. I had no awareness of time. My wound crawled no more but would not heal. I wept every day until I was exhausted. Had I left the girl alone, she might have lived. She would not have endured those final hours of her brief innocent life.

What happened to her was my fault.

I led the fiends to her. And no matter what I had been taught to believe and trained to honor, I no longer considered those men, men. I had believed evil to be a perception. I experienced it as real. That evil lived in me—that power and desire to destroy. I feared myself. I feared all of humankind. I was not spared this sickness.

Makha knew the way into the realm. She had accompanied me before. She led me to the Three. You thought they were myth? They are no myth. I risk my life for their mystery while others mistake the treasure they keep.

So—

I stood before them with my weeping wound. The woman-wisp gave me a potion. The dwarf laid me on a soft bed in a cave. I felt no pain but I was awake. The dragon blew fire on a brand that the dwarf seared into my back and the woman cooled with water and song. This was a ritual meant to cleanse me. The wound healed with a slight leak, and the dwarf crafted a plate to protect my flesh as well as hide my pain.

Prepare yourself.

Look, woman. Look at my body. Never mind the slices and gouges.

Look at the scar that split me in two. My navel is gone, eaten by maggots. The blade ripped only skin and muscle, but the deed tore more, far more.

I awake every day with that child's blood on my hands and in my own body. Every day with the trace of rage I could not conceive I possessed.

A sickness festers beyond our settlements, worse than I ever imagined. I am witness, and now I am carrier.

I looked into the fiend's eyes before and after the deeds. That was a wholly human evil. That was a wholly human choice. And I must endure the rest of my days knowing he and others like him live and befoul—in mundane ways, in secret hidden ways, in the worst ways—what is sacred.

My wound reminds me of what I could not, cannot, protect.

Speech and movement eluded you. A cold sweat continued its creep across your skin. Your heart beat wild. You were in shock. Your mind's eye continued to see the frightened, defiled, dead child.

Then you were four, five. Your brother was crying again. Your mother was silent. Your father was a shadow. You hid and screamed a wordless petition for escape. Take me from this place. I don't care about the cost or the trouble or if someone dies, even if it's me. Take me far away. Please.

Leit slipped on his tunic. He put his head in your lap. You touched the welts on his neck. You smoothed his hair. All you could do was smooth his hair. Later you cried alone all night. So many tears, endless as the suffering you caused and endured.

Not long later, you went to his bed.

The invitation was unspoken.

The night was one of ice and fire. You walked to his home after a late meal with friends. He stepped ahead of you to block the force of the wind. Snow and ice covered horizontal planes. A world of white silver black. You loved the bell-chime flutter of falling snow.

Makha split through the darkness when you crossed the

threshold. You felt intimate space before you saw its corners. He lived in a small two-room hut with no other person. He invited you to sit on the high bed near the hearth. It was warm from Makha's heat. She jumped next to your hip.

Leit placed logs and struck flint. He knelt at work until flames leapt. The space echoed with a sharp noise. You thought that cracks of fire and ice sounded much alike. A release, a giving way.

He removed his cloak, a fur-lined hat, a wool overshirt, and a tunic. You could discern welts that reached from his waist to his neck.

He stoked the fire. This is where memory loops, the first and the last | you think the last | and unions between. A precise steward of an efficient fire. He returned to you with his face and chest blazing on their own. Transferred to you. Oh, you move in and out of this memory because these were moments before | and after | Wei. Strange, the stray details that cling with such tenacity.

He gave a short bark to Makha and pointed her to the floor. She jumped down. He took you in his arms. Warm. You were so warm.

You asked him to sit with his back to the fire. You looked at the brand. He had not shown it to you when he revealed the scar. The shapes were not random. They formed an image. You swept his dark hair away from his neck. He was marked with a dragon.

And this didn't hurt? you asked.

No. I received merciful care, said he.

You asked him to lie on his back. The darkness beyond the fire spared you full sight of the gnarled knit but you could not avoid its texture. With gentle hands, you touched the scar for the first time. You reached the place where his navel had once been. He choked with a cry. He grabbed your wrist.

Allow it, said he.

You understood. You placed both hands where his life had begun.

He held your arm as if it were a rope. He wept. You wept. Makha whimpered. You kept one hand on his belly and stretched at his side.

Where are you now? you asked.

Leit looked into your eyes. His hands twisted into your hair. His mouth sealed yours. He remained solid and he became fluid.

You were unprepared for the transformation. He abandoned himself to you. You, surprised, abandoned yourself to him. The cold beyond the bed gave love an edge. A border to contain it. Despite his scars, he was in other ways whole. There were places where sharpness had never touched him.

As you curled together to sleep, your hands rested each upon the other's healed skin. The one flashed through your memory, touched where your thighs met, and was gone. Aza and your daughter would later help you purge him for good.

YOU WERE NOT FOOLISH ENOUGH TO ALLOW THE SOWING OF AN UNwanted seed again. All of the women of the settlement knew where to get aids to continue their cycles. You visited a midwife who had special knowledge of these matters.

You thought of your life before. There were rumors of those who had plant wisdom. Discouragement of all kinds kept women away, including you. There were coercions, and there were lies. The wish to fill the womb was natural and welcomed. This was the female's highest purpose. As well, you, all of you, were told, in one way or another, that you suffer your mistakes. This had been ingrained in you without your knowing how. The inevitability of consequence. You resented it. Yet the twins were proof of how you embodied the lesson.

The old woman sat next to you in a cushioned chair. She asked if you'd had children. You could have lied. No one knew. But you stated the facts. Yes, twins. Did they survive the birth? Yes. How old are they now? You became blank and mute, then said, They would be five. Are they still with you? No. When did they die? They didn't. Or haven't, I believe. I had to leave them. | the truth |

I feel sorrow to hear that, Aoife, said she.

Yes, well, some time has passed, you said.

She stood to prepare two cups of tea. She closed the door to the hut.

We must have a talk about our ways in matters of new life, said she.

We are the only beings, at least to our knowledge, who can choose to create another, said she.

The beasts and we are driven by our bodies, but we have greater faculties. Unlike the beasts, we are aware of what these impulses are. This must be important, otherwise we wouldn't have this awareness.

The human can be long-lived. We rarely die in large numbers. We have no predators as the beasts have among each other. Nature seeks to balance itself. We are part of Nature, but we can manipulate it. We have no natural enemies—except one another, it seems. If we crowd, we can sicken each other. Some maladies are of the body. These correct with loving care, rest, and wholesome food.

Some believe wars are a way to thin our herds. The old woman believed violence was a sickness itself.

Without awareness, humans could strain, even break, the balance of which they were part. The land, the water, the beings whose lives were taken for food could be in peril.

The old woman said that the Guardians understood most people desired to have children. They also believed that none should be denied the joy that children bring. She reminded you of the myths of Azul the Orphan. Love transcended the body and all that came of it.

You gave birth to two children who survived, Aoife, said the old woman. You continued the cycle of young and gave your legacy and that of another man.

She said she could not and would not forbid you to have

another child. It was not her place to decide for you. Her responsibilities were to share knowledge of their ways and treat you to bring you health and comfort. Before you left her hut, she gave you a pouch of herbs and told you how to use them.

Never once had you considered bearing another child. However, the visit sparked thoughts you didn't expect. You had no dispute with the striving for balance. The view was practical, although you knew of the instinctive forces that fought against it. The woman didn't speak of such impulses.

Neither did she mention dangers no beast considered. You thought of Nature's uncertainty. The Guardians, like you, were subject to drought, cold, famine, disease, and predators. All were brought forth in risk. Born to die. But the principle remained the same. Life repeats itself. Life wants to be.

You had replenished. Because of that alone, perhaps you should have considered no more. You could have waited for a foundling.

Still, the instinctive animal in you stirred. You had the prospect of a virile mate. You were not yet too old, almost in your thirtieth year. You felt your body warm in waiting.

You chose to pair yourself again. You left your room and your housemates. Leit's small hut was enough for you and the silver wolf. By mutual agreement, you decided to have the bonding ritual. You chose spring for obvious reasons, and one significant for you. It would mark your fourth year in your chosen home.

Any elder could have the honor, but you asked Edik to perform the ceremony. He smiled and held you close. He took unexpected joy in your happiness and your inclusion of him. His delight made you cry until your heart hurt.

You acquired a simple silk gown from the stores. A gifted friend cut and stitched it to fit. You had no mirror to see yourself at once, but you felt beautiful.

Leit reflected your feelings in his eyes when he beheld you

that day. His gaze was transcendent. He was handsome in his new clothes. Three embroiderers had worked long on the elaborate vest that covered his linen shirt.

As agreed, you didn't exchange rings. He surprised you with a narrow sapphire bracelet with a center crystal of Guardian blue. You gave him a gold torque decorated with beasts of the forest. Neither could have chosen a gift more suited to the other. Yet that night, after the celebration, he brought to the bed you shared | room, house, life | one last token.

I smithed some fine pieces and traded well the last time I was away. Here, said he.

You opened a wooden box. Inside were several vials of ink, a clutch of feathers, and a stack of writing sheets. You had never seen the latter. They were made of fibers, not skin. They were so thin that light glowed straight through.

I thought you might like to try this for your writings, said he.

He knew about your records of the Guardians' history and ways. He encouraged you, although he didn't fully understand the purpose.

The ink and quills I'll use soon, but I will save most of the sheets for a special work, you said. You kissed him with pure affection.

FOR ALMOST A YEAR, THE DECISION TO HAVE A CHILD WAS A MATTER OF discussion. Not so had it been with Wyl. This had been a given in your life before, not an option. The awakening to bear another was a mystery. You were fully aware of it but confused. Your body seemed to want one thing, your mind another.

Yet one thing you did know. You had to tell him the secret.

I gave birth to two children. Twins, a girl and a boy. I left them in my exile, you said.

This was the truth, beyond the facts. You weren't overcome by the admission. This was a matter to settle. No tears came to your eyes. No lump swelled in your throat. Whatever guilt you felt for your lack of guilt kept itself hidden away.

His eyes flashed with surprise, then understanding. You realized he had long sensed a secret in you and thought you now revealed it. Leit took your hands.

Do you wish to speak of them? asked he.

You had anticipated no such response. You had practiced for shock, dismay, and sympathy. Even anger. Instead he broke you open with the unexpected. A brief summary was what you had prepared to share, but that wasn't what you said.

He listened as you told of the unintended result of your ardor. The pregnancy prompted the wedding, although Wyl | yes, you spoke his name | was intended for another. Their birth was long and painful, but the children were healthy and strong. Short of forbidding, Wyl denied your intent to return to mapping the kingdom. So you cared for the infants with the help of a nursemaid. They were sweet children, no more fussy than expected. The girl had an eagerness about her. The boy, a watchfulness. You took them into the forest often. They liked to explore and share what they found with one another. They preferred to sleep face-to-face. When separated, they became distressed.

You paused. The thought that formed didn't escape your mouth. They had each other. All those dark months in your womb, the girl and the boy weren't alone. You felt comfort. You felt sorrow. You acknowledged what a barren place your body had been. Only after Wei could you understand.

Leit clutched your hands.

What are their names? asked he.

Then tears came. You didn't know why. His thumbs stroked the water away from your cheeks.

The invocation of their names in your native tongue made you quiver. Then you told him.

Does their father love them? asked he.

I think he does. Yes, you said.

They are fortunate, said he.

You thought of Wyl with the newborn twins, their hands in his. Then of how he had grabbed them when you returned from warning the settlement. They are mine, said he. Was his love pure or possession? you wondered. You had neither for them. You'd left them without a struggle, protest, or plea.

Your ambivalence is clearer now, said Leit.

You nodded. I've told no one else except the midwife. Please keep this between us. It's too complicated to share. You are my witness, Leit. Help me carry it, you said.

YOU WEREN'T ALONE IN YOUR RETICENCE. LEIT, TOO, QUESTIONED whether to sire a child.

He was the one to speak to you of the forces the parents bring to bear. These were patterns that determined hair, eyes, skin, shape, and voice. Still more mysterious were tendencies, aptitudes, and afflictions. There were behaviors learned, rote, from one generation to the next. Yet he thought other matters, unseen, transferred as well.

My scar is external proof of a greater disfigurement within, said Leit. I felt my body fibers warp. What I witnessed isn't only on my flesh and in my memory.

You thought he exaggerated.

Notice how few warriors have children who resemble them. Some among us feel our patterns have been twisted and fear the damage this could do, said he.

Edik told me a child can endure much if it feels beloved, you said.

That depends on the child's nature and the conditions into which he's born, doesn't it? asked he.

Under and aside from his fear, Leit wanted a child of his flesh. He acknowledged the primal urge. He wished to know the swell of a woman's body was due to his part. To love a child didn't require biological paternity. He loved the children he tended in the nurseries. But he admitted that he wanted to experience the blood mystery of fatherhood, his connection to a child as both root and branch.

And you? What was your reason to bear, again?

Tell the truth.

You questioned whether you could be a loving mother. You wondered whether circumstances had impinged upon your feelings for the twins. This was a terrible risk to take. Your decision was selfish at its source. If you were flawed, incapable, the child would suffer. There was little consolation that the babe would be in a community based on love.

It was also a repeated pattern of your own. What you gave to Wyl, you could give to Leit. The difference? Wyl wanted an heir. Leit wanted a child.

You both chose to have Wei. In spite of it all.

THERE, IT WAS DONE.

No concoctions taken before, or after, you moved away from him. A beginning in the womb, alone in the dark.

You went to the midwife again. You told her you were pregnant. She asked what you wanted. Her question's ambiguity shocked you. You complained of nausea and dizziness. She asked when you last bled. When you told her, she grasped a knife and gouged one of thirteen sticks that hung on the wall. She told you to expect a winter birth.

What have you shared with the little one? asked she.

Shared? you asked.

What have you told the babe of your stories and wishes?

You thought of Leit. He placed his hands on your belly every night and talked through your skin. You thought his actions silly but didn't discourage him.

I've told it nothing, you said.

Why not?

Why indeed? What grows is a dumb thing.

She turned to a wall of shelves with ceramic jars painted various colors. On each were small symbols that had meaning to her. She peered among them and then said:

A seed has its own map of being.

Its simple shape holds within a design greater than its size would suggest.

But will it become what it could be? Will it find its way to sandy soil when it requires loam? Will it find itself in the dark when it needs sun? If it sprouts, will something haplessly crush it? If it begins to grow, will it live where the roots can grow wide and deep, the stem strong and straight, the leaves broad and open? In what ground will it begin its life? Where it is planted makes a difference.

No matter what, it will continue to live, to try to live, no matter how inhospitable its environment, no matter how deformed it may become, how sick it is.

And here is a greater mystery. It may be deformed and propagate. The new plant may bear no obvious evidence, but somewhere in its memory, it carries the wound, one that takes long to heal.

The new seed is set. You are the soil now.

No warning. You burst into tears. The old woman sat across from you in silence. You wept a confused grief, utterly sourceless, it seemed. A grief you didn't know was there and could not name.

Your babe feels your sadness. She feels what you feel. You

cannot hide the truth from her. Place yourself within the child. What would you wish to feel and know? Begin there, Aoife.

YOU WERE BETTER PREPARED FOR WEI'S BIRTH. THAT YOU HAD GIVEN birth before was not the reason. Your friends and the midwife who cared for you embraced the dark secrecy of new life. Of course, without the man, the being could not begin. However, without the woman, it could never take form. It would never be. The Guardians honored this mystery as a sacred act of giving.

They acknowledged but didn't dwell on the dangers to the mothers' bodies and babies. They trusted an innate intelligence that began the moment two forces conjoined to bring forth a new being. Your body, said they, understands what your mind cannot.

The midwife chose herbs to give you strength. She visited you and Leit to teach you how to breathe. You laughed at the absurdity. You remembered the endless brutal bellow of your lungs before.

Holding of breath is common to block pain. Think for a moment. Do you remember an instance when you were hurt or frightened and stopped your breath? asked the midwife.

You looked at Leit when he suddenly took your hand. He held you in his eyes. You felt afraid, then braced yourself against it. His other hand went to your back. You had no clear images, but you clearly had the memories.

I'll teach you to move through pain. Leit will learn with you to help, said the midwife.

No such care was given to you before the twins. You remembered nothing but stories of horror, of endless screaming, of membranes ripped, of blood, so much blood. Oh, but when you see the babe, the pain will be worth it, said the women. You wondered if that was a lie or a consolation.

Pregnant with Wei, you felt loved as you had never been before. Your friends embraced you with tenderness you felt in your physical body. Their love for the unborn child flowed through their hands when they touched your belly. You know Wei sensed this. She seemed to reach through your flesh to return the affection. The babe's joy spilled into you. Leit, although not stingy before, kissed and caressed you more often. He rubbed your aches away and weathered your moods with sweet patience. For several cycles of the moon, you knew bliss.

You never knew this was possible.

Leit's turn to go back on the trails came, but he didn't leave. No warrior left the side of the woman who carried his child. Every morning and night, Leit spoke to the babe. | still he did not sing | Wei kicked at the sound of his voice, then became still as she settled to listen. He told her the myths, and fanciful tales, and stories of his life before the war. He repeated the names of ancestors and relatives, with titles or descriptions of what they had done. His mother had served as a smith. His father had been a fletcher. There were his grandparents, maternal and paternal, and their parents, and their parents. He named cousins, aunts, and uncles. He named the people of seven generations, each one connected to Wei through Leit.

Before you, child, your mother was Aoife, a mapmaker, who braved the curve of the world to find her home. What might she call herself now? asked Leit.

Content, you said.

You were. As well, you were happy. You couldn't remember many periods in your life before in which that had been the condition for long. Moments when you were a child and free to roam the forest. The apprenticeship with the old mapmaker, despite your undertone of desperation. The return home with Wyl, until.

Then inertia set into your body. Wide and round, you moved with difficulty. A rock budged with oxen will. The child would be born soon enough, but not soon enough. You felt the happiness slip to give way to deep sadness.

You weren't a monster, you knew at last. You loved the babe as surely as you loved her father. You anticipated the joy you would feel to see her face, to hold her warm new body.

Yet your pregnant stillness forced you to sit with old wounds. You bore the twins in fear, and you would bear Wei in grief. You wept as you remembered your mother's suffocated shame for the twins, who came too soon. You wept as you thought of your duty to the infants, who were needful and wanting when you needed and wanted something else.

You looked at your spouse's scar, sealed but somehow always open. You wondered what you had done. You were of two worlds. The one you left and the one you joined. You made a deliberate choice to bring her between them, although the latter would be her home.

Tell the truth, old woman. Name the grief now.

You had abandoned the girl and the boy before they were even born.

You were not ambivalent. You did not want them. No matter that the decision to give birth to and care for them suggests otherwise. Their presence in your body was an unwelcomed curiosity. You dreamed of them. They were one, sometimes two, sometimes three, birdlike serpents that bit your insides and sucked you dry. Parasites, you thought one morning, then banished the thought. You knew you shouldn't think such things. But you did.

You felt punished for your pleasure. A woman's fault yielded evidence that no man could ever bear. She took full blame, although only half of it was hers.

Your mother had said, Be grateful they are so young. They will not remember you.

You were not spared the memory of them.

HERE YOU SHALL LINGER. HERE IS WHERE YOUR LIFE TURNED ON ITself.

You awoke at night. The moon was full. Leit slept while you breathed through several waves. You roused him when you knew the duration between lessened. He put on his heavy cloak to alert a neighbor. That person left a warm bed to awaken the midwife and ring the nearby bell. The rhythm chimed to tell the others a woman's labor had begun. Your labor.

Leit fed the fire. He prepared the floor with a cushioned pallet, large pillows, and soft linens. He covered your feet with wool socks and helped you into layers of simple shifts.

You wanted to pace. You paced. The midwife arrived to see about you, then went to the adjacent room. You were prepared for this. She was near if she was needed. Otherwise, Leit was to see you and his child through the birth. This was their way. Nature's wisdom was within you both. You were encouraged by your friends to believe this was so.

The singing began outside. The welcome song repeated several times. Different gentle melodies followed. You could ask them to be silent or to resume any moment you wished. Their presence was meant to comfort. You had joined the welcomes for other babies. Then you felt the warm swell swirl among the singers. As the mother, you felt a loving heat penetrate your body to the waiting babe. You were surprised at the tangibility.

Makha paced. She loped at your side. You wanted her present. This was decided some time before when you discussed your wishes for the day of Wei's birth. You didn't tell Leit the reason, however. You didn't want to refer to the wound. Makha was welcomed because she had saved him. The wolf's healing instinct and her bond to your spouse ensured her wise attendance.

The waves intensified. You draped yourself over a mound of pillows. Leit rubbed and pressed your back until that no longer soothed. You crouched on hands and knees by the fire and slowly rocked. He was close enough to touch. He breathed with you, rhythmic as the sea. In a cessation of the pain, you became aware of what was outside you. Beautiful singing outside the door. Your spouse's quiet presence. The freedom to move and use your voice as you pleased. | such noise, woman! lie there and be brave! |

An unexpected pulse of desire streamed from your thighs to your mouth. You kissed him long until the next pang doubled you over. A horrible throb rippled through your abdomen as if something had escaped, violent with fear. You crept to a cold corner and pressed yourself up. You wept with hopeless grief. Leit's hand pressed on your shoulder. The midwife's hand was suddenly on the other. You demanded to be left alone. The pain of labor was minor compared with what now seized you. You wailed and keened. The midwife spoke into your ear.

Let it through, Aoife, said she. I know you're afraid, but you will not rip apart. Let it through. Let it out.

Because you trusted her, because your child wanted to be born, you screamed although you didn't understand why. You let the nameless rage have its way with you. Its power threatened to rupture the wet web of your flesh. Then Leit slipped himself between you and the wall. He held your exhausted body. He took that old pain in his arms.

Listen, said he. I love you. I love you. I love you. This he repeated until you calmed enough to say the words back to him. The midwife gave you a bittersweet drink. Within moments, the furious grief that had possessed you was a memory. You returned to your body in all its fullness. The midwife secreted herself away.

You asked Leit to remove your shifts. You knelt on the pallet with your hands on your thighs. You looked at him. He sat with his legs out. He balanced back on his arms, his scar exposed. You reached out to him. He came to you with a kiss. His body was relaxed. You felt the trust he had in himself that he could see to your labor and the birth of his child.

Sit here and support me, you said.

He sat with his legs wide. You leaned the whole of your weight into his shoulders and chest. You felt him tense to hold you upright. His hands moved across your body in soft, long strokes. His touch and your breathing together were soft currents against the cresting pain.

In a moment when the tension eased, you asked, How did you know to do this?

I didn't, said he. The men told me to try whatever felt right and to try another means if I was mistaken.

You moved away after several waves. You knelt on the pallet, aware of the ground below you and the child within. The sounds in your throat were not human. Makha sat up on her haunches and stared. When your body commanded you to push, you trusted the urge. Leit stood behind you with his elbows under your arms. You moaned. You bellowed. You howled. You reached down and touched a moist, unfamiliar curve.

Then you felt tremendous relief. You gasped. Leit guided you back to the cushioned floor. He reached between your legs, lifted the newborn, and placed the infant close to your chest.

We have a girl, said he.

The child moved but did not cry. You felt panic.

She's silent. What's wrong? you asked.

Leit took your hand and placed it on the babe's abdomen.

Feel, said he. She breathes. There's no cause for her to scream. She'll cry when she's ready.

The infant opened her eyes. She peered with an intense gaze that seemed to pierce you through. Your body flushed with warmth. She was beautiful, with fine dark hair and rosy skin.

Welcome, my daughter, you said.

He covered you both with blankets. He slowly stroked his

hands along the baby's calm body. He left her connected to the cord. | the girl and the boy, out, cut, cleaned, packaged | When the membrane left your body, he wrapped it in a thick cloth close to your hip. He spread fresh linens under you. Makha curved her muzzle above your head and looked at you and the babe. The wolf's nostrils twitched.

Leit knelt near you. His fingertip traced the infant's cheek.

Beloved Wei, said he.

He kissed his daughter, then opened the front door. Cheers and bells rang for several moments. They knew Wei had arrived.

The midwife twirled a knot of dried herbs, which smoked. The smell was sweet and vibrant. She swept the smoke through the chamber, then tossed the rest into the fire. She tended to Wei as the child remained on your chest. Strong, with a good heart, said she. She tended your body and asked what you wanted for comfort. Broth and bread and a bath. Leit helped you into a shallow tub. He held you and draped you in a heavy quilt. Your breasts ached against his dark chest. The midwife cleaned Wei with cloths in front of the fire. You watched Leit cut the cord. Wei gasped and began to cry for the first time.

She isn't hurt, said the midwife. Wei felt the separation.

Leit led you to a warmed bed with comfortable linens. He helped you into a garment you had seen other mothers wear. The bodice was loose and open. The midwife placed Wei on your chest. Without a word, you shifted the infant against your arm. She turned with purpose to nurse.

The midwife served food a friend had delivered. She kissed you all, Makha as well, and left to enter the cold and the morning light. Leit secured the curtains around the bed. Your friends who were skilled with cloth and thread had made them, embroidered with animals, plants, and symbols. The gift was a traditional one. Leit peeked into the bed space. He asked whether you wanted to be alone.

You were exhausted, but you wanted him near.

Then the twins were in the room in cribs out of reach. For a moment, you were alone when you did not wish to be. Wyl hadn't been allowed in as you labored, only a brief visit after you had delivered. You had wanted him but were told it was better for each of you to rest apart.

Leit touched you. You knew where you were. He had been present every moment for every breath. He let you be. He let you cry moan scream with his full attention. Within, you had felt the fullness at the depths and edges of your flesh. What contained Wei, from which Wei would spill. You were aware of the being who liked her father's voice, rhythmic drums, and sunlight experienced through your skin.

He fell asleep before you did. He lay on his side. His arm cradled your neck. The other stretched over your stomach, under his newborn's back.

Wei slept. You wondered what she thought of the journey to your arms.

A QUARTER MOON OF SOLITUDE WAS WHAT YOU ASKED TO HAVE. Friends came with food and clean clothing and went with brisk warm kisses. You felt no urgency to leave the house. You felt no compulsion to leave Wei alone. Where you were, among the Guardians, you were willing to be Wei's mother because you didn't have to be.

Among the gifts you three received, one surprised you above all others. The gift was dolls within dolls.

A woman you didn't know had crafted them with her own hands. They were carved, painted, magnificent.

She said a meaningful encounter had occurred with you a few

months after you arrived. You didn't recall. She did, vividly. She was learning to use a lathe. She was slow at the skill. You appeared at her side for a moment. You asked, Do you want to be adept? She said she did. You said, Then you will be. Your kindness touched her and encouraged her to find her confidence.

They nest within one another, said she.

She separated the two halves of the first one. You revealed the ones hidden.

We were both born away. I was a foundling, said she.

You asked if she remembered her life before. She did not, in mind. She had been an infant.

I made this to honor you and your child, those who came before, and those who will follow, said she. I made this for you because I did become adept at the lathe. I have you to thank.

You hugged the woman and kissed her cheeks. Thank you for sharing your own gift, you said.

YOU WEREN'T DISTRACTED WITH WEI. NO OTHER WORRY OR DUTY gnawed for your attention. Had you wished to, you soon could have resumed your work in the bakery. She could have slept near you. She could have stayed with tenders in the nurseries. Instead, you chose to be with her day and night those first weeks. Your friends taught you how to wrap her against your chest. Wei rested with contentment. You experienced deep peace, unexpected and welcomed.

She was a calm, cheerful infant. She enjoyed being with others and hearing their voices. In the evening, Leit built steady fires and gave her his full attention. He soothed her skin with ointments and massaged her tiny limbs. Wei lay between her father and Makha and played with her toys.

You watched him with her. Your spouse, a man of extremes, so gentle with his child. He loved her with a fullness of heart. You didn't linger, but you wondered if your own father had looked at you, or touched you, the way Leit did with Wei.

You wanted no more than you had in those moments. Loving spouse, beloved child, a safe and peaceful place to live. Your needs met, your wants granted. You sensed this would not change but somehow would be shattered.

THE DREAM FROM WHICH YOU ROUSED WAS NO DREAM.

You were no longer asleep, yet not quite awake. Clearly, you heard the unmistakable singing of notes. A melody high and sweet as birdsong. You were alone in bed. At the window stood Leit. His naked branded back and shoulders were rounded. You knew he held Wei. Yet you couldn't discern the song's source.

You called his name. He turned with your daughter against his bare chest. The song quieted to silence.

What do you know of your mother's mothers? asked he.

What do you mean? you asked.

What were you told of them?

Little. Nothing. My grandmother died before I was born, you said.

How?

I was told she was found dead one day.

What was she like?

My mother said she was clumsy and quiet. She often left for long periods of rest.

Come to the window, said Leit.

You wrapped yourself and stood next to him.

Our daughter is a Voice, said he. See for yourself.

Wei seemed unchanged. You stroked her cheek. She blinked and lifted her face.

Her eyes turned to violet in the night, said he.

A baby's eyes don't set color for some time. She's far too young, you said.

Hers will not change.

How do you know?

Sing for your ahpa, Wei, said Leit. He cleared his throat and strangled forth the melody you had heard. His tone was thin, wavering, but the sounds were on pitch. Wei pursed her pink lips.

The song trilled through her alone. Wordless and beautiful.

You reached for your infant. She quieted at your breast. She rooted for her morning meal. You sat in a cushioned chair to feed her.

You have Voices in your blood, said he.

Leit told you there were women in your past who'd had the gifts your daughter would soon reveal. They knew the father of such a child must have Guardian blood as well, but no one had determined how thick it had to be. The mother's bloodline held the promise.

He tucked a quilt around you and the baby, then dressed himself. He placed a kettle on the hook in the hearth. He stoked the embers that had survived the night.

My daughter is a Voice, whispered he, through tears.

YOUR FAMILY MOVED TO A LARGER HOME WITH AN EXTRA ROOM FOR Aza. You remembered the Voice from the settlement far away and the little girl in her care. So it would begin for your daughter, a life you couldn't imagine.

Soon after she began to sing, she started to babble in a way unlike any you had heard from a baby. Aza explained those were the languages coming through. You were to speak to her as you would any other child. She would learn which tongue to use with those around her.

Wei grew well and happy. For years before she was born, you had watched others with their children. You tried to learn from observation. You wanted to be a loving mother.

You had come from a place where people thought children were animals to be tamed. Willful savage creatures who required sternness and punishment. The Guardians treated their children with love and guidance. They believed them to be born full of joy, compassion, and kindness. The brutal part of human nature wasn't denied. There was patience given for the dark moods and nurturance for the light ones. They were shown how to treat others by what the adults did and said, and didn't do or say.

Despite your embarrassment, you asked friends to help. I wasn't born among you, you said. Please show me how to raise a peaceful child.

So often it was a matter to pause and breathe. Think before you act. Consider how new the experience of life is for the child. Understand she must test her will to discover what it is. Wei was an older girl when you finally realized she wasn't yours to control but to love.

WEI SAT UPRIGHT BY HERSELF. YOU RECLINED NEAR HER. HER HANDS explored what you gathered along the way to find rest in a forest glade. Stick stone leaf petal. She burbled quiet sounds. Streams of language converged. She chose one.

Ma Ma Ma Ma, said Wei. She patted your knee.

Wei Wei Wei Wei, you said. You clapped her feet together. She laughed.

The story returned as you played with her. Your mother had told you few as a child. One you had long forgotten resurfaced when Wei began to babble. You sensed a connection no one in your family remembered.

An ancient tribe wished to have a weapon so powerful that they could not be defeated. So one of the leaders made a ring of stones surrounded by a shallow circular trough that he filled with dried grasses and set aflame. His wish was to have spear points that seared like fire through an enemy's flesh. Another leader arranged an elaborate pyre in the shape of a tree and burned it with the hope that the spears and clubs made from wood could bend like boughs and never break. Another leader drew the shape of a man against the face of a hill and wished that the warriors were as strong as the forces of nature.

The stones were left alone, the ashes allowed to mix with the wind, and the shape on the hill to blend into the grasses. The shape remained as clear as the day it was dug into the hill. In summer, along its head, draping from its crown to below its shoulders, were beautiful yellow wildflowers. On the morning that the leader noticed that the drawn man now looked more like a woman, a girl child was born to his wife.

A great drought forced them out of their village two years after the child was born. They began to travel to find a new place to live. It was during this time that the girl child began to speak strangely, not a baby babble, but another tongue altogether.

A sickness fell upon the tribe the following year, which all blamed on the strange new child. But on their travels one evening, the child approached an old woman and spoke to her in a language that no one could understand. The old woman nodded and spoke back to her in the same tongue. As the old woman gathered the women and began to point to plants they were to harvest, the child's father realized that their wish had been granted. The weapon was words.

WEI LEARNED TO CRAWL. HER MOVEMENT WAS UNPREDICTABLE. SHE collided with obstacles as if she had no awareness of them. Other instances, she stopped as if startled. Her coordination seemed delayed.

You wondered about her unusual gaze. Wei looked through or past what was in front of her. She followed a moving object with ease one day, difficulty the next. You didn't remember the twins' development this way.

You shared your observations with Aza. Her response shocked you.

Wei is blind, as you understand it, said she. We Voices don't see as you do.

Some mothers feel sadness for their children, said Aza. I understand they wish their children could see as they do. I assure you, Aoife, Wei sees the same world but with different senses.

She explained her experience of vision and her sensation. With her physical eyes, Aza perceived broad gradation of light and dark and movement of shapes. She touched the skin between her eyebrows. Her point of focus was there. She received images within that space. Colors were distinguished by temperature. Wherever she was, she noticed flows of air currents and sounds. Both gave her indications of space, what was near or far, what was open or closed. All physical objects vibrated. Those that were inert, such as walls, furniture, clothing, or tools, were less intense. She said you might have noticed that she moved slower than most people. She did so to accept the sensations around her. She had to orient herself to act with purpose. She could move with ease among water and rock, plants and trees, animals and people. Those vibrations were stronger. Her awareness received more feeling.

But some see the unseen as well, you said.

Aza nodded.

Tell me of my daughter's mystery, you said.

She sat next to you.

The Voices announced themselves with singing before they could talk.

They spoke languages they had never heard.

Most had the gift of insight into hearts and minds.

Some had the gift of foresight into what could be.

All had a gift to heal. Some were great listeners. Some sent light through their hands. Some used sound and song.

An uncommon Voice was born with a rare gift that required much restraint.

Only the strongest among them were invited to serve on the trails.

You glanced at your sleeping daughter. Your blood carried the possibility of a child like her, and there she was. What other secrets within would be wrought upon her, from you, her unwitting mother?

When will Wei show her abilities? you asked.

Sooner than you might wish, said Aza. We reveal our gifts by our seventh year. You will have an adult Voice to help you at all times. We will guide and teach Wei. You and Leit will be taught as well.

What do I do until then? you asked.

Love her, said Aza. In most ways, she's no different from any other child.

She told you to give attention to Wei's emotional reactions in your presence or that of others. Your daughter would begin to show her sensitivities to others soon. You were not to be surprised if she spoke to you in your native language. You were cautioned that Wei might say strange things or ask odd questions, as if she knew your thoughts, your secrets.

So it was. When you were pregnant, you gave thought to the kind of child you might have. Healthy, you hoped, with a good disposition and ready mind. You hadn't cared whether you had a boy or a girl. You hoped Leit was wrong about the dark legacies you might bear.

For several weeks after your talk with Aza, you felt numb. Tricked, almost, as if you were the object of a joke. How could you have a child like this? How could you raise a daughter you thought you would never understand? Why you? You kept your silence, then shared your feelings with Leit, Aza, Edik, and close friends. Aza and Edik assured you that you wouldn't be alone. If you and others recognized Wei's abilities as gifts, not afflictions, she would grow into them with confidence.

Tell the truth.

At first you wished Wei had not been born that way. A typical child was what you wanted. Instead, you received a little being who defied reason. Then on impulse you spoke to your daughter in your native tongue. | you had not forgotten it | She squinted her eyes as if they were pierced by a bright light. You asked her a question. She smiled and answered in the words of your life before. Impossible, but there it was. You couldn't deny what you heard.

You resolved to accept her as she was and would be. You would do your best to remember the promise you made in your heart.

BY THE TIME WEI WAS THREE, YOU OFTEN WITNESSED WHAT AZA HAD prepared you to expect. Happiness was her usual condition. But in the presence of others that could quickly change. Wei became tangled with other people's emotions. Aza and Edik explained that she perceived the feeling as part of her. She couldn't separate as most did. Wei collapsed in laughter as well as tears. She ran away in fright or screamed with rage. You often couldn't determine the impetus. Aza told you what stirred under people's skin was as powerful as what Wei could observe.

The Voices were aware of what cannot be seen. Most people understand what is said beyond words. They apprehend an expression or posture or tone of voice. For Voices, the experience is deep within themselves. They feel within their bodies sensations like ripples in a pond or a strike against a hard surface. The Voices perceived that most people had the potential to experience in this way. Most, however, were distracted by what they saw and the discomfort of intense feeling. The Voices couldn't see as others did. They had to learn to move with the feeling rather than block it. They had to learn it was not theirs to keep.

Wei's earliest lessons were for centering and separation. All Guardians were taught to focus themselves, and you learned the power of pause breathe repeat. However, the Voices needed to concentrate on the practice with urgency. Aza taught Wei as well as you and Leit. In calm moments, the training mimicked play. When Wei was upset, the training was part of her survival. Wei had to become still and breathe. She had to place her feet on the ground and look at her hands. She became aware of herself and those around her. Aza told her to notice how far her feelings reached away from her. Aza told her to observe if she felt too full. Wei learned to imagine herself as a large pot that could hold much water but preferred enough for one cup of tea only for herself. What was too much left her in a vision of steam. Wei's little body and mind became quiet. She remained calm.

You needed the same skill on the days when Wei's behavior wore you thin. In the beginning, you had outbursts of your own. If you didn't catch the moment before frustration became poisonous,

Wei faced a screaming mother. You could barely contain the urge to shake her. Your reaction worsened hers, and you knew it. Ashamed, you spoke to Edik. He asked what you thought she needed in those moments. Patience, and love, you said. Respond with that even as the anger fills you, said he. You must practice, as everyone does. Every time. You practiced and practiced for your sake and Wei's.

Soon after she turned four, a new stage of training began.

When Leit told you | warned you | of what was to come, you thought it cruel. You protested to him and Aza. You wanted to protect Wei from the worst of human feeling, the worst of human horrors. Leit understood. He, too, wished his daughter to be spared. Yet her encounters would be inevitable whether she joined the trails or served within the settlements. As a warrior, he knew this well.

He explained the warriors' role in the training. The men reached into their memories to recall specific sensations and emotions. The young Voice stated what she felt from them. What would trouble you, Leit knew, was the task that followed. The warriors remembered experiences of their lives in detail. They were given no restrictions. The young Voice's response would hint at the depth of her gift. Some could feel emotions only. Others could describe pieces of the event. In any case, no child could comprehend fully an adult experience. There would be mental blanks, although the emotions could be overwhelming. An adult Voice gave immediate care to heal any wound to the child.

You hoped Wei had a limited ability. You suspected she didn't. Since she could speak in sentences, she had said strange things to you on occasion. | Ahma, you liked to look with one eye closed | You spoke little of your life before. No matter. She seemed to know of objects and experiences that the Guardians didn't possess.

You asked to be present. Aza and Edik accompanied you. She guided Wei. He attended you. Leit watched but did not participate as he had done before.

Several warriors, young and old, sat on the ground. Aza and Wei sat across from them. Aza bowed her head at the group. The men closed their eyes and placed upturned hands on their knees. Wei was told to touch their hands and tell Aza what she felt.

Your daughter knelt before each man for a moment.

Bright, said she. Warm. Empty. Soft. Cool, with air. Happy.

Aza praised her effort. She turned to you and Leit. She nodded.

Wei perceived what they felt with accuracy, said Leit.

The same effort repeated several times. Wei sensed emotions from light to dark. She seemed to take pleasure in her efforts.

The task we spoke about is next, said Edik. Remember, Wei is safe. Aza has done this before.

Leit clasped your hand in his.

Aza instructed Wei to center herself. She told the child that she might feel something different from the men. She told Wei to tell her what she sensed. The child could touch the men or not. That was her choice.

Wei stood within arm's reach of each warrior. She stood straight and calm in front of the first man. She kissed his bearded cheek. He laughed. Aza asked what happened.

Turtles hatching from eggs. He was a little boy, said Wei. He knows I like turtles, too.

You were relieved the man had shared a pleasant memory. You were conflicted that your daughter had such a gift. Edik offered his hand. You accepted. Your spouse and your kind old friend kept you anchored.

The other warriors shared their silent memories. Wei connected to the emotions and the images. They weren't joyful. One man couldn't keep distance from his own pain and wept. Wei rubbed his arm. Aza intervened then. She whispered to your daughter and hummed a soothing tone.

The warriors hugged Wei as they departed. She kissed their cheeks and squeezed their necks. Aza sat with Wei alone. They talked while you sat in silence. Wei ran to you and Leit.

Ahma! Ahpa! Their bodies are full of stories, said she.

Are they? you asked.

Full of them, said she.

You shivered. For an instant you recoiled at your daughter's strangeness. You didn't wish to. You did not intend to. Before and then again, you wondered how human she was. Yet she came from your flesh blood bone. You could look at her. Feel her hair and skin. Clean what she soiled. Hear her voice and see her smile, dance, laugh. What doubt in that could there be, that she was different from any other child?

A deep breath filled your lungs. You smiled at her as you exhaled.

That is fascinating, Wei. You've worked hard today. Would you like to play outside now? you asked.

She did. The door opened. She ran into the twilight.

Aza dismissed the warriors. She asked you and Leit to stay. The older Voice said Wei's response showed her expansive potential. The child described the warriors' memories with accuracy of emotion and image. In some instances, Wei claimed to see perspectives that were not the warriors'. These your daughter referred to as the outside stories. Aza prepared you that some Voices could perceive thoughts, emotions, and actions of those connected to a person's memory. You wondered how that was possible.

Tell the truth.

You questioned your child's truth, and that of those she stood before. You questioned her sanity, and that of those who said she knew their stories. What delusion did they agree to share? Yet none of them had a clear motive to lie or dupe. Still, you wondered whether this was all elaborate trickery. If not, you speculated whether Wei had imagined the outside stories. No one, of course, could dispute what she told.

AZA WAS CORRECT. IN MOST WAYS, WEI WAS LIKE ANY OTHER CHILD. THAT she was yours made her remarkable.

She grew into a little girl unlike the one you had been. Wei took great delight in billowy skirts and dresses. She and her young friends traded adornments. They draped themselves in jewelry, belts, wraps, and hats. | your sapphire bracelet wrapped twice at her wrist | Her hair was black like her father's. A white streak grew near her temple. She liked to comb her shiny straight locks. Then Leit would plait her hair in elaborate designs. He had learned and practiced the skill in the nurseries. His dexterity surpassed yours, and Wei knew it. She laughed at your clumsy attempts.

Her movements were a perpetual dance. You had never seen a child so graceful. She learned to use her senses to flow among all that surrounded her. Sometimes she seemed to defy air or accept its gentleness. You loved to watch her with the children at the Wheels. She swayed and kicked in harmony with the twinkling music. She led them to join hands and form ribbons of mirth.

As all Voices did, she had a beautiful voice. The sound was soft and warm, with uncanny depth. She discovered its power when she sang. She shared sweet wordless melodies and renditions of the old and new songs of her people. The beauty overwhelmed others more often than not. Listeners wept without shame. You joined them in their tears.

How much love was in that child? you wondered.

As you witnessed her gifts strengthen, you worried what Wei would see in her father. You both knew that some of her outbursts had occurred when she was alone with him. Leit had told no one except you the circumstances behind his scar. He seemed somewhat unburdened after your witness, but the inner struggle was not gone.

He didn't return to the trails for long periods when Wei was young. His service lasted only weeks of a given season. Instead, he remained in the settlement to train young warriors or to work in the smithy. Those brief times away stirred him, but that wasn't the only provocation.

You were watchful when the darkness emerged from him. It came and went without announcement, without a pattern. You did what you could to protect Wei. You tried not to leave her alone with him. If his mood was especially black, you sent her to play or spend the night with friends. She knew, she felt, so in a way this attempt to shield her was pointless.

Leit knew when he was taken by the furious gloom. He was fully aware. A rupture in him loomed on the worst days, but he never lashed out.

Don't fear me, and don't teach our daughter to fear me, said he.

While you tried to avoid him | dead father, old fear |, Wei tried to heal him. He sensed when his daughter hugged him with affection and when she held him to soothe his old wound. He pulled away, as he did with you, when he wore the pain as a skin. You watched Wei persist.

Ahpa, what hides in there? asked she once. Her innocent hand lay on the center of his chest.

A terrible story. Leave it alone, said he.

She was vigilant in a way you could never be. You were afraid of that wound. You were afraid of what Leit might unleash if he could no longer contain it.

Wei couldn't help her impulse to comfort. This was an attribute of most people, but it was acute in the Voices. The instances were spontaneous. Pain or unease reached her, and she wished to help release it. Until she learned to ask permission, she approached neighbors and spoke for a moment or touched them. Despite the feeling of violation, the people acknowledged she had relieved them. They understood they had a role as well to help Wei learn to use her gifts.

Wei knew when to warm Makha's aged hips or her father's

sore right shoulder. She rubbed your wrists, which tightened from kneading. Yet you knew she went deeper with you. She explored your complications. Then, unexpectedly, she would soothe a wound. She was five when she sat in the bathhouse with you and placed her hand on your left arm. Wei covered the scar. You trembled and resisted tears. Ahma, you fought the best you could. Believe no longer you could have done better. You were very strong and brave. Your daughter smiled, your arm became hot under her touch, and you wept with relief. How could she know, but she did.

Now and then, she spanned the limits. You had no comprehension of how she learned what she did. When Wei extended her impossible sight through you, you could doubt the truth. But you could not deny it.

LEIT RECEIVED AN INVITATION TO THE ASSEMBLY. EVERY SEVEN YEARS, representatives from all the settlements across the known world met in Egnis's realm. They discussed observations from the trails and their own communities. He had attended the meeting for his first time before the war. | the year of your quest | You were in the same house by the time he attended his second Assembly. Wei had not yet been conceived.

He said he had listened without comment at the last gathering. His thoughts were unsettled. Never had he questioned the Guardians' ways before. Since the war, and from what he had seen on the trails, he had begun to doubt what once had seemed immutable.

He noticed more violence and chaos while on his duty. He thought the war had had a virulent effect beyond the places where the battles had been waged. Leit pondered the safety of the Voices and whether their service was worth the risk to them. He wondered whether their presence on the trails mattered any longer. The warriors' protection of the realm was passive. He considered that that might have to change.

We know people slip into the realm to loot the hoard, said he. They rarely steal more than a few items. They're afraid of the unknown—oh, they've all heard tales—and get away quickly. We see the pieces traded on occasion. Sometimes, a Voice can determine where they gained entry if we know where the loot takers came from. We often chop down the links in the event luck strikes the same place twice.

As long as their fear of the dragon is stronger than their greed, this is a reasonable loss, said he. What's concerned us is that someone will become bold and organize a way to maim or kill her. The hoard is only metals and jewels. Nothing essential to life. Egnis's mystery is. If enough armed men stormed through at once, our response may not be quick enough to help.

What would happen if she was harmed? you asked.

We speculate. A suggestion comes from one of the tales when she wouldn't raise the sun. All realms fell into darkness. Without light, nothing can live. The connection of one life to the next is broken, said he.

You pondered the conversation long after it was done. The Guardians perceived cycles, not finality. Far later in your life, you realized that their hope for the future was twined with this view. They had not what other peoples did. They had no eschatology.

Leit believed there was grave danger, though. A cruel darkness had begun to deepen outside the settlements. An infection of the mind, he thought. The Guardians were human. They might be protected, but he didn't believe they were immune.

Leit felt deep concern about those born away coming into the settlements. He had reservations about the foundlings, but he had serious worries about the adults. He knew some adults born away felt led or drawn to their new homes with the Guardians. Others stumbled upon them as a place of refuge. Regardless, Leit thought, the adults had not lived with the gentleness and cooperation natural to the Guardians. He believed those born away would bring greater strife now, worse than the individual troubles they had brought before. Like a blight on a crop, the darkness could spread, threatening the ways of his people. He would recommend that adult newcomers be led to neighboring villages instead, to protect the settlements.

So why did you come to us, Aoife? asked he.

I was compelled to be among you after I visited the settlement near the kingdom where I lived. I had never felt such peace. Such safety and acceptance, you said.

That peace is meant for every person, but now I doubt it's possible. I consider myself a man of courage, but I fear this contamination to my bones. It's inside of you, Aoife, because of your origins. It's inside of me because of what I've seen. It is likely within Wei, through no fault of her own, said Leit.

These thoughts preyed upon him. Leit spoke to you often about what your birth home had been like. He had taken no such specific interest before. You tried to love each other as you were, where you were. He didn't deny you had a role in what had come about. A catalyst. The Guardians didn't shun or persecute or, so it ever seemed, blame you. Many influences bear on one moment. Your intent had been to protect them, not to invite invasion. You couldn't have imagined what horror emerged from the war. You loved your new people. | you rarely thought of the others |

You wondered what would have become of you had the Guardians refused your stay. Had you not found work as a mapmaker, what would have been your fate? A new struggle took root. You believed Leit. You knew well the strife beyond the settlements and what you had escaped. Despite the gratitude for your welcome, your impulse was to deny others what was offered to you. You wanted to protect the Guardians' ways, too. Yet a deeper wisdom urged the opposite. Grant others the chance you were given.

Leit was away only a few days to meet with the Assembly. He returned uncertain about the results. He wasn't alone in his counsel, but he was among a minority. Each representative agreed to observe whether matters improved. They chose not to be hasty. There would be no abrupt change to their customs. No one who wished to live among the Guardians would be denied residence. You felt relief. You saw no reason to disturb the balance that had long been held.

SEVERAL MONTHS PASSED AFTER THE ASSEMBLY.

The early spring of Wei's sixth year, she began to prove the depths of her gift.

My brother and sister don't believe their father is their father, said she.

You froze. Of course, you had given her pieces of your life before. Facts. The two of you shared a love of the forest, and in the forest's quiet, you gave her the fragments. Far away, a father, mother, brother, and another spouse. You had to leave them because of a terrible disagreement that could not be resolved. The twins were a subject you intended not to mention until she was much older.

Who told you of them? you asked.

No one. I've known about them for a long time, said Wei.

How?

Oh, Ahma, said she.

You breathed. With calm, you said you had had a girl and a boy in your life before. You had put them in the care of your first spouse when you left after the disagreement.

I know about him, too. He's their father.

Curiosity had its latch, but fear had a stronger grip. You knelt in front of your daughter and nudged her chin to face you. I don't wish to speak of this now, Wei. What happened is complicated. Respect my thoughts and theirs. Stay away, you said. Please.

Don't you want to know what troubles them? asked Wei.

No.

But, Ahma—

I know you don't understand. I'm sorry. This cannot be discussed.

Wei's face was sorrowful when she walked away. You wondered if she glimpsed your true feelings, the ones you never spoke.

Late that spring, Makha came to her last days. She was impossibly old. As long as she was able, she kept to Leit's side. She sat with him on the plateau. She took slow walks through the forest. When she could no longer hunt for herself, Leit did for her. Makha had her fill on what he killed | hare heron deer boar | and the rest went to the stores.

Her frailty slipped into lethargy. She left him slowly. She gave him time to let her go. Leit lay upon the floor with her body against his chest. Her once-silver fur was white but for the shimmering streak from her forehead to her tail. He whispered to her. She wagged her great tail and licked her old teeth.

The night of a full moon, Wei sat between Makha's outstretched legs. The wolf lay on her side with Leit at her back. They petted her with tenderness. Wei placed her two small hands at the beast's heart. Later, Leit told you he felt Makha relax with a peaceful sigh. You both watched your daughter kiss Makha's face and accept a kiss in return. You both heard her speak into the wolf's ear:

Don't be afraid. Your body is a shell that will crack to set you free. I love you, Makha. Thank you for saving my ahpa.

Leit rushed his gaze to you. You nodded. He burst into tears. You contained yours.

Makha licked Wei's face until your little girl laughed.

They slept with Makha on the floor. You awoke to Leit's hushed keen. His wolf was cold and stiffening in his arms. Wei hugged her father. You knelt near them. Leit touched her callused paws and rubbed her thin ears.

My loyal friend, where is the forest where you now run?

Makha's body was placed on a cart near the Wheels. The children asked to have songs played for her through the day while they sang. They covered her with flowers. Leit's companions built a pyre for her on the plain. Her body was burned as a warrior's.

You and Leit didn't ask Wei what she had meant. Her words might have been innocent. She knew Makha had protected her father on the trails. You hoped that was the extent of her knowledge.

Then came summer. The three of you had enjoyed the day. Wei spent the better part of it with friends helping a potter. You spent the morning in the bakery and the afternoon chronicling a history you had heard from a storyteller. Leit worked in the fields and returned home with a simple meal. That evening, you added notes to what you'd written. Leit polished his weapons. Wei played with the dolls within the dolls. Each one spoke a different language.

You heard Wei ask:

Why are you bleeding?

You turned to see her run to her father. He stood to catch her.

You're bleeding, Ahpa! So much blood!

She screamed as if she were being tortured.

Leit cupped Wei's shoulders. You ran toward them. You were grateful to Aza at that moment. She had trained you well. You knew what to do.

Wei, settle down. Breathe, you said. She couldn't hear you over her howls. She threw herself on the floor and began to pound her forehead against it. Panic flushed you cold. You had never seen her so out of control. Leit lifted her in his arms and braced against the blows from her tiny fists. When Wei began to cry, he let her go. She shook where she stood.

Wei, listen to me. Listen to the sound of my voice. Yes. Stand still. Breathe. How full are you? Release some if you need to. Now, where is Ahpa standing?

You looked into Leit's eyes. You both realized the fullness of Wei's sight.

Ahpa is near you at this moment. Leit, may she touch you?

He nodded.

Wei, touch him. You'll feel he is unharmed.

Your daughter touched her father where his navel had been. A gentle press. She pulled her hand away. Her palm was covered in blood. Neither Leit nor you could see a stain or drop on his shirt.

Your mind became blank as a stare. Your body constricted with fear and grief. Poor Wei, you thought. What have we done? you thought next.

I'm sorry, Ahpa. I'm sorry, said Wei.

She wrapped her arms around his thigh and wailed.

Get Aza, said Leit.

You ran through the door. Each person you saw, you asked to get word to Aza that she must go to your home with haste. No one asked for an explanation. They responded. You ran to Aza's house | before then, she had left your home to pair | but she wasn't there. You trusted that the people would share the message. That Aza could help.

When you entered your house, Aza was sitting on the floor with Wei between her legs. She hummed. She held your daughter with crossed arms. Wei seemed entranced. Their eyes were closed.

Go to Leit, said she between breaths.

You found him at the house of the elders who had sheltered him upon his return. The warrior had died when Wei was a baby, but his spouse survived, ailing but strong. She led you to a small chamber. Leit lay on the bed on his side.

Beloved, you said.

She knows, said he.

You stroked his hair. You touched his arm.

Not my pain alone, said he. That of the children. That of the fiend.

You knew she can see the others in memory, you said.

Leit turned and met your eyes.

No, said he. She said she faced, then entered them. She knows their stories as well. From the inside. That's why she was screaming. She said the rage wanted to kill her.

The elder crept into the room. You were too stunned to ask her to leave. She took your hand and pressed her other one against Leit's temple. She began to sing a lullaby. She was suddenly ageless. He tried to join her, desperate to match the tones. One phrase, one phrase, formed in perfection, then he strained until he stopped.

Grief leached from your bones. You had just heard the voice he'd lost to the war. You mourned the missing piece of him. You lamented what had been wrought on Wei.

BY THE NEXT EVENING, AN ELDER VOICE FROM A FARAWAY SETTLEMENT came to assist Wei. Aza didn't feel she could serve your daughter as she needed. What had occurred was rare. She didn't share Wei's ability. She didn't know what to do to guide your child.

You had never seen a human as old as Sisay. She stood strong with a slight bend in her limbs. Her black skin rippled against her bones like bark. Her teeth were worn and yellowed. Her coarse hair was white and trimmed close to her skull. Within two deep slits, her eyes were waning violet moons. Her voice made the arches of your feet ache, your body heavy.

Bring me the child born without the cloud, said Sisay.

You stepped outside to call Wei from her play. Whatever Aza had done the day before had soothed her. She had no signs of shock and slept well through the night. Aza said no one could be sure how much Wei remembered. The trauma might have been more than she could hold.

You introduced Wei to the woman. Your daughter's face brightened as they regarded one another. She hurried into Sisay's arms. They twined together and laughed. Their bond was immediate and mysterious. You felt a sear of jealousy. You gave her love, but the ancient woman offered understanding.

Leit fumbled with his composure when he met Sisay. He had heard tales of her. She was the oldest living Voice. She was known to be as ruthless as Nature, one who saw what was beyond all appearances. Her presence was another adjustment for you but a portent for him. He bowed to her, a rare gesture among the Guardians. The old woman took his broad hands in her thin small ones.

Your warrior heart beats in your daughter's chest, said Sisay. Prepare yourself to confront that strength again.

He nodded. He couldn't speak. His awe almost frightened you.

That night, Leit held you to the curve of his body.

You realize there's little chance now that Wei won't be asked to join the trails, said he.

I know, you said.

You remembered a conversation with Aza sometime before. The most gifted among the Voices were asked if they wished to serve in the wider world. Their role was to accompany the Guardian warriors who traveled as traders. Voices who were boys didn't have gifts as strong as the girls', so only girls walked the trails. They weren't ordinary children. They could feel into people and places. What felt peaceful, what felt unstable, what felt dark. Because they were so young they were often overlooked. They appeared small and weak, therefore unthreatening. Most people were less guarded around them. They forgot their tongues because they thought what they said was over a child's head.

You've been brave, Aoife. No mother, even one born among, could have been more resilient, said he.

I feel shame to say this, but I sometimes wish she was like any other child, you said.

As I have in rare moments, said he. But to require that of her would crush what makes her Wei.

SISAY HAD COME TO DEEPEN WEI'S TRAINING. SHE ALLOWED YOU TO watch several sessions. You would have to understand how to help Wei with a new skill.

For your daughter to center herself would no longer be enough. If she had this greater gift, she risked being pulled apart, mind and soul. She could get lost in another person's story. She would forget she had the ability to help a person heal.

You watched Sisay teach Wei to find the space between herself and the memory she confronted. If she did, she didn't risk a merge with another's pain. She was taught to root herself in her physical presence. She had to connect with her feet and hands, with any sense she wished. Sisay told her to let her body choose a gesture to ground her focus. You saw your daughter move in a tuneless dance. Every part of her swayed. Her hands and arms twined and parted. Wei stood firm when her fingers laced together at the webs, each digit straight and firm.

When Wei mastered her ability to root, Sisay taught her another skill. An elder warrior who no longer walked the trails sat with them. He had resolved a painful experience but could still reach into the feelings if he tried.

Wei stood near him. She told Sisay what she felt and saw. She cried. Sisay told her to find her root. She calmed but quivered. Sisay told the warrior to stay in the moment.

Wei, find the gap that spans then and now. Know you can cross it or leave it alone, said Sisay.

Your daughter nodded.

Leave it alone. Observe from where you are. Do nothing but observe.

She nodded again.

Wei, you are a witness, said Sisay. Repeat what I say. I am a witness.

I am a witness, said Wei.

Now. Brighten, said Sisay.

Your daughter didn't move. Her focus seemed impenetrable. For an instant you thought the whole of her blurred. As if she escaped the corner of your eye.

Sisay stood at Wei's back and whispered to her. You couldn't hear what she said or see what she did with her hands. Sisay walked away. Wei approached the warrior. She placed her small palm against his broad forehead. He inhaled with force, held the breath, then exhaled with a long blow. When he looked at her eyes, his face relaxed.

Remember, Wei. You helped the moment to open because he was ready. If it is closed or dark, you must not cross the gap and use force. Guide, but allow them to see the truth for themselves, said Sisay.

Each day, your daughter and the ancient Voice went into the forest. A small group of warriors accompanied them at times. If you stood at the margin, you could hear human sounds. Screams, wails, shouts, laughter. Of course, singing. Sisay's sonorous tones pulsed like a heartbeat through the trees.

You knew some days Sisay took your daughter away. There were other Voices for her to meet. Wei had lessons to learn that couldn't be taught at home. When Wei and her teacher returned before dinner, they were tired but in good moods.

Each evening, Sisay took to her bed at twilight. You, Leit, and Wei visited friends, played games, or sat in quiet company. When you embraced your daughter, she vibrated with a noiseless hum. Her father had noticed as well.

There's a slight tickle when I hold you now, Wei, you said.

Sisay sings the pain out of my body. It gets caught, and she makes it go away. Then I tickle.

Whose pain? you asked.

The world's pain, Ahma, said Wei. She's teaching me to do it, too. I can use sound, but I'm better with light.

You looked at your spouse. He shook his head as he smiled.

Sisay taught me a word for what we do. Transmutation.

Transmutation, you said.

It means to turn into something else.

The mystery of your child deepened. You were told little. It was impossible to comprehend anyway. Wei wasn't forbidden to tell you, Leit, or others what she learned, but she was cautioned. Sisay, like some Guardians, believed everyone was born with the Voices' abilities. These were buried and unformed within the mind. If they were released without guidance or discernment, grave harm could be done.

SISAY LIVED WITH YOUR FAMILY UNTIL WINTER APPROACHED. SHE trained Wei with intense focus. When she left your home it was only physically, because Wei understood how close she was. Your daughter was not as alone as she appeared.

Before she left, Sisay invited you to walk in the forest with her. You felt tenderness for the ancient adept who apprenticed your daughter in the Voices' esoteric gifts. She surprised you when she took your hand.

Aoife, said she in her low firm voice.

Yes, Sisay, you said.

Wei has her father's heart and her mother's forward mind. You have shown courage to allow both to thrive in her. The proof will come to bear, if Wei follows her own will and moves past efforts to thwart her.

As before, you will not get to keep this child. She must leave you. The journeys ahead will clarify her purpose. Wei has the potential to be an eminent leader. If she chooses this, she will be misunderstood. You share this fate, and this is the legacy you have given to her.

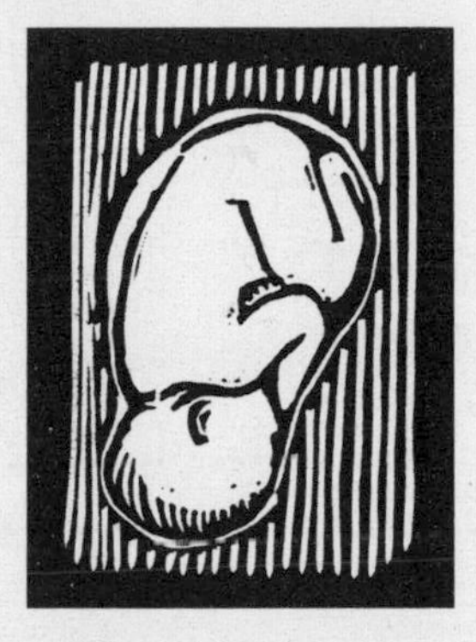

In an era yet to be born, you will speak to a grandchild. With this child, and others whose time has come, beginning in the land of your exile, a great hush will force a reckoning between lies and truth. The future will depend on those who survive.

Sisay hummed softly like insects.

You thought of Wei, then of the twin, the girl. Her weight against your leg. The boy was a shadow. Sorrow welled into you. As before, you will not get to keep this child. You had no doubt Sisay had peered into you. You could not conceive how she made sense of what she saw.

The old woman halted near your favorite stand of fir trees. She grasped your palms. Her gaze, fierce and loving, focused on you.

Had they not been, Wei could not be. This is a truth beyond fact.

Why? you asked.

That is beyond our understanding, said Sisay. You have served her well. Have no doubt.

After sisay was gone, you decided to ask Wei how she experienced her gifts. She had never spoken of the glimpse beyond her father and the horror of his scar. Aza's intervention was meant to spare her memory. If she retained any vestiges, she didn't speak of them. That instance had been the most extreme. You knew her glimpses didn't always yield physical proof like blood.

The two of you took an afternoon walk to the lake.

When you find your root and witness, what happens? Explain to me. I want to understand.

Look into the lake, Ahma. What do you see?

The reflection of the trees and sky around us.

She took your hand and led you to stand in another place.

And now.

I see the shallows below. A small cluster of fish. If I turn my gaze, I also see the trees and sky again.

Wei knelt on the bank and plunged her hand into the water.

Nothing has changed, but I'm in both places at once, said she.

An echo tingled your bones.

When you were a little girl, Ahma, you knew, but you didn't know what it meant.

How do you know that? you asked.

I peeked. I apologize.

A hardness formed inside of you. Wei flinched. In moments like that, you were afraid of your daughter. Still. To be guarded all the time was impossible. You did your best to accept her gifts and that she was a child still learning to use them. Yet when she penetrated your life before, you feared what she could know. You willed yourself to take her hand with gentleness. Wei's fingers hummed in your grasp.

Wei, remember what Aza, Edik, and Sisay told you. We discuss this now and then.

I must respect every person's sheath.

Yes. Do you not have thoughts you wish to keep to yourself? you asked.

I do.

As do I and Ahpa and everyone else.

I mean no harm, said she. But sometimes I can help when I glimpse. If people let me.

WINTER SETTLED ON THE LAND. THE LONG WAIT FOR SPRING HAD begun. The wait to learn Wei's fate ended.

Edik and an elder visited your home one afternoon. Leit fed the fire as they sat with her. They told her she had been chosen to be a Voice on the trails. She would translate for her Guardian companions when that was needed. Her role was to protect them and Egnis through her awareness. If she heard or felt that any persons were in danger, she was to tell her companions. They, not she, would be responsible to thwart the possible harm and settle all into balance.

They explained that she would be away from her home, family, and friends for seasons at a time. There would be long visits in between to rest. She may withdraw her service if she no longer felt fulfilled. She wouldn't be asked to serve past her fourteenth year.

Wei sat still as they spoke to her. She paid close attention. She smiled and nodded. They said she was to make the decision from her heart. She was to talk to her parents and friends if she wished, but they were not to interfere. She must decide for herself.

No surprise. Wei was a decisive child who consulted but did not depend on you or Leit. You tried your best not to influence her about the trails. In truth, you didn't want her to go. The separation from you was one matter, but more serious were the dangers she would face. The mothers born among knew by hearsay what was beyond your peaceful borders. You knew by experience. You had not forgotten.

Leit was as conflicted as you. He loved his daughter with

affection, respect, and tenderness. He was proud of your little girl. As to her gifts, he confessed to awe. Leit had traveled with several Voices and knew Wei's abilities far surpassed theirs.

In the quiet of your bed, Leit admitted that he wished Wei wouldn't go. He knew the pain Wei would feel. The people felt sorrow for what the warriors sacrificed, but the warriors felt a unique sorrow for the Voices. The girls sacrificed their innocence to confront the neglect, cruelty, and violence away from their homes.

He hoped she would serve as Aza and Edik did, safe within a settlement. He still believed the war unleashed a darkness that would claim more than it would spare. He worried that the world away had the power to shatter a child as beautiful as Wei.

Some nights, Leit sat next to your sleeping daughter. The past crept into the space he left next to you. You thought of your father. He didn't encourage but also did not deny your mapmaking apprenticeship, then duties. He acknowledged you served a greater purpose, whether he liked it or not. Your beloved spouse understood Wei was called to higher service as well. You wondered, for a moment, what these two men would think of each other.

Leit returned to bed and pulled you against his chest. He held you while he could. His time to return to the trails approached. Your daughter's entry would follow in his footsteps.

I WILL, SAID WEI.

Not, I want to, or I wish to. I will.

Settled, then. Your daughter had chosen for herself. Leit gathered her in his arms. Wei kissed his wet cheeks.

I'm brave like you, Ahpa, said she.

Braver, said he.

Soon after Wei agreed to be a Voice on the trails, she turned seven. You and Leit had pondered a gift for her. You decided to give her the dolls within dolls, presented to you at her birth. She played with them more than with her own toys. Wei jumped with glee.

Thank you, Ahma, said she. They are so beautiful, like you and me.

She celebrated the day among friends. She asked for musicians to entertain. You provided players on string, pipe, and drum. The children danced with joined hands, snakes and circles in the snow. You loved to watch her in those moments. She was fluid and graceful. The love around her made her buoyant. She ran to you and pulled your hand. Come, Ahma, said she. Join the dance. You surrendered to her joy.

The next time you danced with your daughter, it was before her good-bye.

You were told of the ritual to honor Wei's new role. She and you had parts to play. Wei needed a simple white frock. You required a specific costume. A young man known for his skills with cloth and thread was elated that you asked him to provide the raiment. He gathered talented friends to help him complete the task. When they were finished, you studied their effort with amazement. The costume lay before you full of life.

The ritual was held on a beautiful cool spring night. All the people of the settlement gathered on the plain. Hundreds of men, women, and children ate, drank, sang, and danced to celebrate your daughter's duty. They hugged, kissed, and thanked her. Nothing in your life prepared you for their sincere love.

Leit drew you from the perimeter of the wide swirling circle to the center. He stood ahead of the ranks of warriors. They wore their ceremonial best. In front of them was a mountain of wood that rose toward the sky. Aza gave you an unlit torch. Leit opened a tinderbox red with the want of flames. You placed the moss end of the torch inside. The fire took its breath. You touched the tongues to the wood and watched the pyre ignite.

So it begins! Aza shouted.

She led you and Wei to the forest margin. Your closest friends separated you to prepare each for the ritual. They sang songs of joy and songs of mourning. They gasped when you moved within the costume, animated that arcane skin.

A drum chorus resonated in your organs. The enactment began. A corridor opened from the forest to the fire. You felt the balanced weight of the red wings on your shoulders. You flapped with grace as you approached. The people who clapped fell into a hush as you walked among them.

Egnis, she who first saw All.

On the ground within the fire's glow was a child. Its skin was blue from head to toe. It wore a loose white garment. You brushed your giant head from its feet to its crown. The child jumped up, alive.

Egnis and Azul danced. They circled the flames opposite each other in perfect orbit. The drums beat faster, and the witnesses hummed. The drone became a force that drew them together. The Red Dragon and the Orphan linked hands. They twirled around the fire until the dragon took the child in her arms. Azul disappeared in Egnis's embrace, then rose again. The child tossed jewels into the circle around them. A rain of stars.

Leit ran toward Wei. He lifted his daughter on his shoulder. He wore the warrior's blue tunic with a gold breastplate embossed with a coiled dragon. | made by Ingot | He placed Wei on the ground where you knelt. Wei took off your mask. She kissed the full moon of your face as you held her.

Aza and the council of elders stood before Wei. Edik opened a small box. He withdrew a pendant on a chain. Circle, triangle, square. Everyone, everyone, knelt as he placed the object around her neck.

Forged by Ingot, kissed by Incant, hallowed by Egnis, this gold amulet marks your transition. You danced in the skin of the Beloved Child, and you will continue within your own to keep our promise to the Three and the promise they asked of us, said he.

To the reign of love, shouted Wei.

To the reign of love, echoed all.

IN THOSE WAITING DAYS BEFORE THEY LEFT, YOU WATCHED LEIT PREpare his belongings. He packed and unpacked, unsure of what he wanted to carry. He hadn't been indecisive before. He brought his weapons to the smiths to hone. He hoped he would have no need for their edges. You mended a blue tunic and splayed it on your bed as he often lay. You asked Wei what she wished to pack but couldn't bring yourself to gather it. Her dresses fell limp in your hands.

You felt muddled. Wei's departure was inevitable. That you mourned openly. Another matter plagued you but you didn't know what.

You went to the plateau to be quiet. The plain changed with the seasons but had not changed at all. You felt the landscape of your body in its shift. You were no longer the child who mapped hidden worlds.

To see a spiderweb was a matter of awareness. You noticed that you shared a space with the creature. You had a choice to leave it alone, destroy it, or engage with it. You assumed you engaged. You studied, and if you drew a map of the hidden world, it was to see the space for yourself. As well, you imagined what lay beyond or within what you could see. When a spider abandoned a web, where did it go? You knew it went to build another web, unless it died, but there was a gap from web to web. You were peculiar. You imagined the little beings could go to places you could not. Each creature had its own perspective based on its body. Where it could go, what it could build.

You watched the ants enter their nests. Like any child in its brutal inquisitiveness, you crushed several to see what was inside. Sometimes you did so to feel power, the gratification of destruction. Sometimes you ravaged their nests for the sheer pleasure of watching the ants rebuild. A grain at a time, moving the eggs and young to safety, an automatic response.

The bees. Yes, the bees. The first time you'd seen a wild hive. The hollow of a tree torn out. Its sapwood little more than dusty splinters. A bear had found the hive and ripped it to pieces. Some remained in the tree, golden wattles so strangely intricate and formless at the same time. You watched workers patch a hole that the bear had made. You found pieces on the ground still moist, some cells unbroken. | and ate one | What order! The bees didn't seem to fight or argue among themselves. Neither did the ants. We have young to protect. There is damage to our home. Let us fix it.

There was no way to save the young in the cells that had fallen to the ground. White ghoulish not-eggs, not-bees. You placed a section of the comb back in the tree. A hopeful act.

In your imagination and on your map, the bees built a bridge. They walked between the broken pieces. You listened to their attentive buzz. You felt the sun and the wind. Honey sweetened the rose of your lips. You studied what you had drawn. In that moment, you were completely yourself. The wholeness was no more complicated than that.

Who you were in that child was what you became. That essence was behind your exile and escape. It proved stronger than every other force that urged you to be a girl daughter sister wife mother woman on terms other than your own.

You understood Wei's decisiveness as a higher form of reason. Your daughter could not deny her purpose if she was born with the power to honor it. No matter how much you would miss her, you had no right to take away what belonged to her.

But you did. You lapsed and panicked.

Before she left, you cut her hair and dressed her like a boy.

You told Leit what you wanted to do. The very idea horrified him. You reminded him of the danger. You didn't invoke that of which he would never speak. Instead, you spoke of the boots, leggings, and cloak that once obscured your form. Your hair was worn long, but not too long. From a distance, you were mistaken for a man. The costume assured you safer movement.

We require no guise of the Voices, said he.

This would lessen the chance that someone would notice a girl among you, you said.

You forget some of our warriors are women.

And how do they dress on the trails?

Not as they sometimes do at home.

Ask them why that is, besides comfort, you said.

You consulted no elder or Voice. Leit didn't fight you. He disagreed and resisted on principle. He deigned because he feared you were right. You gave Wei no choice.

For the first time in a long while, you spoke aloud of your life before her. You explained that where you came from, in most places beyond the settlements, girls were confined in what they could do and where they could go. Almost everyone seemed to agree to this. The girls who didn't follow the rules were punished.

Sometimes by their own family and friends. Sometimes by strangers, who had learned the same rules and believed them to be true. When you were a mapmaker, you had dressed as a man to look like the other members of the group. The disguise hid you from people who might think you didn't belong with the men and try to hurt you. The women who walked alongside Wei's father chose a similar costume.

Wei asked for no explanation. She seemed to accept the idea of a costume to perform her work.

Then you said her hair must be cut. She was outraged.

That is a part of me, said she.

It's only hair. It will grow back.

It grows from inside of me. It's mine, said she.

Wei, you won't be able to wash as you do here. You would be uncomfortable.

Is that true, Ahpa? asked she.

You will not often bathe with the same comforts, said Leit.

She paused, considered the inconvenience, and stared at you. No, said she. No.

Sit here now. Do as I say. This is for your own good, you said.

You spoke those shame-filled words from the past. Your will held her down. Your hands whispered sharp violence below her ears. No blood was drawn but it drained from Wei's face. Her black and white hair dropped lifeless around her feet. What was left framed her chin.

Wei, in time you will understand this action, said Leit.

Until then this will be a hateful thing, said she.

She pierced you cold with her uncommon gaze. Before she could see into you, you pushed the old resentment away. That was what had troubled you. That was the source of what you did to your daughter. Aside from the necessity, under the justification you despised the dangers no man would face. Outside the settlement, your daughter was a carnal prey. A lamb for slaughter.

I mean to protect you, you said.

Why do I bother to wear this? asked Wei. She held the gold amulet away from her neck.

That has power only with those who recognize it, you said.

I will have warriors with me. Aren't they supposed to protect me?

Yes, but they will not be with you every single moment.

You did this to me out of fear—not love, said she.

You breathed. An old part of you wanted to lash out. It wanted to assert a parental right to her blind obedience. You had no claim. The Guardians granted even the smallest child her truth and its say.

I hope one day you'll forgive me, you said.

I feel very, very angry. I'm going to the forest now. I will ask Aza to go with me, said she.

You nodded. You knew you had wounded her deeply, and she knew she needed to tend that pain before it burrowed and festered.

The two of you achieved peace by the time she left for the trails. You held each other and wept. She covered your face with kisses. She placed her hand on your heart and warmed you through.

I will be with you again soon, Ahma. Be brave, said she.

Leit settled her on a cart. She and Leit would travel a short distance together, then separate for different trade routes. He lifted you as you clutched him around the neck. You pressed your lips to his throat's pulse. He kissed you as he slipped you off his body. You expected to feel Makha's kiss on your hand. For an instant you'd forgotten she was gone.

You watched the warriors in their blue coats begin another long journey. Wei turned to wave. You hardly recognized her until you realized she reminded you of yourself.

THEN YOU WERE ALONE FOR SEASONS AT A TIME. YOU MISSED YOUR spouse and daughter, but you also welcomed their absence. The focus you had devoted to Wei shifted. Of course, you had your duties to fulfill in the bakery and fields. When you left that work, you resumed another. Attention went to the manuscripts.

By then you were fluent in the Guardians' language. You had developed a written form that satisfied you. Before, your collection of histories and tales was sporadic. The effort became a devotion. You were allowed to observe the storytellers' training. Each young apprentice spent years with the elder adepts who repeated the legacy of their people. You listened, then scribed their words.

As well, you observed your neighbors and gathered their wisdom. You noted how they performed their work, where, and when. You spoke to them of the ways they learned their peace. You wished to glean the secrets that weren't meant to be so.

Your friends saw you less often when your spouse and daughter were away. You showed them examples of your work to explain your absence. They were curious. None had ever seen a map or a written page. Although they encouraged you, they didn't comprehend the purpose. We must only ask and we are told, said they. I don't understand the need, said some.

This is a means of memory, you said once. The statement startled you and puzzled friends. The words you wrote were not static. They had the power of conveyance, if one could comprehend the language. In your life before, you used texts for their facts. Yet you knew they could contain falsehoods, deliberate or unintentional. Regardless, the words became a form of memory that outlived the witnesses. They spoke for themselves.

Yes, as Sisay's words suggested, you, too, were misunderstood.

Nevertheless, you continued.

You offered to teach those who wished to learn how to read and write. You had few students. They enjoyed the novelty but to them these skills served no practical purpose. Why write when they could speak? Why read when they could listen? The immediacy of their lives required no record. They remembered what they needed to remember.

THOSE SEVEN YEARS WEI WAS ON THE TRAILS, YOU ACCOMMODATED THE cycles. You worked with determination while Wei and Leit were away. You welcomed the rare nights when Leit slipped through the gaps to join you in bed. At dawn, you walked with him | and the wolf | to the hollow then back to the settlement in time to knead. When your daughter and spouse arrived for their rest, you felt missing pieces had been returned. You remembered how you pined for their love and affection and the chance to give yours to them. The discovery surprised you at each reunion, like a well full again.

Wei's emergence into womanhood was abrupt for you. She returned home taller, the shape of her face sharper. The older she became, the more difficult it was to disguise her. She was no tawny little bird. Wei was a striking beauty. Her physical being and essence were feminine, soft as they were strong.

Each return, she told of her adventures. The warriors she accompanied treated her as loving uncles and brothers would. They allowed her periods of play. In safe villages and distant settlements, she made new friends. You were grateful the warriors didn't deny her simple childhood pleasures.

For all of Wei's joyfulness, she was a serious girl as well. She shared some of what she had encountered while on the trails. As a younger girl, she told stories of people and places. As she grew older, she began to speak of what she discerned.

There is so much pain, Ahma, said Wei. She told of the children she found and the adults who crossed her path. She had learned to treat others as friends, but she and her warrior companions were often met with suspicion. She glimpsed lives full of cruel words, bitter silences, and harsh whippings. There were resentments and grudges that lingered long. She had felt unease and witnessed strife and poverty. With her own hands, she touched children who had endured treatment that left them sad, hurt, and confused. They all blamed themselves. They believed themselves to be bad and deserving of punishment. Wei did what she could to help them, children and adults, assure them. You are more than this pain. You are beautiful. But the wounding was too profound. These matters affected everyone to some degree, but some far worse than others. The harm of it twisted people deep within themselves and they hurt others in return.

So many believe the toil and trouble of life is all there is, said Wei. They believe this is how life is meant to be, that it will always be so, and they have no understanding that it can be different.

You nodded. You listened with your full attention. She said she was confiding this to you because you had been born away. You knew the consequences of these experiences. | all too well | If she asked questions about your life before, you replied as best you could. Some you simply could not answer. The most difficult was, Why? How does one explain a beginning no one remembers?

She didn't know then | or perhaps she did | that she was about to name her purpose.

As for Leit, he appeared more worn with each return. He was older than many of his companions. The exertion of travel was enough of a strain. He knew, and told you, that his endurance waned. He admitted he was rough in situations he might have once managed with a lighter touch. He couldn't discern whether the incivility had become more common or his tolerance for it less strong.

You watched his darkness loom like storms, then blow away. The man he was at essence would return for periods, then slip into hiding. You encouraged him to speak to Aza or Edik, but he refused. He thought his wound was beyond their healing. The dragon's brand didn't have the power. How could they? He wouldn't dare risk this pain with his daughter.

Despite this, you had more days of contentment than not. When Leit and Wei were home together, they played and walked in one another's company as before. Their shared experience of the trails drew them closer.

Wei was ever gentle with her father. Her affection for him was expressive and frequent. She still took his hand and kissed his cheeks. When he was occupied with a task, she sometimes looked at him with love. She knew what the warriors suffered. You wondered if she glimpsed into his wound, waiting for it to open.

Once, Wei came to you when you were alone.

Ahma, said she. He cannot forgive himself. Do you understand?

You stared into her violet eyes that saw beyond seeing.

The child's desecration and death were not at his hand. He intended no harm to her, said Wei of what had never been spoken aloud between you.

You didn't ask how she knew. You didn't ask why she spoke when she did. Wei had her ways and reasons.

I don't understand why he clings as he does, you said.

He wants someone punished for what was done. He only has himself to inflict with the pain. He judges himself unjustly.

What of . . . You paused to build your courage. What of the man who did the deed? you asked.

Listen, Ahma. He suffered before and continued to do so afterward. What is no consolation to the little girl, or Ahpa, or anyone else who suffered at his hand, is still heavy with consequence. His lifetime is a limitation but not the end, said she.

Wei embraced you. She tingled in your arms. You accepted the light she offered. You let it slip, for a moment, into the hard holding cells within yourself where forgiveness couldn't reach.

As she grew older, Wei had great compassion for as well as conflict with her father. She had always discussed the Guardians' ways with Leit. However, her observations on the trails deepened her inquisitiveness.

She was thirteen when she began to deliberately challenge him. Wei questioned why the settlements remained remote and why their | our | people had rare contact with others. Leit reminded her that new settlements were built when populations needed to be dispersed. She knew that but wondered why those born away weren't invited to join. He explained how often those born away struggled with their ways, even those who were mysteriously drawn to the Guardians.

That's not how it always was, said she. Remember, Azul gathered friends at first to build the early settlements.

We don't reject anyone who comes to us, said Leit.

We don't openly welcome them to stay, either, said Wei.

You cringed when the two of them slipped into these discussions. If the Guardians had a means for peace, why was it not actively shared? Wei wanted to understand. Your small daughter sat without a flinch in front of her giant father. The disagreement simmered. You waited for it to boil over. You waited for Leit to declare his authority but he refrained. He spoke to your child as an equal.

You haven't seen what I've seen, said Leit.

I have seen what you have not as well, said Wei.

She told of a child she'd found in the forest. The girl wept piteously but without sound. Wei asked the child why she cried but she wouldn't speak. Shame wrapped her like a cloak. She had been beaten without mercy with a belt. She had dropped an egg. Her father had beaten her as her mother kept her back turned at her bowl. No supper for you! Get out of my sight! he had screamed at her.

An old wound split open. A cry thrust itself against your clenched jaw. Wei regarded you for a moment, then looked at her father.

I sang to the girl, and she crept into my open arms, said Wei. I saw how often she'd been beaten. I also saw her father find dark corners and pound his own head with his fists. He is ashamed of himself and doesn't want to beat her but believes, as he was taught, a child learns through punishment. I saw her mother knocked senseless because of her child's beatings, although no hand had touched her. She goes through the motions of the day and says nothing until it or the next one is done. She believes without him she has nowhere to go and she and the child will starve.

She's right, Wei, you said. This was a truth for every woman of every station in your life before.

Her fear is frank in her circumstances, said Wei.

I know this story. It's a mundane horror by now. Our Voices and warriors hear, see, and feel it told in all its forms over and over again, said Leit.

Do you know in their deepest hearts they wish to know better? asked Wei.

The cry whimpered from your lips. Wei turned one palm toward you. You felt your pulse change.

They know better, said Leit.

In most cases, they know what they do is cruel and hurtful. For those who wish not to be, they've never been taught other ways.

She's right, you said to him. You remembered all you had to unlearn when you found your new home. You knew there were still matters to unravel.

Ahpa, I must share the truth as I see it. We've waited for the world to join us but they don't have the knowledge to do so. Our example is here, but few notice. Our warriors have protected Egnis from the fear and misunderstanding of others. But we cannot expect our warriors to protect us from those who fear and misunderstand us and our promise. The war wasn't the first or the last—nor was it the one that must be fought. Your scar bears proof, said she.

Leit flinched. Wei invoked what no one, no one, dared speak.

I know your wish to deny residence to those born away is meant to protect us. You want to preserve the integrity of our ways. That's noble, rational, and sound. But, Ahpa, we can't expect love, cooperation, and peace to reign if we contain our knowledge as we do.

What are you saying? asked Leit.

We must begin to live among those born away and welcome anyone who wishes to live with us.

That is a beautiful but naïve idea, said Leit.

Dangerous and hopeful, too, said Wei. She smiled.

You wept from grief and pride. Had you spoken that way to your father, he would have slapped you for defiance. You looked at your daughter and your spouse passionate for the same ends, differing in their means. Theirs was a higher love too rare beyond your borders.

Ahma, what do you think? Our conversation has clearly moved you, said Wei.

I'm of two minds about the matter. I don't know, you said.

They tried to secure your opinion, but you had no firm one. You were a Guardian then, by choice, and wanted the ways protected. You once, by birth, were not a Guardian, and wanted another way to be. Your own house was as divided as your heart. The latter caused more strife. Knowing what you knew, how could you choose?

Well, you don't have to decide now, do you? said Wei. I didn't have my ideas together for the last Assembly. I intend to speak at the next one.

You have six years to prepare, said Leit.

As do you, said she.

She kissed your hand then kissed her father. Her light loose dress fluttered at her side as she walked across the room and through the front door.

What a formidable daughter I have, bold as her mother, said Leit.

WEI ENDED HER DUTY ON THE TRAILS THE WINTER BEFORE SHE TURNED fifteen. Your little daughter came home finally as a young woman. She enjoyed the company of friends and the admiration of young men. From a distance, you watched her consider the handsome options. You discovered an unexpected well of envy that sprang from the memory of your life before. No young woman of your station was given the latitude allowed your daughter and her friends. | had it been, would you have sat at Heydar's table? | Leit basked in the nostalgia of youth even as he glowered at the boys who stood on your home's threshold.

Your daughter knew of the collection of histories and tales you had worked to gather through the years. She agreed to chronicle some of her experiences as a Voice. You asked to teach her how to write them herself. She tried, but the attempts were frustrating. Her unusual sight as you understood it hampered her dexterity and precision. She tried to comprehend your texts through touch. She discovered she had little sensitivity to do so. She was sorry to disappoint you, but she wished to concentrate on the abilities she possessed.

This gives you pleasure, Ahma. Continue. I think there's a reason you persist.

And what is that? you asked.

Oh, the passage of seasons will tell, I suppose.

During the next few years, Wei served as Aza did. | beloved Edik had died | She had a reputation as a great healer, young as she was. Yet Wei expected more of herself and her gifts. She continued to ponder the possibility of showing others the Guardians' ways. Wei traveled to other settlements to speak to Voices and elders across the known world. She used the gaps, but sometimes she didn't. You understood to leave her alone when she sat in her room with her palms open.

You respected what you didn't comprehend.

There is interest, Ahma, said she. Others feel as I do. Not many, but enough to matter. The next Assembly will have a vibrant debate, I think.

She was fearless, your Wei. Courageous and inquisitive. What was, was not what would always be, she believed. She believed this as if it were her next breath.

The Guardians would be the least of her worries by comparison. You had been born away. You remembered what power, no matter how weak, others cherished. To release that called to chaos. Without might—over one's will or body, that of another person or a group—what control could there be? You had learned the power of love and trust. You were long suspicious of the lessons, trained as you were to accept the means of dominance.

When she was nineteen years old, Wei asked you to join her at the Assembly. This was a surprise. You had not been invited by the leaders. Neither was she, she reminded you. She had requested an audience. Such appeals were rarely denied, and hers was not. That she was Leit's daughter and a Voice must have made the leaders curious.

I wish for you to serve as witness, said she. You were born away and can speak to the difference between the ways.

But I'm torn, you said.

You were grateful for the Guardians' welcome despite your origins. Wei knew by then, from your own words, what role you'd had in the war. The inherent peace you'd felt was what you had intended to protect. You hadn't meant to threaten it. When you arrived at the settlement, you had been rent apart from all you'd known. You were willing to surrender to another structure of order. You were desperate but also humbled. You availed yourself of another way of being.

I was drawn to these ways, but I was also ready for them, you said.

Wei asked you to explain.

My daughter, you were born into a life where fear was not ever-present, you said. You have never experienced lack of any kind. Those around you understood the meaning of love. When you served the trails, you witnessed the opposite. Remember the man who beat his child who dropped the egg? To him, his world is the real one. Ours is a fantasy. We could show him our ways, but he would resist. All of us born away do, to some extent. What were held as truths are revealed as lies. We have to confront those who ruled over us, what agency we ourselves had in our lives, what possibilities our physical bodies and ancestral lineages held open or kept closed.

I admire what you want to do, Wei. But I think the approach must be gradual. The shock would be too great for everyone if many new people moved into the settlements. The suspicion could transform into real danger if large numbers of our people tried to move into other villages.

I hadn't considered that, said Wei.

My caution isn't meant to temper your zeal but to hone it. Go to the Assembly and explain your vision. Regardless of their response, be true to yourself. I know all too well the consequences of regret.

You didn't accompany her. She said she understood but that she was disappointed. You would have given persuasive testimony. While she and Leit had been away, you'd thought of Sisay's portent. Wei was now taking the first steps toward her great purpose.

SOON AFTER THAT ASSEMBLY, LEIT WAS ELECTED TO SERVE ON YOUR settlement's Elder Council, one of nine members. His known opposition to opening the settlement to outsiders echoed the wishes of many neighbors.

This wasn't as contentious as it might have been elsewhere. Everyone struggled with the possibility. Wei's proposal challenged the Guardians' understanding of themselves. Had their wish for peaceful communities become an act of isolation? For generations, they had built new settlements when needed. They had little contact with the villages closest to them. The war had only deepened their desire to be left alone. Wei openly questioned the wisdom of their practices.

You held the tension of all sides.

Leit contended that the risk was too great to allow in large groups of those born away. He cautioned those who wished to leave about the circumstances they would encounter.

After Wei had returned from her first Assembly meeting, she was ardent. She was admired for her compassion and intention. However, the plausibility of her proposal raised questions and worries. She began to organize discussions within the settlement. You watched your daughter listen more than speak, but when she spoke, you felt her power. Her force was like water. It was constant—at times slow, at times swift. As some came to share her ideas, a small group of them traveled to other settlements. Within a few years, Wei had friends across the known world. They advocated a new perspective on how to bring peace.

One of her new friends became her spouse. Olen was a young farmer. He had been born away, welcomed as a foundling. You had already known him from your help in the fields. You expected the couple to remain in the settlement. They were among the first young people who moved.

Leit struggled with a sense of betrayal. The village Wei and Olen had chosen—an easy three-day walk away—was the one that had revealed the settlement's location during the war. Wei and her Guardian friends had visited on several occasions. Their gesture was one of reconciliation. The agreement was for a temporary stay. Skilled people from the settlement would teach and learn from their people.

I know most neighbors here prefer to leave customs as they are, said Wei. One day that may change. Right now there's another place willing to try. And I want to try.

Wei and Olen packed their belongings and moved with fifteen other Guardians. Aged though you were | alive and healthy still, fifty-five | you traveled to see her, and they back to you. They seemed happy and purposeful, although their work was difficult. They discovered tempers they didn't know they had. Wei found the abuse of authority painful to witness and resistant to suggestions of kinder means.

That doesn't surprise you, does it? asked Wei of you.

Not in the least, you said.

When they had Katya, you hoped they would move back to the settlement. They did not. However, Katya spent seasons at a time with you and Leit when Wei traveled to other settlements. With her ahpapa, Katya roamed the forest to see its surprises. With you, her ahmama, she learned to read and write her mother's tongue. She was excited to learn and took materials back with her to her home. Upon her visits, she would read to you chronicles of her childhood days. As she grew older, you allowed her to read your collection. Some texts were recorded before her mother was born.

Then you began to do what the old do. You told stories of your life before. Rare were thoughts of the people and places where you lived the beginning of your life. Nearing the end, they returned to you. Not all was laid bare. Not all did you reveal. You told of how you became a mapmaker as if it were a wonder tale. You explained how you found the Guardian settlement far away and how you wished to protect it. The quest and the exile surfaced with moments of beauty and curiosity. As Katya became older, you spiraled through the accounts again. You threaded into them details you had spared before.

Tell the truth.

You didn't tell the whole truth. You tried not to speak ill of those presumed dead. For those for whom you had affection, you emphasized the warm feelings. Some you would not mention at all.

You have great stories, Ahmama. You should write yours on the sheets, said Katya.

They're of no interest but to you, you said.

Then do it for me and your grandchildren to come.

You smiled but gave no answer.

There was pleasure in the telling but also sadness. When you were alone, lost grief traveled to find you. It took you by the throat and refused to tell you its name. You were needful of Leit's old arms at night. He couldn't shelter you from what lurked within.

THE LATCH LIFTED FROM THE BOBBIN. THE DOOR OPENED. YOU EXpected your spouse but saw your daughter. You stood to greet the surprise. You put your hands on her silver black white head and kissed her.

Later, she would tell you she knew you would have refused. She was correct | perhaps not | but the risk was nevertheless one she thought worthy to take.

Ahma, said Wei. I've brought someone to see you. She had to repeat what she said three times. You hadn't heard your native language in so long. As you stared at her, she stroked your forehead with gentleness, then kissed the skin. Wei disappeared outside.

Through your door walked the image of your father. An elderly specter, gaunt, but bright-eyed. The shock made you wonder if Wei had defied reason and brought back the dead. The image spoke your name.

Aoife.

Your name spoken the way you remembered it by your people, your tongue, and his voice without the brittle strain of old age.

Ciaran, you said.

You embraced. You had missed him and had no idea how much until he stood there. He carried a satchel on his shoulder.

My wife believes I'm away on a brief trip. She has no clue of the distance, said he. Unless this is a dream.

You assured him it was not. Welcome to the mystery.

The old tongue came back to you but it was slow, slow. A creature roused from sleep to emerge in words. You encouraged him to speak first, to accustom you to the sound again. You exchanged the pleasantries of strangers while you made tea. Then you sat close enough to touch him.

He said your parents had been dead many years. You assumed so. He said he married not long after you were exiled and thought you would like her. The pairing was fortunate and complementary. She came from a good family, well propertied. She kept a cheerful home as best she could.

So this wife I took abed but nothing came of it, said Ciaran with a slight grin.

You thought he was making a joke, but he was not. He was to give you a revelation blunted by humor.

We had children. We raised the twins.

Thoughts failed. You couldn't imagine what had happened, so he told you everything.

Painful, Aoife, to tell you, said he, but this is the truth. I want you to know. We may never see one another again and for so long I've missed you.

Ciaran had believed you were dead. As the kingdom prepared for the war, Raef gained power within the ranks. There had been talk of your imprisonment, but the official public decision was for exile. Raef himself arranged for the escorts out. The younger prince never said so, but even then Ciaran suspected a hidden intent. Wyl seemed more distraught than angry, as if he'd been swept away and dazed by the lack of footing. He agreed to the exile because it meant your life would be spared. Your father claimed he understood the reason for exile and supported it with no objection.

Your mother keened at your loss. Where will she go? she asked her son. Where will my lamb go? | my lamb, she called you her lamb in sweet moments | Ciaran did his best to comfort her. Mother, remember that she lived roughly and through all manner of terrain. If anyone can survive, it's she. Your mother imagined horrors beyond death. Milkmaid. Washerwoman. Chambermaid. Beggar. Used woman. Ciaran couldn't bear to tell her the truth. The night of your exile, he was told the escorts had been instructed to kill you and bring your heart as proof of the deed. Wyl wasn't informed until it was too late. Days later, even your father couldn't bear the sight of the raw leathery organ one of the escorts held as evidence.

They were so ordered, but one of the men let me go, and I ran, you said.

He burst into tears. You took his hands. He tried to pull away but you gently held on. How long it had been since you'd felt the pain of seeing him cry. Finally, as you never had before, you were able to comfort him.

Soothed, Ciaran continued.

Not soon after you were gone, the twins became an issue. Wyl was free to marry, properly. It wouldn't do for him to be saddled with the children of his traitor wife, exiled in shame. The Queen had little affection for them. Sweet children though they were. As if they had been responsible for the troubles that had unfolded. Ciaran knew Wyl didn't wish to give them up. However, even though he was King, he couldn't hold out against his brother and his mother and their aspirations for the kingdom. So he relinquished them to your mother's care. Father was furious. He didn't want the bother in the house. Old man. Too old. Mother was glad to have them and seemed joyful in their presence. Wyl went to see them, but Mother said he shouldn't. It was selfish to confuse them. If he wouldn't stand for them as the legitimate issue they were, better they were told they were orphans than treated like bastards. This Mother told Ciaran and King Wyl himself.

By that time, Ciaran had married, and they didn't know of the barrenness. His wife was a largehearted woman who took pleasure in her niece and nephew. Ciaran told her the truth of their circumstances. It was harder to disguise the truth from those in the inner circle of relationships. Among those outside, the troubles were abandoned to the past. For good. Eventually Ciaran learned the written chronicles had been altered. He suspected Wyl had given orders but had no proof.

Your place in history was expunged.

To the matter, his wife suggested they take the twins as their own. The girl and boy were young enough that they'd grow without recollection of either blood parent or the strife of their infancy. Ciaran loved them as well. Like you, the boy was serious and the girl spirited. Like Wyl, the girl had natural charm and the boy literal-mindedness. Their father relinquished his claim. Unimaginable, but he did, thinking it best for all concerned. So they took the twins, which pleased Mother, for she could have them call her Grandmama still. By all accounts, they knew no different. They called Ciaran Father and his wife Mother. She was gentle and kind and cuddled them like puppies.

As this transpired, Ciaran traveled to the opposite bank to assess what had been claimed. What was left after the battle, to be sure, because the whole settlement had been looted, including the road that was rumored to be made of gold.

It had been. When I returned there after my escape, it was gone, you said.

Ciaran continued. He brought his envoys and tally sheets and walked every foot of ground. He required a survey of the land that had been seized. So much of it was supposedly unclaimed. The neighboring kingdoms to the north and east had long respected the space of the strange people who lived there. It was Raef who set about to convince those kings what threat must be thwarted. He lied about the Guardians' cache of weapons and ample riches. The wealth was in the gold road and in their possessions. In truth, Aoife, it was a slaughter. They weren't armed enough. The kingdom's forces overreacted.

Then why did the war spread? you asked.

It was believed the people moved what had been stored there, said he. It was a contagious distortion. A mania I'd never before seen, and it consumed me as well. It was as if the leaders, army, and people of our kingdom became crazed with the idea that those people were stalking from a distance, waiting to destroy us all. Neighboring kingdoms joined the madness. Villages that knew of their presence suddenly feared them and led troops to their borders.

And what was gained? you asked.

He said the kingdom's domain doubled in size. After the Queen died, Wyl decided to move the seat of power across the river. The flat wooded land was an inappropriate place for a fortification. He ordered the land cleared in the settlement, as well as acres of the forest that surrounded it. An earthen mound was built, and the castle atop that. What ground was spared proved fertile and full of game. Wyl took great pleasure in the claim.

What of Raef? After the war, which he had viewed, by all

accounts, from promontories and margins, he took to his own quest. No magnificent stores that rivaled the hoard had been found in any of the settlements. This enraged him, for he had convinced himself that what he had seen in the first settlement was sure to be found in the others. He wanted the hoard Wyl said he had seen. That, Raef wanted as his conquest. Wealth not to be meted out by royal custom or law or his brother's grace. There was no secret in this. He spoke of it often, to the point most thought him obsessive, perhaps deranged. One day he disappeared, with no attempt to cloak where he'd gone. He left with a fortune in gold and the map you drew.

The map is a lie, you said.

Ciaran suspected so and thought Wyl did, too. He knew Wyl had seen the map because he was there when Raef unfurled it in the great hall to behold. Your father, Ciaran, the Queen, and members of the Council were present. You were locked in the house with the twins. Ciaran stood among those who witnessed the work you'd done. It bore your hand. He confessed he had to hold back tears. It was beautiful, Aoife, with the tender touches you gave to the playful ones of your girlhood. This one had so many animals, and the bold *X,* too bold, as if it were a joke on us all. But Raef asked Wyl to study it right then. Brother, what say you? asked he. Wyl gave a fine performance with his knitted brow and folded arms and close peering. He declared it accurate and sound, as far as he could tell. Such a long journey it was, such a long journey.

Raef ventured out with a copy of the map and returned home for a time, penniless and exhausted, only to try again. He had not traveled far enough. He'd misstepped. There was always an excuse or a thwart. If he believed the map was false, he never said so.

The stranger lie was yet to come. Wyl married again, a princess from a kingdom that had participated in the war. A shallower little creature didn't flit on a puddle. Kindly in disposition and pure of voice, as you can imagine. Not near so beautiful as a king is promised. But there was his match, the price of allegiance. Together, they had four children, three boys and a girl. One of the boys was afflicted with fits and died, poor thing. The rest of the children grew strong. When the oldest boy came of age, the people chose his feat. And what do you think they deemed?

A quest, you said.

Full of imagination, they were. The vicarious thrill of battle and adventure was revivified in their minds, although almost thirty years had passed since. They were proud to be led by stouthearted men. The people sent Wyl's son for the same feat as his father's, to bring proof of the dragon. Wyl gave him the amulet you had given him and, upon Raef's latest return, required the copy of the map he carried. No more were to be made. So off the son went in full regalia as if going to war. A handsome young man, much like his father, but not as thick, not as credulous. He left, was away for months, and arrived looking none the worse for wear. Almost refreshed, to be exact. He went before the Council as his father, the King, had many years before and upon the table laid a scale.

From what? you asked.

The prince claimed to have fought the dragon. He raised the sleeve of his shirt to expose a burn scar above his left hand. A swift sword swipe drew dragon's blood and loosed a scale from its body. He declared the hoard as well-stocked and awesome as his father had said it would be. The prince had detected and heard of no imminent threat as he bided his time near the lair.

There was later a welcome ceremony with the people. A feast. Until his death, Wyl had been a generous king, Aoife. What he lacked in wisdom he made up for with boons. But to the matter, there was a fuss about the scales, a display made to be kept in the King's private chamber. Ciaran saw for himself the difference. The scale Wyl had brought back was colorless. His son's was red, through and through.

It's a fake, you said.

Which one?

The son's. The scales are transparent.

How do you know?

My spouse and my daughter told me so.

Then you had a turn at your tales. When you were finished, you sighed. You felt released. You felt forgiven, although you had not asked that of him.

During his stay, your brother accompanied you to see the whole of the settlement. To those who asked how he had found you, you responded simply, Wei. No more needed to be said. You led him through the forest and into the plain. He saw the mine, fields, lake, and river. He slept in the small room you kept for Wei's family. He joined you, your spouse, and your daughter for meals and amusements. Genuine affection emerged among them. Too soon, he had to leave. Neither acknowledged you would never see one another again.

The peace I feel. I didn't understand you then. That's what you tried to convey so many years ago, said Ciaran.

Yes, you said.

We mistook the treasure. We sought the obvious. What a terrible pity.

You nodded. Ciaran held you in his arms with love. When Wei led him to the forest, you didn't follow. She alone would return her uncle home.

LEIT DIED TWO SEASONS LATER. HIS DECLINE WAS RAPID. THAT DIDN'T startle you. He was elderly. What made you quiver was his dying. The scar began to split open. It bled a slow weep like water through a rock. You had a Voice summon Wei. She arrived with Olen and Katya.

They helped you care for him as his life leaked away.

Wei's light soothed him, calmed him, but she couldn't save her father. She curled against him as she had as a child. He whispered to her. Beloved Wei. Beautiful beloved Wei.

One morning, when he was still strong enough to sit, Wei knelt at his side. She was silent. Her expression showed conflict.

What is it? asked Leit.

I know something, but I don't know whether you wish to be told.

An understanding crossed between them without words. He nodded. She took his hands.

The tree that shared the wounds. A crack grew long and a hollow formed deep. The tree has died. When the hollow is through and through, what is left will be a link, said Wei.

Leit grabbed her wrists.

This you glimpsed? asked he.

Yes and no. I've been to it. The links are not all random. Some stand on hallowed ground.

He dropped his head and her arms. She stood behind him with her hands crossed over his chest. Wei began to sing a song of welcome. One for a coming newborn. Innocent, remind us what is pure. Innocent, remind us what is true. Innocent, awake from the great sleep. Behold what waits for you. Leit splayed his limbs. He fought no longer. As tears flowed, he sang with his daughter.

The beauty of their voices awed you to silence.

He sang with his whole voice again, at last.

That afternoon, he insisted on a walk through the forest. He sat on the plateau until the moon rose. Then his bodily strength left him.

His friends streamed in with comforting touches for you all. As always, they met your needs, especially for love.

The flow quickened. He was not afraid.

I weaken but I'm in no pain, said he.

You slept next to him. You awoke in the mornings touched by his blood. In those last days together, you remembered, cried, and laughed. You held one another with your eyes when his arms became too weak to surround you. Once strong, scarred with fire from the smithy, with violence from blades.

He became so pale. His family gathered around him. Each of you held on to him. You lay stretched at his side with your hand on his belly. The red wetness was part of him. Was him.

Leit smiled into each person's eyes. Then he closed his for the last time. You kissed him, then pressed your lips to his neck. The throb, once so steady, slowed slowed slowed. He gasped once, as if surprised, then exhaled.

Ahpa, wailed Wei.

The sound of her cry shattered your heart where it was already broken.

Wei's spouse left to announce the death. Within moments bells rang throughout the settlement. You asked to clean Leit's body alone. You would never touch him again.

On the plain, young warriors prepared the pyre. Companions arrived to carry the corpse. Leit was shrouded in a fine blue cloth. It was woven by certain weavers and stored for use only for those who walked the trails. He was laid upon a bed of boughs. The ritual cauldron consumed offerings in flame. For two days and nights, warriors kept watch over the fire. On the third day, one of his closest surviving companions lit the pyre.

You thought of winters past and fires he tended to keep you warm.

Leit's ashes were brought in a beautiful urn. He had said that you may choose how to release them. Wei wanted to give him the honor he had earned. Long ago, the Guardians received agreement to scatter each warrior's remains in the realm.

So you stood before a dead hollow tree at twilight. Your

daughter spoke the incantation. A bee bade entry. You were here, then there, within a few steps.

It is always this close, Wei? you whispered.

She opened her arms wide. She bent her elbows and brought her flat hands toward her chest. Her left palm faced the sky. She turned her right to face the earth. Wei placed her palms one upon the other.

A thin space separates realm from realm. Some places allow both to meet, said she.

You stood at the foot of the mountain. Leit's ashes were heavy in your arms. Blue swallows gave chase across the valley. The clouds blushed pink rose crimson. The billows revealed contours. You gasped as the shape became form and drifted to the ground. You looked at her wings, tail, legs, head.

The winged beast, so red, bowed to meet your eye. You stared long at your reflection, the darkness in the light. Your mind spiraled with images. The glimpses spared nothing. Revealed everything. The entirety was beyond comprehension. The flood was ruthless—then stopped. You blinked. That moment, you thought you understood why they guarded her.

She was the witness of the world, future present past.

Egnis huffed. She turned toward the open land. You and Wei followed. Wei broke the urn's wax seal. Together, you tipped the vessel and spilled the dust. The dragon blew a warm breath. The ashes lifted into the air. She beat her wings to urge the dust upward.

Then she took flight with a great plume of flame from her mouth. She danced with grace through a breeze. She flew higher until she disappeared beyond the rise of the moon.

Gray powder covered your hands. Bone shards lay scattered at your feet. The empty urn held the peace of his release.

YOU DID NOT SPEND YOUR LAST YEARS ALONE WITH LEIT'S LOSS. KATYA and her own family remained in the village, an easy three-day walk away, but Wei returned with Olen. You shared a house together within sight of the Wheels. The children's joy and voices gave brightness to each new morning. After the music, some of them came to your door for lessons. To them, it was play. Some sat with compasses and straightedges. Others held only quills. What you taught had little purpose in their world, but it bound yours together.

Alone, you sat at a table. You clutched an incomplete chronicle, one written in fragments on scraps. You stared at an open box of writing sheets. You had told Leit you would save them for a special work. On several occasions, you attempted to begin. Too much came at once. The thin pages could not endure the furious scratches. You contemplated your quest and exile. You realized there was one last journey to take.

Wei closed her eyes when you made the request. You reminded her that she had found her uncle. She had brought him to visit. Wei said she sensed Ciaran had the strength to see you arisen from the dead. In your hearts, both of you had wondered whether you knew the truth of past events.

She admitted she had seen the twins many years earlier. She was young, testing the gaps and her sight. Her brother didn't yet have a wife and was in service of the King, | the boy, the heir inapparent | Her sister was married and not yet with child. Boldly, she spoke to them but did not tell them who she was. She said her friendliness confused them. They found her strange.

What do you want? asked Wei.

One last look with my hands free.

She cautioned you to keep yourself removed. You assured her you didn't wish to speak to them. Wei asked you to be mindful, to spare them their lost memories. You understood. From your daughter you had learned words were not necessary for knowing.

First, Wei led you to the boy. She told you he was a widower with three surviving children. Ciaran's late years were marred with dispute. A good portion of what he'd held had been given to another. The boy managed what was left of his uncle's | his father's | estate. What had once been the boy's grandfather's, and that man's father, and so on. The reward for loyal obedient service. He had no interest in courtly affairs or fighting. Those who lived on his land worked it hard, which covered the costs of supplying the King | his half brother, consider | with armored men and steady taxes.

You stood at the edge of the forest. You looked at the house where you had lived as a child. Repairs kept it free from decay. No noticeable changes captured your eye. You stood where once you had worn a path. It was gone, overgrown. An old woman clothed in wool and drudgery went to the well. You crouched like an animal to watch the day's activities. No urge pressed you to creep upon the house's windows. You remembered. You suspected few differences within.

Your presence there felt as unwelcomed as ever.

Later you ate a simple meal. You drank from a bladder. Wei returned near sunset to take you to the hut of an old woman. So much time had passed since you had crossed such a threshold. You convinced Wei to let night come.

Candles burned in the chamber that once had been your father's. With caution, you approached. The boy sat with a drink in a polished goblet. The light revealed few details. He was tall, with a balding head fringed with dark hair. His profile was pleasing. You imagined, hoped, he resembled Wyl. You studied him as if he were a stranger, because he was.

Tenderness swelled your heart. You seized the open warmth for a moment, mistaken. No, the mother in you did not recognize him. The human in you did. He had come from your flesh but you had no claim to him. You had relinquished that by choice, no matter the forces.

Suddenly he shouted a name. You jumped. He leaned forward to peer out of the window. You hid deeper in the shadows. Two voices mingled in brief tense conversation punctuated with the slam of a fist. When all was quiet, you touched the stone wall once, one last time. Your footsteps walked an old hidden path back to the trees where you always felt more at home.

Morning brought rain but across the gap there was sun.

The girl lived in the new territory on the other side of the river. The conquered lands. Wei said she had been married well before Ciaran had lost favor and prominence. That she did not choose her husband was no surprise. Women were makers of heirs, not choices, among most born away.

There was no forest in which to hide. You wouldn't be so bold as to knock upon the door. A worn dirt road bisected an orchard of fruit trees. You pretended to be a weary traveler. The simple clothes you wore gave no hint of your life before. You rested in the shade of an apple tree. Alone, you were alert. You were no longer young and quick. You felt sorrow for the awareness of danger. The feeling you remembered too well had been buried for so long.

Several days you spent this way. You strained Wei's patience. You almost relented and returned home.

Then one morning, a little girl of four or five appeared on the road. She ran back to join an older woman. You sat with anticipation. They approached, and you pushed yourself up to stand. The woman was the girl. Your second daughter was correct that you would recognize your first. She was stout like your mother, with her thick brows and pinched mouth. The woman and the child were dressed in great finery more appropriate for a banquet than a walk.

Old peasant, pick me an apple, said the little child.

You flinched at her words. You looked at her, seeking a resemblance. The little one had blond hair, green eyes, and pleasing features. The girl was too old to have a child so young. The girl's granddaughter, you thought. | your great-granddaughter | With a tolerant smile, you twisted a fruit from the tree.

There you are, child, you said.

The little one took a bite.

The girl nodded at you. Not a gray hair was out of place.

Good morning, you said.

She scowled and nodded again.

Your sudden confusion diffused your anxiety that she stood almost within reach. Her response had been less than cordial. Then you realized the error. You clutched the sides of your skirt in your wrinkled hands. The curtsy was empty but heavy with humiliation. Ages had passed since you'd bowed to anyone.

My lady, you said.

What brings you to this road? asked she.

I'm traveling to see my daughter and stopped to rest.

Well, it is a lovely day for a walk.

Old peasant, get me another apple, said the child.

You reached high for a large ripe one. When you held it out for her, she grabbed your wrist. She touched the sapphire bracelet Leit had given you instead of a ring.

What a pretty sparkling bracelet! said the child.

Yes, it is. Wherever did you come by such a dear piece of jewelry? asked the girl.

A wedding gift from my husband, now at rest, you said.

And who was he?

A great warrior.

The girl stared long at you. She turned her aged face to play the light against yours.

Do I know you? asked she.

No, my lady.

Should I know you?

No, my lady.

Then might it not be best for us strangers to part and continue along our own ways? Come, said the girl to her granddaughter.

Once more you curtsied. | your body remembered | They

continued on their stroll and vanished in the distance. You searched yourself for remorse, guilt, shame, love, acceptance. The unforgivable acts remained unchanged. Your deeds were done. Your choices were made. The consequences rippled before and beyond you.

Tell the heinous truth.

The twins had freed you.

Your worst fear had not come true. You hadn't been forced to lay aside your compass and straightedge to marry an intolerable man and bear his young. Instead, you married their father, who welcomed them as you could not. His esteem for you, their mother, spared you noose and blade. You left them without a struggle. No matter that they were his issue to keep and give away. They were your terrible innocent ransom. Their little lives opened the window of chance that allowed you to flee at all. You did, but you could not escape them.

They revealed you fully to yourself. You were a woman unwilling to be what others expected of her. A person unable to love without condition. A human being who wanted peace regardless of the price.

You stood on the road in the land of your birth. No longing, no regret. You exhaled a sorrowful gratitude. Your life before had given you the gift of your life after. Beautiful, horrible both, and all points linked between. There in that place, you waited for Wei.

A gentle hand touched your left arm. Her lined violet eyes looked within you.

Take me home, my beautiful child, you said.

ACKNOWLEDGMENTS

My most sincere thanks extend to—

my circle of family, friends, and acquaintances who shared kind words and encouragement—particularly Nolde Alexius, Martin Arceneaux, Tameka Cage Conley, Penelope Dane, Ava Leavell Haymon, Jamey Hatley, Susan Henderson, Judy Kahn, Karla King, Ben Lanier-Nabors, Jandy Nelson, Ariana Wall Postlethwait, Joe Scallorns, and Emilie Staat;

the online literary magazine *The Nervous Breakdown,* which spared me of one because of its supportive writer community including founder Brad Listi, Robin Antalek, Matthew Baldwin, Sean Beaudoin, J. M. Blaine, Jessica Anya Blau, Richard Cox, Joe Daly, Kristen Elde, Gina Frangello, Marni Grossman, D. R. Haney, Cynthia Hawkins, Nat Missildine, Don Mitchell, Quenby Moone, Uche Ogbuji, Greg Olear, Zara Potts, Judy Prince, Erika Rae, Simon Smithson, Angela Tung, Kimberly M. Wetherell, and Irene Zion.

the readers who first saw the strange beast—Katy Powell, McHenry "Dub" Lee, Kate Suchanek, and James Claffey;

the talented artist, Kathryn Hunter of Blackbird Letterpress;

a true friend and solid anchor, Alison Aucoin;

a grounding force and thoughtful reader, Madeleine Conger;

a writer soul mate if there ever was one, with fierce editing chops, Mary McMyne;

the hosts who provided places of respite when the words finally showed up—Lisa and Maurice Werness, Angie Ledbetter, Gary "Doc T" Taylor, and Janet Taylor;

the experts who generously shared their knowledge—Dr. Jon Campbell, Elaine B. Smyth, and Michele Piumini;

the magic places that always seemed to have what I needed—the East Baton Rouge Parish Library and Louisiana State University's Middleton Library and Hill Memorial Library;

those authors, translators, and visionaries whose books confirmed I was on the right path and showed me the way—Anne Baring, Jean Shinoda Bolen, Lloyd A. Brown, Joseph Campbell, Jules Cashford, Riane Eisler, Marija Gimbutas, Jonathan Glover, Edward T. Hall, Seamus Heaney, Buffie Johnson, Robert A. Johnson, Thomas Kinsella, C. G. Jung, Alice Miller, Robert L. Moore, Parker Palmer, Wilhelm Reich, Edward Tick, Eckhart Tolle, Edward R. Tufte, Marie-Louise von Franz, and Marion Woodman;

the stellar creative team at Atria Books which *yet again* amazed me;

my agent, Jillian Manus, and publisher, Judith Curr, for embracing the leap;

my editor, Sarah Branham, who guided the journey's completion with insight; and

my beloved, Todd, who waited at the end of the tunnel.